HIS MASTER'S SUMMONS

CASSIE SWEET

DSP PUBLICATIONS

Published by
DSP PUBLICATIONS

5032 Capital Circle SW, Suite 2, PMB# 279, Tallahassee, FL 32305-7886 USA
www.dsppublications.com

This is a work of fiction. Names, characters, places, and incidents either are the product of author imagination or are used fictitiously, and any resemblance to actual persons, living or dead, business establishments, events, or locales is entirely coincidental.

His Master's Summons
© 2016 Cassie Sweet.

Cover Art
© 2016 Brooke Albrecht.
http://brookealbrechtstudio.com
Cover content is for illustrative purposes only and any person depicted on the cover is a model.

ISBN: 978-1-63476-363-9
Digital ISBN: 978-1-63476-364-6
Library of Congress Control Number: 2015945888
Published February 2016
v 1.0

Printed in the United States of America
∞

This paper meets the requirements of
ANSI/NISO Z39.48-1992 (Permanence of Paper).

Author's Note

My original vision for *His Master's Summons* had more in common with soup made from a broth of Mary Shelley's *Frankenstein* mixed with a seasoning of the Brontë sisters. As the book began to simmer, an unexpected and intriguing character popped into the scene and decided to take over. I let him. Doing so opened an entire world in this series I wanted and needed to explore, and begged answers to questions of exactly what it is that makes a person creative. Is it an intangible part of our essence, or created by external forces? And though I may not have posed any true answers, I sure had fun uncovering the possibilities while discovering the fae realm.

So to my readers, I give you Azgarth.

Chapter One

Teatro La Fenice, Venice Italy—1897

DR. MIKHAIL Stanslovich huddled into the darkness of the private box. Sounds of the other patrons finding their seats created a gentle rumble through the acoustically perfect room. Voices echoed and carried to him in a wash of emotion. Excitement vibrated through the theater, taking on a living presence. One Mikhail could almost taste and feel.

Spirits always ran high whenever Andres Valentine took to the stage. A true virtuoso in every sense of the word, Valentine made love to the audience through his music. Passion, love, sex—all the base emotions were present in Valentine's concerts. For this reason alone, Mikhail had traveled so far to see him play.

Cloying scents of too much perfume and men's pomade wafted up from the floor below. He tried not to take in too big a breath, lest he gag on the fumes. Women had a tendency to overplay their hand. Was it beyond their comprehension that the musician whom they came to hear would not single them out from the stage by scent alone?

Dante Savoy, Mikhail's best friend and fellow scientist, shifted in the seat beside him. He pulled at his white waistcoat and made a face. "You'd think from the price we paid for these seats they'd be more damned comfortable."

Mikhail shot Dante a withering glance. "This is one of the world's premiere opera houses. It is everything grand and fashionable."

Dante's mouth quirked up at the corner. "You said that about Vienna, London, Paris, Rome, and even New York."

"Because you've complained about them all. You are an absolute Philistine." There was no malice or even much heat behind Mikhail's words. He loved Dante better than anyone in the world and knew him to be a cultured and sophisticated man with discerning tastes in music, art, and science.

They had met in medical school and formed a friendship that lasted for over ten years. Both of them worked tirelessly researching the art of reanimation. As music was a passion to Andres Valentine, science and medicine were to Mikhail.

Other than traveling the world to see Valentine perform, but then who could blame Mikhail for having one or two vices.

Mikhail scanned the audience, wondering how many others had gone far and wide for the pleasure of hearing Valentine make auditory love to the masses? A slight burn of jealousy heated his veins.

He doubted any of them were as loyal a fan as himself. Not even Dante.

The lights dimmed. A hush fell over the audience. The curtains opened. A lone man walked across the stage. His presence heightened anticipation throughout the room: Maestro Wilhelm Kering, the symphony conductor and man who brought Valentine from busking on the street corners for change to a celebrated world-renowned artiste.

Rumors circulated that Kering was a cruel and nasty taskmaster who kept his musicians under his thumb as the devil imprisoned the wicked and unjust. Mikhail brushed off the idle comments as gossip. As any great man knew, there were those who strove to diminish another's success by railing against his accomplishments. How well Mikhail knew the scourge of quarrelsome tongues.

Kering tapped his baton against the music stand, and the musicians played the first strains of the opening piece. The tune was unfamiliar to Mikhail; the orchestra had not played it at any of their other concerts.

Dante leaned back in his seat, his expression guarded and gaze troubled. "At least we'll be treated to something new." The words were incongruous to his demeanor.

Mikhail ignored him and listened intently as the various instruments joined in, giving rise to a full spectrum of chords in perfect harmony. It was a melancholy tune that hearkened back to dark times. Ghosts from Mikhail's own past rose up to greet him. The memories uncomfortable while seated in a theater with hundreds of other people.

A solitary figure stood in the background, hard to see in the dimness near the rear of the stage. Then a bow moved across strings, and Mikhail's heart took flight.

Valentine.

The song went from sad to heart-wrenching within a few notes. Sorrow, agony, loneliness rose on the air and filled the hall with the power to make angels weep. This was Andres Valentine at his best. He poured all of his emotions into his violin, letting the audience hear his pain and allowing them to bleed along with him.

Why would the maestro open with such a gut-twisting tale? The story of the composer's anguish was tangible enough to touch. It floated over the crowd and whispered weeping words in their ears.

Mikhail turned to study Dante, who had gone terribly still beside him. His dark brows were pulled together in a frown, and his mouth turned down at the corners. His eyes were fathomless pools of disquiet.

For once it seemed Dante was as moved by the music as Mikhail.

By the end of the last movement, people all over the theater were dabbing their eyes with expensive handkerchiefs. Valentine held the last note out, milking the moment until the sound died a natural death.

The audience erupted into thunderous applause.

Valentine walked to the center of the stage and started off a lively melody, more suitable for a gypsy caravan than a world stage. He worked the bow across the strings as a desperate man works a fervent lover. He moved his hips and shoulders in a seductive dance as he walked back and forth across the stage, daring the audience to join in on his musical mania.

Though the selection seemed inappropriate for such an audience, it proved too much to ignore. People sat spellbound, their gazes wide and expressions eager. Mikhail wondered at the thoughts moving through their collective heads. A glance around the private boxes showed more than one being used as a dance floor for those who refused to remain in their seats. There was no question about their reactions to Valentine's music.

A steady thump came from beside Mikhail. He turned to see Dante keeping time with his foot. If even the immovable and dispassionate Dante became affected by the music, then there was surely magic in the air.

Dante raised a brow in challenge, then went back to watching the stage. He'd never really understood or appreciated Mikhail's fascination with Valentine's enormous talent, and yet he'd sat beside Mikhail in more concerts than Mikhail even remembered.

Mikhail had come to believe it was all a diversion for Dante. He enjoyed traveling and exploring different locales, and if he had to sit through a concert he'd heard several times before, it was considered a small price to pay. He was a true friend—more of the brother Mikhail never had.

The music spun on, painting tales in the air with sensuous rhythms, compelling harmonies, and interesting styles. By the time the lights came up for intermission, Mikhail had run the gamut of emotions, all the way from sorrow and despair to elation and joy.

Dante rose. "I need a strong drink."

Mikhail waved him away, wanting a moment to sit quietly with his feelings. This lonely obsession with Valentine was beginning to overtake his entire life. He'd not been home in weeks or even set foot on English soil. He had experiments to perform, research to conduct, and lives to save. None of them seemed to matter when he heard Valentine play. The rush of chemicals into his bloodstream was as addictive as opiates. Getting clean from them was going to take a strong constitution and iron will. Fortitude.

He curled his hand into a fist.

Perhaps if he had a chance to meet Valentine face-to-face, he'd feel differently. Oftentimes the illusions of a person—the fantasies drawn from smoke and mirrors—paled when introduced to reality. Mikhail didn't want to be disappointed, but feared Valentine was as eccentric as his musical tastes suggested. Not that it was a bad thing to enjoy variety, but there were rumors Valentine was also a bit of the prima donna.

Anyone who played with such unrestrained passion had to live with gusto. It made sense.

Perhaps that was the draw for Mikhail. He loved to see passion burning in the eyes of another human. To know he wasn't the only one whose body burned with an inner fire to create more than the world had to offer.

Dante returned to his seat, handing a glass of Scotch to Mikhail. "I thought perhaps you might need one."

"Thank you." Drinks weren't allowed in the boxes or anywhere in the audience, but Dante had never let rules stop him from doing exactly as he wished, and for once Mikhail was thankful of the personality quirk.

"Why do you look as if your last drum of preservation fluid leaked all over your lab?" Dante took his seat but turned to face Mikhail. His dark eyes were full of annoyance.

"Contemplating Valentine and how I would feel afterward if I had the opportunity to meet him."

"I believe the purpose of admiring an individual is to become excited with anticipation at the thought of being able to speak with them, to let them know of your existence." Dante gestured with his glass, moving it up and down to indicate Mikhail's demeanor. "You look like a man who'd rather wear the noose than meet the object of his infatuation."

Mikhail started to make a protest but knew better than to do so. It wouldn't wash with Dante. "I only thought that I might be disappointed if I met him. The illusion shattered."

Dante gave Mikhail a sage expression, nodding. "You have a point. I have very rarely been impressed with persons whom I've built up in my mind. It leaves a rather sour taste on the tongue for such things. Personally, I've decided they are better avoided."

Mikhail frowned. "When have you ever been intrigued enough by someone to build them up in your mind? You, who disdains everyone and everything?"

"Now. Now. Let's not get testy." Dante took a deep sip of his drink. "I'll have you know I am a man of many lusts and varying talents. Sometimes the two intersect."

"Sounds to me as if you're harboring some dark secrets, my friend." The thought of which made Mikhail uncomfortable and rather warm.

Dante shrugged in a dismissive manner.

The lights came down, and the rush for people to take their seats began. The end of intermission always had that look of the stockyard to it. People stood around the lobby too long, talking, gossiping, waiting to be seen by important people, and usually missed the first indication to make their way back to the theater proper. A mad rush ensued that clogged the aisles.

The second half of the concert was even darker than the first.

As the orchestra began the first strains of the finale, Valentine walked to the edge of the stage. "I want to thank you all for allowing me into your hearts tonight. This concert is a very special one for me, since it will be my final performance with the Kering Orchestra."

Shocked murmurs started around the audience.

Mikhail sat forward in his seat. He'd not heard correctly. Valentine leaving the most important and influential orchestra of the age? Leaving his maestro? For what? For where?

The answers were not forthcoming as Valentine placed his violin under his chin, drew the bow across the strings, and began to play a song that tasted of freedom.

Every note, every chord spoke of the spirit soaring higher, of reaching full potential and rising up to dance in the heavens. No one hearing the song could ever be anything but moved. It was both call to action and cry of triumph.

In all the concerts, and as many times as Mikhail had heard Valentine play, he'd never experienced the full thrust of that talent when allowed to express itself unhindered by convention.

Emotions too big to remain contained in the theater flowed out of the opera house and flooded the canals and sidewalks of the city. Venice came alive with the song of uninhibited liberation.

ANDRES CAME off the stage and headed straight for the dressing room while Herr Maestro accepted his accolades from the crowd. A slow chant of "Valentine" rose up through the theater to echo through the halls.

They wanted an encore.

For once in his career, he had no intention of paying the audience the compliment. Unkind payment for their years of devotion, but he meant to stand behind his decision.

The Great Valentine was no more.

He had enough money invested in ventures throughout the world to keep him in a comfortable style for the remainder of his life. No need to live frugally. Now he had only to collect his luggage and make it out of the opera house before Herr Maestro came off the stage, searching for him.

He'd arranged for a boat to take him to the port, where he'd booked passage for New York. Opportunity and greater anonymity awaited him in America. He didn't intend to squander it.

Nor could he live under Herr Maestro's thumb a moment longer.

Giving up the world stage was a small price to pay to reclaim his freedom. For too long Herr Maestro's puppet strings had strangled instead of supported Andres. Creativity and imagination had been pushed to the side to make room for avarice and greed.

Music had never been about money for Andres—it had been about his spirit. Back in his childhood, before Herr Maestro ever found him busking on the street corner, Andres's talent had soared on the wings of the wind. He had only to close his eyes and draw the bow across the strings to become transported to another world. One where notes rode the air in brilliant colors, dancing waltzes, polkas, and reels. In those days, he'd not known the art of reading music, nor placing his compositions on lined pages.

Form, instruction, and discipline had crushed his creative expression—his magic.

It had also introduced him to the world of the dark fae, and he had no desire to live in that realm or move within those circles any longer.

Andres shoved what few articles he'd allowed himself to take out of his trunks and placed them in one small black bag. He'd have no need for others. Everything he required already awaited him in New York. Oh, he'd been so careful in his plans, waiting for the precise moment of Herr Maestro's greatest triumph before sticking the knife in his ribs.

The man deserved so much worse.

Both he and his master did.

Andres pulled an extra hat and cloak from a hiding place behind the wardrobe. He'd stashed the articles there the day before; careful to conceal them from anyone who might be inclined to snoop through his belongings.

The nondescript brown wool would transform him from Andres Valentine, world famous violinist, to Andrew Etine, immigrant and music teacher. No one seeing him dressed as a common working-class man would believe him to be the premiere violinist in the world. Nor would they expect him to book passage in the steerage compartment on a steamship bound for America.

His humble beginnings had prepared him for much worse than any shipboard inconveniences might offer.

Andres started for the door, his hand on the knob, only seconds away from escape, when an angry voice shouted down the hallway.

"You ungrateful bastard! I'll rip your heart out for this."

The threat made Andres swallow hard. His heart beat in sixteenth notes. Blood sang in his ears. Time to pay the devil, and there was no demon worse than Wilhelm Kering and his master.

No. He'd not face another punishment for disobedience. He was a grown man with thoughts and dreams of his own. He no longer wanted to live in fear of masters who took and gave nothing in return.

The door burst open. Herr Maestro's face was livid with rage. His eyes glowed with anger. Even his hair stood up in violent disarray. He was the very image of a man beyond the reach of amendment.

Herr Maestro lifted a beefy arm and pointed a shaking finger in Andres's face. "Betrayer!"

Andres took a step back, cursing himself for showing fear. "I only want my freedom."

"I've given you more than that. I've given you the world—two worlds—and you've thrown it back in my face!" Herr Maestro pushed Andres back a few feet.

The blow nearly made Andres lose his breath.

He dropped his luggage, hat, and coat on the floor. He scrambled to his feet. Before he could retrieve the fallen items, Herr Maestro kicked them out of Andres's reach.

"You are never leaving my service. I won't let you."

"I won't be enslaved forever. I'd rather die first." Andres dove for his bag but caught a kick to the chin from one of Herr Maestro's shiny black shoes.

A maniacal light, both dark and awful, lit Herr Maestro's eyes. "Do not tempt me."

Andres swallowed.

Herr Maestro laughed. "What? Did you think death would release you? It will only ensure you never leave *his* side."

Andres's breath came harshly. Not even death would set him free.

He tried to step around Herr Maestro and got another shove for the effort. He tried not to cringe, to fall into old patterns. His body remembered too many nights of beatings until he was too weak to play the songs Herr Maestro wanted him to perfect. If Herr Maestro had opened his rotted heart, he'd have heard the *real* music Andres had played from the time he was old enough to hold a violin.

Andres should have stayed on that street corner busking for a few coins to buy a meal or earn a place to sleep. He should never have sold his soul for the price of fine clothes and luxurious surroundings. Andres knew what the so-called civilized world had yet to learn—no amount of money could turn a human heart to gold. Not a heart as black as pitch. Not one touched by the dark fae.

Herr Maestro stalked Andres across the room. None of the corners served as a good enough place to retreat until Herr Maestro's anger was spent. If Andres waited, pretended to acquiesce, he might be able to slip out in the early hours of the morning and still make his boat.

One look at Herr Maestro's eyes and Andres knew the anger wouldn't be gone anytime soon. His entire future hinged on this moment.

He waited until Herr Maestro moved to the left. Andres stepped to the right. For a large man, Kering was surprisingly quick. He caught Andres around the waist and pulled him around until he faced the window—and pushed.

Glass shattered. Wood splintered and broke, falling to the stone walkway beneath. People standing below, waiting for the gondolas to take them to their lodgings, screamed in panic.

Weightlessness.

Andres had never known plunging to his death would bring him a sense of peacefulness. He closed his eyes in complete acceptance and begged God to intervene on his behalf.

Maybe then he would be free.

Chapter Two

THE PRESS of people exiting the opera house moved in a slow surge. Tar flowed quicker than the patrons of the Venice Opera House. Women craned their necks in all directions, hoping for a last, fleeting glance of Valentine.

Stunned, Mikhail walked beside Dante. Numbness suffused his body. His arms hung limply at his sides. Why would a man on top of the world, the premiere musician of his kind, shuck it all to fade into obscurity?

The music told the story. Sorrow hung on every note until his announcement.

Dante bumped against Mikhail's arm. "Cheer up. Perhaps he'll go to London and join the symphony. It will be closer for you to travel."

Mikhail raised a brow. They had finally made it to the door and were headed to a gondola when screams rent the night.

"*He's dead! Valentine's been murdered!*"

"*I saw someone in the window. Herr Maestro killed him!*"

Mikhail stilled. Shock vibrated through his body seconds before his legs engaged and he ran, following the crowd. Dante kept pace behind him. They turned a corner and encountered a small knot of people.

Mikhail pushed through the crowd. "Let us through. We're physicians."

Spectators parted, allowing them access to the fallen man. Valentine lay broken on the stones. His head hung off the sidewalk, arms outstretched. Mikhail crawled out to the edges of the sea wall. He extended his arm and placed his fingers where a pulse normally beat strong and sure. There was nothing.

He glanced up at Dante, who gave an imperceptible nod.

"He lives," Mikhail lied to the crowd. "We have to get him where I can treat him."

Dante stood. He flagged down a passing gondola.

"Help me move him. Gently. Gently."

Several of the spectators helped Mikhail and Dante transfer Valentine's body into the gondola. A small window separated a subject who was beyond the reach of Mikhail's skills and one who might benefit from reanimation. More favorable results occurred if the initial serums were administered before the body cooled.

Mikhail felt Valentine's hands. Calluses created hard skin on Valentine's fingers, but the palm remained relatively warm. Not much time had passed between the murder and when they had pushed through the crowd.

A clock ticked in the back of Mikhail's brain, making him ever conscious of how long it took to navigate the waterways to their rented villa.

Light from the moon shone down into the boat. Shiny slivers of glass glittered in Valentine's hair. However much the moonlight shimmered around them, it was not enough to physically see any injuries, so Mikhail was left to do a tactile examination. Crushed skull, broken bones, open wounds, all could be assessed by feel. So far he hadn't felt the sticky telltale gush of blood to suggest there had been a fatal external puncture. That did not mean there wasn't one that bled him internally.

Mikhail felt around the back of Valentine's head. There was a slight depression in the occipital lobe, and mushy, spongy skin where blood pooled between skull and skin. He moved his hand down, feeling the neck for any unnatural movements of the cervical vertebrae, but found nothing of note.

He'd wait to examine Valentine's torso when they were in better light. A lacerated liver or ruptured spleen would spill blood into the peritoneal cavity. Without the heart pumping, blood tended to ooze instead of flow. He'd have to open up Valentine's belly and search for injury before reanimating him. Once the heart started beating, and blood poured through the veins and arteries, any injury to the vital organs or intestines might see the subject bleed to death. Mikhail found it prudent to ascertain all injuries before restarting the heart.

The gondola eased up to the villa entrance. Dante remained low as he moved to the back of the boat to help Mikhail get Valentine to the stairs.

"Henri!" Dante called to Mikhail's assistant. "We need assistance!"

Mikhail stood. "Let me get him under the shoulders. You get his feet."

"Wait for Henri."

The gondola rocked, nearly tipping. The gondolier began to shout at them in rough Italian. Dante turned and shouted back a few choice phrases that were better suited to someone living in the gutter than a man dressed for a night at the opera house.

Mikhail pretended not to hear the exchange, and in truth his attention remained focused on the man he tried to pull from the boat.

Henri hurried from the villa. He pulled a jacket on over his nightshirt and tucked the tails into his pants. "Good God, what happened to him?"

Mikhail looked up at his assistant. "Doesn't matter now. Help us get him into the villa."

"Hold on." Henri turned and ran back inside, then came out a few minutes later with a litter.

Henri placed one end of the litter into the gondola. "Slide him onto it and we can pull him across rather than lifting him out and you two trying to balance."

"Good idea." Mikhail lifted Valentine's shoulders and laid him on the end of the litter. Henri reached over and grabbed Valentine under the arms, then placed him higher on the device.

Dante stepped out of the gondola and helped Henri to get the litter up onto the stone walkway. Mikhail climbed out and met them on the dock.

He stayed at the foot and bent over. "On three. One, two, three."

They lifted as one and carried Valentine inside. Other gondolas had begun to ease up to the residence.

"Henri, get the servants out there to shoo them away. I don't want anyone trespassing or trying to get in here."

The last thing he needed was a bunch of curious admirers breaking into the villa and discovering his workroom. Unfortunately he didn't travel with all his equipment, only a few necessary pieces to conduct small experiments that might attract his attention while abroad.

"Take him into the laboratory. I want to perform a thorough evaluation on him."

"We're running out of time. He needs the serum."

"Prepare for surgery, and I'll get the syringes ready." Mikhail looked around for a place to put the litter. "We'll put him on the floor for now, then move the credenza into the middle of the room, and I'll use that for the operating table."

Under the circumstances allowances had to be made for less than perfect conditions. If he managed to restore Valentine to life, all the years of hard work and dedication would have been worth the sacrifice.

They lowered the litter to the floor with great care. Mikhail hurried to the small brown trunk he carried with him on all his excursions. He lifted the lid, then opened the side doors. Hinges unfolded to show row upon row of small vials. Anyone seeing the bottles would assume he was some sort of charlatan trading in snake oil and astounding cures. He reached into the trunk and pulled out one of the vials. Clear liquid left an oily residue on the side of the bottle as he spun the contents between his palms, bringing the liquid inside to body temperature.

The bottom drawer of the trunk contained various sizes of glass syringes with long needles of differing gauges. Quickly he assembled his materials and walked back to the credenza.

Dim light made it hard to distinguish between shadows and lividity. If blood had already begun to pool under the skin in places, then they had a real problem on their hands.

"Light! I need more light."

Mikhail didn't waste time. He held the syringe in his teeth as he ripped open Valentine's shirt. Soft golden hair covered his chest, growing into a trail that disappeared inside the waist of his well-tailored pants.

Using his fingertips, Mikhail felt along Valentine's breastbone, going just underneath the lower aspect. When he found his mark, he plunged the needle deep, going directly into the heart. He pushed the plunger down, delivering the serum directly into the area it would have the greatest impact.

"Henri, start cardiac compressions."

Henri climbed up on the table, straddling the inert Valentine, and began to push up and down to get the serum circulating. Since the heart was not pumping on its own, external forces had to be used in order to move the serum throughout the body. During the course of his experiments, Mikhail had determined this to be the best method for getting the life-restoring drug into all the systems and organs. However, if blood had already begun to pool and congeal, it complicated matters considerably.

Mikhail lifted Valentine's long golden hair off his neck. The barest edges of a deep purple bruise lay right below the skin. That might have been from the head wound. He'd have to do a more thorough assessment in order to determine if it was lividity in the true sense of the word or merely from the injuries.

Damnation!

Not only was he going to have to give multiple doses of the serum straight off, but he'd have to administer an anticoagulant as well. Doing so with a head injury was extremely dangerous.

Mikhail ran a hand through his hair. The sooner he got Valentine into the resurrection tank, the better off he'd be.

Sweat began to run down Henri's face.

"Hold." Mikhail prepared more of the serum. Henri wiggled back a bit to give Mikhail room to administer the second dose. "Resume."

Henri wiped at his forehead with the back of his sleeve before returning to his duty. Dante brought a rolling drinks cart over. The decanters, bottles, and glasses were gone, replaced by a tray covered in various sized scalpels, saws, and sutures. Mikhail doubted he'd need half that equipment, but it paid to be prepared.

"Keep going, Henri. I want to make sure the serum has gone throughout the body before I start to cut."

The special serum, once infused, would begin the process of regenerating cells, though it was only one part of the equation. Bringing a dead body back to life required time, care, and stages. No amount of serum, no matter how well administered, was going to do the job alone. Each stage prepared the body for the next level of care.

Mikhail stripped off his jacket and untied his neckcloth. He slid the garment off and threw it in the direction of the counter. An apron hung on a hook by the door. He hurried across the room and grabbed it.

"You can stop now, Henri. Take off his clothes and prepare him for surgery."

Henri climbed off the table and then slicked a hand through his short dark hair. "Where do you want to start?"

"I'll start with his abdomen. It will be a quick slice to see if there was any internal bleeding. If there wasn't, I'll close up and move to his head."

The thought of cutting all that long, beautiful hair off Valentine's head squeezed Mikhail's heart. Freedom sang in the shiny strands. If this was all Valentine got from announcing his intention to quit the Kering Orchestra, then Mikhail would be damned before he'd allow such a symbol of independence to be spoiled in a bid to reanimate the dead. He'd find a way to work and keep Valentine's hair intact. There was going to be enough of a shock when Valentine woke and realized he'd been plucked from the grave.

Naked, Valentine was an even more impressive specimen of manhood than he'd been on the stage. Mikhail tried not to fantasize over how it might be during the musician's recovery phase, or his gratitude for saving his life. Concentration had to remain on the task at hand, not daydreaming over future scenarios. A possibility remained that the process might not work on Valentine and all this would be for nothing.

Mikhail took the scalpel and made a midline slice down Valentine's abdomen. The layers of skin, connective tissue, and muscle were all separated very delicately. He peeled back the layers and looked around. All the organs were intact, no surface blood pooled anywhere within the peritoneum.

Gently he moved some of the organs aside to see down to the bottom of the cavity. That too looked clean. Mikhail took his time closing the incision, paying close attention to the sutures to prevent later scarring.

When he finished, he washed his hands in a basin. "Turn him over. I want to inspect the head wound now."

Henri glanced up. His eyes round and vulnerable in the low light. "Do you want me to shave his head?"

Mikhail dried his hands on a towel, shaking his head. "No. I have another idea I'm entertaining that will allow him to keep those golden locks."

Valentine was as famous for his hair as his violin playing. Mikhail stalked closer to the table.

Dante assisted Henri in turning Valentine onto his stomach. "You know you can shave a small swath through the hair and then cut the scalp in a cross section? Pull it back and fix the skull fracture by only exposing the area you need to see."

Mikhail gave Dante a knowing smile. "You've read my mind."

Dante's gaze slid from his. "Would you care for my assistance with the procedure?"

"I'd be honored."

Dante might be a dear friend and traveling companion, but he was also a talented surgeon. He'd preformed surgeries other physicians would never dream of touching.

Dante washed his hands and dried them. He took up a place on the other side of the table. He set to work parting Valentine's hair down the back of his head. "Henri, a very sharp razor if you please?"

Henri sorted through the instruments and found the one he wanted. He handed it to Dante, handle side out.

"Now we shave a small row of hair away, both vertically and horizontal. Widening the row made by the part."

The snick, snick of the blade against scalp sounded loud in the quiet room. Long strands of hair fell onto the floor in golden ribbons.

Dante looked over at Mikhail with a raised brow, and a sly smile. "You might want to save that for a souvenir."

Heat spiraled down Mikhail's body. Such an intimate memento, captured when Valentine was at his most vulnerable.

He glanced down at the strand that landed on his shoe. A desperate longing to pick it up and hold it to his nose, to take in the scent of the man, filled his heart, made his breath hitch. He flicked the fanciful notion away.

When Dante finished, he gave a nod to Mikhail. "Proceed."

The surgery was delicate and intricate. More than once, Dante offered an unsolicited opinion of which Mikhail had mixed feelings. Envy speared him. Dante made it all look effortless.

Mikhail pulled the scalp back to expose the bone beneath. The depressed fracture wasn't as bad on closer inspection as it had initially felt. The cement used to hold the fractured piece in place was made from a base of ground bone. Experiments had proved the compound had little to no side effects and very little infection.

When he finished fitting the skull back into place, he applied the cement, then strengthened it with small brass brackets. An added benefit of the brass in direct contact with the skull came when the electrical charge was added to the resurrection pool. Current would snake through the suspension and find the brass conduits close to the head, exciting the brain to begin bringing back conscious thought.

Mikhail would wait until they arrived home before he performed that crucial step. He wanted his own laboratory and materials, not ones he'd had to procure in a foreign country.

He placed the tiniest of sutures, knitting the scalp back together so Valentine might never know there had ever been an incision. The mission of any good surgeon was to put the patient back together with the least amount of visible evidence. Of course, in the case of an amputation that theory was irrelevant.

Mikhail tied off the last suture and cut the thread. "We can roll him back over and prepare to pack him in ice. I suggest we vacate the villa as soon as possible. We'll not be able to keep his death a secret for long."

Dante dipped his hands in the basin. "Members of the company will want to come and see him. Rich patrons will want to know how he fares and if he will return to the stage. The authorities will want to question us on his care to decide if Maestro Kering is indeed a murderer."

Mikhail looked down at the body lying facedown on the improvised operating table. One thing was for sure: Kering was a murderer, because Valentine as the world knew him was no more.

WILHELM KERING ran a sweaty palm down his face. The patrons were out for blood. He'd picked up Valentine's abandoned disguise and travel case and hurried through the back corridors to exit at the rear of the opera house.

Each heartbeat battered against his breastbone. His breath came in panicky little pants as he navigated the crowded walkways. People cried in protest and offense as he pushed them out of his way. He needed to put distance between himself and the scene of the crime.

A few streets over and he jumped into a waiting gondola. He couldn't return to his villa. The authorities would search there first.

That damn nosy bitch had looked up and recognized him. He had a good mind to find her and push her out a window.

Shock made his hands shake. He'd killed Valentine.

Oh God in heaven how had he given his passions free rein? How could the man have betrayed him in so fundamental a way? He'd given Valentine everything. Left him wanting for nothing. Was this any way to say thank you? By God it was not!

And Azgarth. Jesus weeping, Azgarth would not be pleased.

Wilhelm glanced over his shoulder, afraid the dark fae master moved through the crowds behind him, blowing fetid breath down his neck.

Whistles blew, echoing all through the canals. Not Azgarth, but the authorities who were hot on his trail. They'd find him unless he got lost in the crowd, but he had to think. To plan. Where was he going to go in order to get enough peace to let his mind work through his current problem?

At this point he doubted anyone in the orchestra would give him sanctuary. They would believe the accusations against him.

He doubted they would understand the fact that Valentine had called retribution down on himself. By announcing his separation from the orchestra, he'd declared war.

By threatening to leave Azgarth's patronage, he'd made it clear he no longer wanted protection.

But dead?

Oh God. He was going to be sick. Death might send Valentine straight to the fae realm, but Azgarth preferred to have deaths occur on his own terms, not those of his mortal agents.

As the gondola navigated through the canals, Kering heard the murmurings of the people who lined the walkways and crossed the bridges. Whispers of murder followed him all through the city. Suspicions floated on the air.

He didn't care what they said or how they viewed him—he was perfectly justified in throwing the haughty bastard out the window. The timing had just been poor.

Lights flickered in the distance. A hotel came into view.

"Take me there."

The gondolier made a noise in the back of his throat to acknowledge the command, then began to steer the boat to the opposite bank.

He threw the gondolier a few coins and scrambled onto the dock. Without stopping to look at those in the lobby, Kering sneaked to a seat behind a stand of potted trees. He put the bag on the chair beside him and began to look through the contents.

What he expected to find and what Valentine had deemed worthy to take with him on the run created a great disparity. A few changes of clothes—and rather humble ones at that—simple toiletries, hairbrush, and a ticket.

Kering picked up the small packet and looked inside. Passage to New York.

His shoulders slumped and his heart rose to his throat.

If Valentine had made the ship, he'd have been outside Kering's reach. America was the kind of place where people were able to lose their past and gain new identities. Down deeper in the pocket where he'd found the ticket were identification papers for one Andrew Etine. A new identity and booked into steerage. Valentine had planned long and hard for this. Leaving had not been a whim. He'd not been lashing out after the disagreement earlier in the day.

What had Valentine expected? Demands of any kind were forbidden in Kering's orchestra. Forbidden to Azgarth's chosen. He didn't care how much fame or money a musician brought to the company. None of them were above him. None of them above their fae master. They played for the enjoyment of humanity and Azgarth's pleasure. Nothing more.

Together they had made Valentine. Pulled him from the street and given him the world. Given him the ability to read music instead of merely playing the tunes that erupted from his uneducated mind. Kering had seen not only to Valentine's musical education but his letters and numbers as well. There wasn't a thing Valentine owned that wasn't due to Kering's generous nature.

And this—ticket and alias—were the thanks he'd received.

"...gravely injured. At first they thought him dead, but two physicians arrived and whisked him away."

Kering peeked out from his hiding place and watched as two women dressed in elaborate evening attire and escorted by two fine gentlemen walked across the lobby.

"We will go to the cathedral tomorrow and light a candle for his quick recovery."

Kering started to snarl at the party but refrained when one of the men said, *"Who would have thought that Maestro Kering was a fiend from hell, capable of murder?"*

His eyes narrowed in hatred. They had no idea what sacrifices he'd made to draw Valentine's talents to the foreground. To make him the premier violinist in the whole of the civilized world.

But the conversation did answer why Azgarth had not yet followed him. If Valentine was still alive, perhaps Azgarth waited to see what Kering did to recover him.

Ignorant barbarians.

Kering looked down at the ticket in his hand, then to the lobby door. What to do? Leave using Valentine's ticket and new identity or stay and regain control of the wayward musician?

Chapter
Three

Dr. Stanslovich made the decision to leave the city under the cover of night on the third day. During that time, the task fell to Henri to keep the subject as cold as possible. He had learned, over the course of his tenure with Dr. Stanslovich, to use chemicals as often as possible to affect change. Oftentimes the smallest of mixtures caused the biggest reactions. It was infinitely easier to obtain the chemicals he needed to keep the body cold than it was to acquire enough ice to pack it for the long journey home.

The desire to see London again was a constant ache in his gut.

Dr. Stanslovich had dragged Henri across the continent and across the Atlantic to America, all in the pursuit of seeing Valentine play. Why the good doctor needed Henri to accompany him, he'd as yet to discover. Henri, as Dr. Stanslovich's assistant, had never been allowed to attend the theater to hear the famous violinist. While Drs. Stanslovich and Savoy had gone to parties, balls, and entertainments, Henri had remained at their various lodgings reading, studying, and trying to perfect his vocation.

Becoming a physician was not an easy route for any man, even less so for a poor one. Opportunities were few and must be taken advantage of when offered. Henri knew he'd found a streak of luck when he'd been hired by Dr. Stanslovich. The position allowed him to continue his education, something Henri did not think possible after the untimely death of his former benefactor.

The situation wasn't all bad. He'd learned a lot working in the doctor's presence. The area of study Dr. Stanslovich traveled was controversial and in some places illegal. Papers written on the subject of reanimation were called immoral at best and gruesome at worst. Henri didn't agree with the critics. He found the work fascinating and ingenious, though at times a bit monotonous.

So far, the doctor had yet to allow Henri to administer the serum. He doubted he'd be allowed to on such an important subject.

He narrowed his eyes and considered the man who occupied one of the beds in the guest quarters. Valentine had been moved to the bedroom in case anyone from the orchestra decided to pay the villa a visit.

If so, there would be no hiding the fact Valentine was dead. Though the serum worked on the molecular level, it didn't give the body a false sense of blood flowing through the veins. A decided blue tint of death lingered around Valentine's mouth and eye sockets.

"You have no idea how much trouble you've been." Henri condemned the corpse, needing a way to vent his frustration that did not show his ill feelings to his employer.

Valentine didn't answer, nor did Henri expect it.

The serum held the body in a type of stasis, staving off the process of decomposition. It had fallen to Henri to ensure other methods were employed to assist in this very important aspect of the procedure. He'd seen what happened when stasis wasn't maintained. Horrific didn't even begin to describe the process.

The year before, Dr. Stanslovich had experimented on a cat that had been the unfortunate victim of arsenic meant for a rat infestation. Since the animal was found after it had rested in the arms of death a bit longer than most of the other subjects, the serum did not hold the body in stasis, but actually accelerated the decomposition process. Chemistry, and the science of devising compounds for the advancement of medicine, was often balanced on a razor's edge. A single molecule could completely change a reaction to have the opposite effect than intended.

The poor cat ended up dropping pieces of its flesh as it ran through the estate. Tufts of hair resembling fuzzy, black tumbleweeds rolled through the hallways. So much skin had gone missing that when looked at from a side view, the ribs and internal organs were visible. Dr. Stanslovich was forced to put the animal down again.

Then he'd flown into a rage and smashed half his bottles of serum.

Henri had been stuck with cleaning up the evidence of the good doctor's temper.

Footsteps on the marble floors caught Henri's ears a few moments before his employer entered the room. Dr. Stanslovich clapped his hands together in anticipation. "Are the preparations ready?"

Henri brushed hair back from his forehead. "All except putting Valentine in a box."

Dr. Stanslovich narrowed his eyes. "Do you have to be so crass, Henri? There are more refined ways to state the matter."

"Yes, Doctor."

Dr. Stanslovich frowned and crossed the room to place his arm around Henri's shoulder. "Why so out of sorts today? This is unlike you."

Henri glanced to the body on the bed. Even in death, Andres Valentine was beautiful. Almost to the point of being ethereal. The sight unnerved and made Henri decidedly uncomfortable. Considering he'd never set eyes on the man while alive, it was hard to imagine the impact of seeing him at full strength and impassioned in playing his violin.

He shook his head to clear the fanciful thoughts.

To cover his feelings, he reached for an explanation more understandable to his employer. "I'm worried about the gamble we're taking transporting him all the way to London."

Dr. Stanslovich let out a breath and gave a nod. "It is a risk, but one we must assume. I fear attempting the resurrection here in Venice away from my laboratory and essential equipment is testing fate. With every passing hour we come closer to exposure."

Henri understood that problem, but there were many miles separating the Grand Canal of Venice from the Thames of London. A lot could go wrong on the journey. Calculating every possible problem they might encounter on the way proved a study in stress.

The job fell on his shoulders to prepare the route and ensure all went smoothly as they fled the continent. If things fell apart or went sideways, it was going to be on his head. He had no doubt that Dr. Stanslovich would let him hang while he and Dr. Savoy came out unscathed. How else could it be?

Becoming dependent on a man of power and vision was not without its risks, but it also held great rewards if everything panned out according to plan.

With any luck, in another year or so he'd be ready to open his own practice and could leave his position in Dr. Stanslovich's employ. Where he'd go, he had no idea.

Dr. Stanslovich went to the bed and leaned down. He lovingly pushed the hair from Valentine's face. Henri had long ago suspected that the love of music had translated to an obsession for the musician. Watching Dr. Stanslovich now confirmed his feelings.

"Come, Henri. I need you to pump his heart."

Henri took a place by the bed to artificially move the serum through the blood, as he'd done with each administration.

Dr. Stanslovich inserted the needle under the breastbone, driving it in deep. He pushed the plunger down. Blood flooded back up into the barrel, thick and viscous. "Damn it."

Dr. Stanslovich threw the syringe on the bedside table. "I was afraid of this. Do not touch him until I return."

Henri came around to the opposite side of the bed and picked up the discarded syringe. He held it up to the light. The blood inside had congealed, moving around in the remaining suspension like a couple of blood pearls.

Doubt that Dr. Stanslovich could save the violinist reared its ugly head. What kind of temper would the good doctor show if his favorite obsession was allowed to succumb to something as mortal as death?

He studied Valentine's profile. "You've caused a lot of trouble, you know?"

This time when Dr. Stanslovich returned, he had Dr. Savoy in tow. "The blood is congealing in the veins. The serum isn't working as it's supposed to. It should be free-flowing at this stage."

Dr. Savoy placed his hands on his hips and studied the corpse as if offended the dead man did not acquiesce to his friend's command to cheat death. "Perhaps you miscalculated the dosage. He looks pretty solid. Dense of muscle and bone."

Now Dr. Stanslovich looked at Savoy in annoyance. "I can do something as simple as calculate dosages on estimated weights."

Dr. Savoy put his hand up to ward off the verbal affront. "I made a suggestion to cause, that was all. No need to get your tail feathers wet."

Dr. Stanslovich narrowed his blue eyes, giving his colleague a cold glare. "To suggest I am unable to administer the serum is really beyond the pale, even for you."

"There is no helping you once you're in a mood." Dr. Savoy turned to leave. "Call me if you decide you really do need my assistance. I'll be securing our accommodations."

Henri watched Dr. Savoy leave, his shoes making dull clicks on the marble. At times he really wanted to step out of his role of subordinate and give Dr. Stanslovich a dressing-down for how he spoke to his best and truest friend. Dr. Savoy didn't deserve to serve as the object of ire when all he did was make a suggestion that anyone asked to consult would have done.

Feeling the weight of a heavy gaze on top of his head as he bent over the bed, Henri glanced up. He said nothing, but waited for Dr. Stanslovich to speak first. When he was in this type of touchy mood, it was best to work as silently and efficiently as possible.

"You wish to say something, Henri?"

"No, sir. I'm waiting on further instructions."

Dr. Stanslovich made a noise in the back of his throat, implying great skepticism. "You think he's right."

Henri straightened the blankets over Valentine's inert form. "It has been my experience—limited though it might be—that oftentimes the best solutions are the simplest. Dr. Savoy wasn't suggesting you were incompetent, he was making a rational and educated suggestion based on the subject's mass and bone density."

Dr. Stanslovich let out a heavy sigh. "You're right and I snapped at him like a two-year-old who has had his favorite toy taken from him."

Henri gave Dr. Stanslovich a cheeky smile. "If you aren't careful, he'll book you into steerage on the voyage home."

Dr. Stanslovich's eyes rounded. "Heaven forbid."

Henri stood by to assist as Dr. Stanslovich pulled up more of the serum from one bottle, then filled a second syringe from another. The anticoagulant. This medication was even more volatile than the stasis serum. Too little and the results were as if none had been given. Too much and the subject bled out into the reanimation chamber, ruining the fluid.

Once administered, Dr. Stanslovich motioned for Henri to begin pumping the heart to mix the blood throughout the body. The process became more arduous the further out from time of death, but still necessary. If they were ever to see Valentine back to London and resurrected, all the steps had to be followed in order.

Since coming to work for Dr. Stanslovich, this was the longest Henri ever remembered having a subject outside the reanimation chamber. All the while they toiled for the past few days, he kept coming back to one small fact: there had to be a better way to keep the heart beating artificially after death than to pound on the chest whenever the stasis serum was delivered.

"All right. You may stop."

Henri wiped sweat from his forehead. Yes, there had to be a better way to achieve the same results. He turned from the bed and started out of the room.

"Where are you going?" Dr. Stanslovich called behind him.

"I've had an idea, and if it works, then there will no longer be a need for manual compressions." Henri had the satisfaction of seeing the good doctor's eyes widen in surprise and his mouth hang open in awe.

It paid to keep one's employer off-balance every now and then.

Henri chuckled as he walked down the corridor to the villa's door.

WILHELM HAD spent his last few days in Venice skulking around the villas near the one leased by a certain doctor named Mikhail Stanslovich. He hated he'd been brought so low by his damn passions, but he had to be certain of Valentine's condition. So far, Wilhelm hadn't been able to gain access to the villa either by bribing the servants or breaking in. Iron bars on the windows of the first two floors prevented him from crawling in that way. Servants guarded both the front and back entrances at all hours of the day and night, providing constant security and surveillance of the property.

From across the canal, he watched as a dark-haired man, no older than his midtwenties, left the residence by way of the front door. The man tipped his hat to the servant guarding the entrance, then hurried along the walkways away from the villa.

Wilhelm pulled his hat down lower on his head, disguising his face from passersby. He'd seen the papers and his likeness that had been plastered onto the front page wanted for the attack on Andres Valentine. He should have stayed and stood his ground instead of running like a common criminal. Then he'd have been able to explain to the authorities he'd tried to catch Valentine as the temperamental musician tried to take his own life.

The man he pursued climbed into a gondola.

No! He'd not lose him on the canals. There might be a chance he could pump the man for information of what went on inside the residence. No news had come of Valentine's passing, so Wilhelm had to believe he held on to the thread of life, even if it was as thin as spider silk. If even a small breath of life remained in Valentine, there was a chance to retake control of him and stay out of trouble with Azgarth.

He dropped down into a gondola and pointed at the one ahead of them. "Follow them."

The gondolier narrowed his eyes. A generous amount of coin in the man's hand kept him quiet. Hopefully it also ensured he didn't reveal Wilhelm's whereabouts to the authorities.

The first gondola pulled up alongside a row of shops, one of which looked more like a junk dealer than one selling new goods.

What did he need in such a place?

Wilhelm got out of the gondola, hurrying behind the man. The store was practically deserted of customers. Only Wilhelm's quarry and one other man dressed in a grubby jacket and ill-used hat perused baskets of odds and ends looking for only God knew what.

Wilhelm watched as the man dug through basket after basket, taking items out and placing them beside him on the floor. He crept closer, trying to see exactly what it was that held so much interest.

Thin copper wires, springs, a small crank handle, nuts, bolts, and various other pieces that looked like they belonged to a gutted music box. What would a doctor need with such obscure discards?

The man gathered up his treasures and gave some coins to the shopkeeper. As he started to leave the shop, the man turned and stared at Wilhelm. Recognition went through his body as an electric charge. Wilhelm pulled his hat lower on his head, trying to hide his features, but feared it was too late.

He swallowed. His heart turned a few somersaults before steadying.

This time Wilhelm didn't follow as a hound would a hare. There was no reason. He already knew the good doctor's residence. No sense in showing his hand. No sense in giving the doctor and his household a reason to call up the alert. If he got lost among the warrens of the canals, there was no way they'd find him.

He would wait until the cover of night, and then he'd return. Find a way to get inside the villa and recapture Valentine for good.

Chapter Four

Henri entered the villa. He'd picked up a copy of the paper to compare the picture he'd seen with the man in the shop. There was no mistaking the wild eyes and hollow cheeks, even under the brim of a large hat shoved low on his head.

He dumped his supplies on the workroom credenza.

Dr. Savoy lounged in a chair, pen to lips, pouring over a stack of papers. At Henri's intrusion, he glanced up. "Your employer has been anxious for your return."

"He should be a lot more than anxious. I believe I've just had a brush with Herr Maestro."

Dr. Savoy rose from his chair. "Are you sure?"

"I want to compare the pictures that have been in the paper with the man who followed me into the scrap store." Henri spread the paper out and studied the picture. The likeness was a formal portrait that showed the maestro in his finery, so unlike the man he'd seen in the shop. But then why would a man wanted by the authorities skulk around Venice instead of fleeing?

"If it is, we need to keep the servants vigilant until we can vacate tonight."

"The way I see it, he wants one of two things. To either clear his name when he finds Valentine alive or finish the job he started at the opera house." A well of fear opened low in Henri's gut. No matter what Herr Maestro wanted, the fact remained that Valentine was dead. None of them could afford discovery. There was still a long journey ahead before they were safely inside the confines of Dr. Stanslovich's estate.

"I don't care what the hell he wants." Dr. Savoy raised a dark brow, his expression menacing.

Deflated, Henri gave a shrug and turned away. If Dr. Savoy didn't find it odd that Herr Maestro remained in the city rather than fleeing in light of being seen by witnesses, then Henri wasn't going to spell it out for him.

He'd do what he could for the cause and not get involved in the intrigue. Though he still believed with every fiber of his being if questions were asked, Henri would be the one to hang.

The sun baked down on the villa. Heat radiated throughout the house. A scent of dead fish, raw sewage, and sea brine filtered through the house. This was one place he'd not be sorry to see disappearing in the distance.

Humidity stuck his clothing to his back. He stripped out of his jacket and sat down at the worktable. There weren't that many hours left before they were scheduled to leave. The journey would go a lot smoother if he managed to get his creation to work.

Hours passed as he constructed a box small enough to fit around Valentine's chest undetected, but large enough to keep the heart beating without having to use manpower in the effort.

A shadow fell across his work.

"It doesn't seem like much." Dr. Stanslovich picked up the box. Copper cables dangled from the sides. "How is it supposed to work?"

"Turn the handle and see."

Henri leaned back in his chair, watching as Dr. Stanslovich began to turn the crank. With each turn the spring grew tighter, the handle harder to move. He let it go. A tiny arc of current traveled down to the end of the copper wire.

Dr. Stanslovich dropped the device and stuck his hand into his mouth. His gaze hardened. Anger covered him like a mantle. "You should have warned me it conducted electricity."

Henri gave a shrug. "It's not finished yet."

"What more is it supposed to do?"

Henri took the device back and turned it over. "Two plates will attach here. Once the handle is turned and the tension built, the plates will move up and down simulating the compressions. The wires connect to two conductive pads to deliver current into the heart. Once it starts, it should keep it beating."

Dr. Stanslovich considered the box. "This might prove to be helpful once we get him into the resurrection chamber."

Henri made a face. "Would you risk changing the process? I only meant for this to aid in crossing to England."

"With a working pump, we'll have better distribution of the serum. This might solve a few of our problems." Dr. Stanslovich opened his hand, waiting for Henri to put it in his palm.

Henri obliged.

"This is an inspired invention, Henri."

"Thank you. I do have my uses at times."

Dr. Stanslovich gave Henri a wry grin. "You have proved yourself more than useful. I'd even go so far as to call you invaluable."

Unexpected heat rose to Henri's cheeks. He looked away so his employer wouldn't realize the compliment struck him so deeply. Many years had passed since he'd last felt appreciated.

The instrument in front of him blurred as tears came unbidden to his eyes.

His late benefactor, Mr. Portiss, had been a gentle soul who had been set on by thieves in an area of London he'd no business going to unaccompanied in his fancy clothes and full purse.

Henri had not only defended and sent his attackers away, but had gotten Mr. Portiss medical attention. As a reward, the rich tradesman had sponsored Henri to medical school.

He'd died before Henri had finished, thus the need to find work to complete his education.

Nothing had ever come to Henri the easy way. Every piece of luck and tangible good he called his own, he'd worked hard to achieve.

Henri blinked a few times, careful to keep his head down and avoid eye contact. He didn't want Dr. Stanslovich to see the depth of emotion he'd raised by a simple act of praise. Such instances were few and far between. Always had been.

"Should we test it before Valentine is prepared for the trip to England?"

The suggestion had more in common with an order.

"When it's finished. I still have to connect the plates. I'll bring it up to Valentine's room when it's completed." Henri took the appliance back and set about attaching the various plates and paddles to the device's main compartment.

Dr. Stanslovich stood there for a moment longer before taking himself off to another part of the villa. Good thing too. Henri didn't know how much longer he could hold back his emotions.

He let out a slow, uneven breath before picking up the tiny screwdriver and finishing the work. Most of the packing had been done by the servants. Only the clothes he currently wore remained outside his cases. He'd wear his current suit on the boat. Steerage didn't discriminate when it came to wardrobe.

Even as Dr. Stanslovich's assistant, he'd been relegated to the lower classes. Always a worker, never an equal. Even in the grand estate Stanslovich called home, Henri had a room in the servants' quarters.

One day he'd be able to look on Drs. Stanslovich and Savoy as colleagues. They might eventually look to him as a friend. Or would the disparity in their current stations persist into the future? Would he always be considered the uncultured and unsophisticated assistant long after he'd earned the right to use the title of doctor?

Henri turned the last screw a final time, then flipped the box over. If this device didn't work as envisioned, he wasn't going to lament the fact he'd tried and not provided. A long line of crafty inventors with sheds full of useless items preceded him. The real test of a man was being creative enough to see a need and try to fill it.

He stood from the workbench and then placed his tools carefully in the pack. Those particular items would travel with him. He had no idea if he'd need to tighten or loosen the tension on the spring during the journey.

A bell rang, calling them to the midday meal.

He didn't have time to eat.

"The servants' dining room is in the other direction." Dr. Savoy stood on the landing, adjusting his cuffs. The man was always impeccably groomed, even in unbearable heat. Often Henri wondered if he was real or illusion.

Henri waggled the device at Dr. Savoy. "I have work to do."

"You need to eat while you can."

Henri narrowed his eyes. "Why? Do you know something I don't?"

Dr. Savoy raised his hands. "Not in the way you mean."

Henri watched as Dr. Savoy continued on down the stairs. The wry remark hung on the air in a ghost of possible meanings.

Did he expect trouble in the crossing to England? Feeling that something would go afoul was a constant companion in Henri's gut. He found it oddly comforting that Dr. Savoy might feel the same.

He continued on to Valentine's room.

A sweet scent of flowers permeated the room, trying in vain to mask the astringent smell of the medicinals.

Henri strapped the box onto Valentine's chest, centering the plate over the sternum and the paddles on the upper left and lower right chest. The handle cranked easily at first, then got harder as the spring grew taut.

He let go and watched in fascination as the plate pumped up and down, moving the chest an inch or more. The depth wasn't as great as what he managed manually, but it got the job done.

For the moment, that's all they needed.

"THERE HAS been a change of plans." Mikhail stood in the doorway, watching as Henri made the last few preparations before placing Valentine into the transport container.

Henri glanced up. His movements stalled. "Cutting it a bit close to change plans now, aren't you?"

"There are still too many people camped out on the walkways and bridges watching the villa." Mikhail glanced over his shoulder. Knowing they were under scrutiny made his skin crawl. "We'll dress him in a nightshirt and take him out the front, right past those who will take the story of seeing Valentine to the press."

Henri made a face. "And tell them what? That we're taking him to England to continue treatment?"

"Yes. He's had no family come forward. No one from the orchestra has done more than stand on the walkway and stare at the edifice." Such a sad situation for a man who was beloved the world over. Mikhail's gaze fell to the dead violinist. "As far as I'm concerned, he is my charge and I take that duty very seriously. If it means taking my patient back to England, so be it."

Henri cocked his head. "This might actually work better than our original plan. Who is going to question a physician who keeps his patient in his stateroom? Administers drugs to an injured man?"

Mikhail pushed off from the door. "Help me change him into a nightshirt."

Clothes would only do so much to keep the curious at bay. Other precautions had to be taken to hide the fact Valentine was in a state somewhere between life and death, hovering, waiting for rescue.

Once they had him in nightclothes, they moved him to a litter and placed white bug netting around it to keep the odd stares at bay and the curious from seeing too much.

Two servants carried the litter to the gondola. Mikhail walked solemnly behind. Dante climbed into the boat first, guiding the litter down.

Spectators stood along the bridges, watching the scene unfold. Questions were yelled to him in Italian, German, and French, all asking what was to become of Valentine. Mikhail ignored their pleas. It had to be enough that they saw the procession to the gondola and out of the city.

Teary fans followed them down the waterways and to the expanse of the Grand Canal. Mikhail did not turn his head to acknowledge them or give them any sign of comfort. At this point in the resurrection, the results might go either way—as it would with any serious injury without benefit of his serum and expertise.

Several times on the ride to the shipping port, Mikhail felt the gaze of someone watching, waiting with the intent of malice. It differed from the stares and teary eyes of the true fans. This was something more, something dark. Vengeful.

Mikhail placed his hat lower on his head and brought his coat collar up despite the oppressive heat. Tracked and hunted like the most common of prey.

Dante raised a brow, looking at him as if he knew the reason for Mikhail's distress. Did he feel it too? A quick glance to Henri didn't reveal he had felt any disquieting undercurrents. No, the most faithful assistant was bent over Valentine, seeming to look busy caring for their patient as they paddled ever closer to the port.

By the time they arrived at the port and boarded, Mikhail was ready to jump out of his skin, leaving nothing but his skeleton to face the world. The sensation of thousands of bugs crawling over his body raised the hair on his arms, sent tingles down his legs and made him startle at every noise.

Easy. It's just the emotion of the moment. Of the escape from Venice and the danger of the crossing. You should feel exhilaration, not paranoia.

Once settled in his modest stateroom, with Valentine on one of the beds, Mikhail sat at the small writing desk and took stock of his surroundings. He'd not rest easy until they were on English soil and secured behind the sturdy gates and walls of his estate.

A knock sounded on the door.

"Enter." Mikhail looked up from the blank pages he'd not been able to find the words to fill.

Dante entered and closed the door behind him. "We are about to leave the dock."

Mikhail gave a nod. "I heard the horn."

"Do you want me to sit with you until we are safely into open water?"

Mikhail let out a low, self-deprecating laugh. "You think I'm acting like a child."

Dante took a seat in the chair across the room. "I'd be a liar if I told you I didn't feel something prowling for us on the canal. It was like that time we got lost in Paris and drunk on absinthe."

Mikhail remembered the night in question with crystal clarity. They had gone to Paris for a medical consortium. After drinking more absinthe than they should have been allowed, they took a wrong turn and ended in an impoverished neighborhood with something dark and festering chasing them. The experience was enough to sober them up quickly. Until that night, Mikhail had never believed in the hallucinogenic properties of the drink, but he never could explain where the bruises on his torso had come from or the bite marks on his legs. Other than a brief infection that was easily cured, they'd never experienced any ill effects from the attack—though every once in a while that same sensation of being followed returned.

Mikhail ran a hand through his hair. "I only hope this time we don't wake up with our legs looking like chew toys."

Dante glanced away from Mikhail for a moment. "You were always too pragmatic to believe in what you couldn't see or solve through science."

Mikhail blew out a weary breath. "Not this discussion again."

"You know my feelings on the matter."

"Yes. I do. And I'm sorry I don't share your beliefs." The very idea that a man as educated and brilliant as Dante Savoy believed in beings from what he labeled the shadow realms fascinated Mikhail. These beings could be anything from dark entities such as demons to fairies and beings meant to test man's mettle and cause harm and create mischief.

Mikhail had never believed in anything other than science. He didn't even believe in the teachings of either the Protestants or Catholics, and the fact wars had been fought over that particular separation for centuries baffled him.

People were oftentimes blind to reason when they took stock in the unreasonable.

Truth be told, if anyone offered him proof that something as esoteric as heaven existed, he'd be the first to offer an apology to those he'd offended. The same for magic.

His practices in his lab, for instance, were based on science and chemical reactions, yet anyone witnessing the marvels he'd achieved might swear he'd dabbled in the occult.

Vibrations shimmered through the ship as they began to pull from the dock. A bit of the tension left his shoulders. His breathing eased.

Dante sat across from him. His gaze had taken on a dark, sulky look.

Mikhail felt a pinch of guilt. "Do not be offended by the stirrings of an old argument between us. What purpose does it serve?"

"It serves to show you the other side of the world. The unseen side. The one you feel you are too intelligent to admit might actually be there in front of you." Dante stood and made a circuit of the small sitting room, looking more the caged lion than a man at the moment. "What do you think bit us that night?"

"A dog or other small canine—a fox maybe."

Dante laughed. "The bite pattern wasn't consistent with a dog, fox, wolf, or herd beast of any kind. I know. I've spent years trying to match that pattern to all the known animals and have come up with nothing."

Sympathy for his oldest and dearest friend swam through Mikhail's veins. This of all nights was not the one to lay bare all the old wounds. Perhaps it showed how much the atmosphere had been affected on the canal, if Dante chose to bring up topics they'd agreed to never discuss.

A rumble from the engines hummed gently in the background. Dante stood there staring at Mikhail as if he wanted to say something but debated it.

"You might as well get it out in the open, Dante. What do you want to say?"

Dante gripped the back of the chair, his knuckles blanching white. "Have you ever wondered why your experiments only succeeded after that night? That you were able to resurrect anything at all when up until that point all your endeavors to create a usable serum were failures?"

Umbrage at the audacity of his closest friend pumped through his veins in a hot river. "They worked because I found a mistake in the calculations and corrected it. They worked because I changed to a base with greater stability. They worked due to good science and due diligence, not from some esoteric theory that cannot be proved."

Dante pursed his mouth and gave a slow nod. "Believe that if you will, but I know it was not that simple."

"Has the humidity addled your brain, man?"

"No. These past few months, traveling the globe for the sole purpose to indulge an obsession with Valentine, I've had a lot of time to observe the world." Dante rubbed a hand around his mouth. His eyes were troubled. "There are things at work that we haven't even begun to understand, and they can't be explained away by scientific theory."

With that, Dante offered a small salute and left.

Mikhail sat quietly, contemplating Dante's mood. He'd promised to stay until they were out in the open sea. Their conversation must have bothered him in order for him to walk away with only the most benign of salutations.

Memories stirred, unable to be contained under the tight lid where he'd kept them since the night of the attack. All his reasons for not wishing to dwell on the marks were valid. He'd challenge any professor at Oxford or Kings College to disagree with him.

Tangible and irrefutable evidence leading to a logical and verifiable conclusion were the hallmarks of good, solid research. If he were to do as Dante suggested and give over to fanciful thoughts—well, that way led to ruination and chaos.

He glanced through the bedroom door at Valentine's still form. The only movement was that of the ingenious contraption provided by Henri.

Deep in his soul, the first movement of the song the orchestra opened with at the Venice concert rose. It bloomed outward, a rancid rose with poisonous petals.

The pen slid from his fingers, dropping with a dull thud onto the carpet.

Now he remembered where he'd heard that melody. A street musician had played it the night he and Dante were attacked.

Mikhail curled his hand into a fist and fought down the speculations that arose. No. There was no room for wayward thinking. Coincidence. Pure and simple. The tune was probably an old folk song spread over the continent by traveling players and gypsy caravans. Its origins untraceable, but tradition bountiful.

At length he retrieved his pen from the carpet and returned to the pages, pushing all thoughts of odd songs and past attacks from his mind.

CHAPTER
FIVE

HENRI SAT in the resurrection chamber, writing by the glow of the ultraviolet light. Valentine lay suspended by straps and pulleys, submerged in the reanimation fluid. So far there had been no change in the subject's condition.

He recorded his observations in the ledger under an anonymous case number. For now, Valentine was known as Subject Forty-Two.

How impersonal, to be reduced to a number? Of course documentation must be provided by stripping the subject of all human qualities. Observations were more unbiased when distance remained between scientist and project. Though how Dr. Stanslovich intended to remain distant and unaffected when the nature of the test subject was already an obsession, Henri hadn't the slightest idea. To him, the experiment was tainted before it began.

The question remained whether Dr. Stanslovich would have attempted to reanimate any of the other musicians of that orchestra had they suffered a similar fate. Henri doubted it very much.

Behind him the tank burbled, gurgled, and belched. Liquid splashed over the side, sending gooey drops across the ledger page. Henri turned.

Valentine was awake!

Frantically Valentine tried to break the bonds that held him under the surface of the resurrection fluid. His eyes were wide, and his mouth opened and closed in panic.

Henri jumped from his seat and ran up the scaffolding to the top of the tank.

"Dr. Stanslovich! Come quick!"

Henri hurried to the flywheel and cranked the handle, lifting the straps and, in turn, Valentine from his wet prison. Coughs erupted as he broke the surface.

As quickly as possible, Henri caught Valentine and pulled him to the staging platform, then unbuckled the restraints and rolled him over onto his side. He used his hand to wipe the goop from Valentine's eyes, nose, and mouth.

"It's all right. I've got you. Try to relax." Henri tried for a center of calm he didn't feel, hoping that by hearing the gentle tone of his voice, Valentine might respond.

Valentine tried to grab Henri's hand, but fine motor skills were slow to recover—if at all.

A well of despair hit Henri like a shock wave from an explosion. It threw him back at least a foot, leaving him shaking his head to clear it.

"What in all the blazing hells was that?"

He glanced down. Damn and blast, he'd forgotten to turn off the current from the compressionator. When he reached for the appliance, Valentine hit at his hand a few times.

Henri met the musician's gaze. Fear, confusion, and pain were all mixed in a soup of emotion that tore at Henri's heart.

No. He would not fall victim to those eyes.

Goo coated Valentine's dark lashes, turning them into spikes, framing his eyes and making him look even more pathetic.

Henri kept his gaze locked with Valentine's, hoping that by doing so Valentine might understand the intent of what he meant to do, if not the actual task. "I'm going to remove this last buckle from your chest. You don't need it anymore."

When no protest came, Henri unbuckled the strap and slid it out from under Valentine's ribcage.

"See? That's much better. More comfortable."

Valentine hadn't taken his steady hazel gaze from Henri's. The fear morphed bit by bit into trust.

"That's a good man."

The echo of shoes running on marble preceded the appearance of Drs. Stanslovich and Savoy to the chamber.

"What are you doing?" Dr. Stanslovich started forward with thunder on his brow.

Henri held up a warning hand. "Easy. He woke up and he's frightened. I managed to get him calmed down some, but not entirely. Gentle voices and touches or he'll panic again."

An annoyed huff came from Stanslovich's direction, but Henri didn't bother to break eye contact with Valentine to give him another look. "We need to dry you off and move you to a more comfortable place. All right?"

No answer came.

"We need a bath blanket up here. He's shivering."

Savoy grabbed one from the cabinet and handed it up to him as Stanslovich climbed the stairs.

"This is the doctor who is taking care of you. His name is Mikhail Stanslovich, and he's not going to harm you. Trust him as you've trusted me so far."

Valentine reached out when Henri tried to back away slowly. He opened his mouth as if to speak. No words. The effort only caused him to cough again.

"Dry him off, Henri. Then we'll take him to the exam table."

"He's shaky as a new foal. May I suggest we carry him down the stairs? I don't think he will be able to walk for a while."

Stanslovich glanced up sharply. There were angry words he wanted to say, a reprimand he bit back. Henri didn't rightly care. He'd been the focus of the good doctor's temper before and no doubt would be so repeatedly during his tenure.

He started the process of drying the viscous liquid from Valentine's body, not unlike the blood covering a newborn. In a sense, the resurrection, or reanimation, of a previously dead body was a birth of a sort. The process was consistent with a new beginning, a brand-new life.

As he worked, he felt Stanslovich's gaze on him, watching, looking for fault or… what? Henri had no idea why the doctor had gotten so quiet all of a sudden.

They worked in concert, getting Valentine down from the platform and onto the exam table. Dr. Savoy brought over a nightshirt to put on Valentine after the examination.

Stanslovich felt along Valentine's neck, brachial, radial, femoral, popliteal, and pedal pulse points. "His pulses are strong and good at all points. Capillary refill remains slightly sluggish, but is improving by the minute. Eyes are clear, with very few broken vessels. Hearing appears normal at close range using average decibel levels. Reflexes are slow, motor skills poor."

Henri watched the examination with detached clinical observations. Stanslovich may have pretended the same, but it was clear to Henri that he was anything but clinical. Fine tremors shook his hands as he touched Valentine's skin. His breathing grew harsh and fast the longer he worked. His color had risen quite high across his cheeks. All tells that he was not detached.

This was not going to end well for the doctor. Not at all.

Either his pet project was going to regain his own faculties and begin making decisions for himself, or he was going to remain a burden and be nothing like the legendary Valentine. Both scenarios would prove a disappointment for Stanslovich on a personal level. Henri did not have to read minds to predict the outcome.

All the while he spoke and Henri recorded Stanslovich's observations, Valentine kept his eyes directed not on the doctor, but on Henri.

The assessment might go faster if Valentine had retained any intellect, but it seemed for now he struggled to even understand the context of his surroundings.

The longer Stanslovich worked, the more one thing became apparent: Valentine didn't trust him. He never struck out or pulled away when Stanslovich reached to examine another appendage or asked him to attempt some skill, but he kept that pleading expression turned in Henri's direction, as if to ask for intervention from the examination. Perhaps some of the movements caused discomfort.

Valentine ran a hand over his stomach and frowned when he came into contact with the rough threads of the sutures.

Henri took his hand and gently moved it away from the vulnerable area. "We didn't know if you had internal hemorrhages, and needed to explore. You might have bled to death."

Valentine frowned. His arm started up for his head, so Henri caught that too and guided it back to rest beside his body. "You also hit your head rather hard."

Stanslovich glanced up sharply. "Do not tell him anything more. You'll contaminate his memory, and I want to know how much he retained from before the accident."

Accident?

Henri didn't want to point out that this was no accident, and indeed they had all read the accusations of attempted murder. Read the accounts and speculations in the daily papers. Even the ones in London had reported the incident that had brought Valentine to England's shores.

Unfortunately the reports had beaten them back to London, and too many people had been waiting for their boat to land. They'd had to stay on board a few extra days and disembark farther up the coast, then arrange for carriages to bring them to the estate.

What had made Stanslovich think he'd be able to smuggle Valentine into England without a lot of fanfare or speculation in the morning papers? News that Valentine was alive and convalescing with his English physician was the talk of the London social season, if listening to the conversations on the street and in shops was any indication.

But what would Stanslovich do when he could no longer contain his creation? Surely even a man brought back from the dead was allowed his freedom?

Somehow Henri thought Stanslovich might take exception to that.

"I have some serum prepped and ready in the syringe. Give him a half dose and see if that helps to relieve some of the stiffness in his limbs." Stanslovich made a shooing motion to Henri.

Henri squelched his surprise at being given the task. Coming from Stanslovich, it was a decided honor.

He only wondered what he'd done to deserve it.

ANDRES WATCHED through blurry vision as the man with the kind eyes turned away. He'd awakened in a viscous bath that continued to make his skin itch. How he'd arrived in this predicament he hadn't even a vague notion.

Every attempt to communicate with those caring for him came out as a garbled wail without form or flow. Even his hands refused to move to his commands to get his point across. So many questions and no way to ask them.

If Kind Eyes returned to the bed, he'd try again. The man's gentle voice was patient and soothing, instilling immediate trust. The one he'd introduced as the doctor was too intense and rather frightening. There was an elusive quality to his bearing that reminded him of someone, though at the moment he did not know who.

And the pain.

It tried its best to consume him. Radiating jolts of agony moved from the base of his skull forward to right behind his eyes. Tears leaked down his face and into his hair.

If they'd only give him something for his present relief, he'd let them do whatever else they wanted to his body. He didn't even care.

Kind Eyes worked at a small table. Andres tried to angle his head to keep the man in his line of sight, but the doctor blocked his view.

He raised his hand to try to move the doctor out of the way, only to have the doctor place his hand back on the table.

Oh, the doctor didn't even try to understand. If Kind Eyes was near, Andres felt safe.

The doctor barked a few commands, sending pain ricocheting through his head, a bullet with no target. He tried to make out what the doctor said, but heard only garbled words. Backward. Wrong. Voices sounded as if he were still submerged in the thick liquid. The fluid had probably gotten into his ears, blocking sound from hitting his eardrum naturally.

Kind Eyes returned to the bed. In his hand was a syringe with the largest needle Andres had ever seen. Not that he'd had much experience with them. Or had he?

A slight pinch, a rush of fluid, and feeling began to return to his limbs. Pins and needles sensations heralded that his feet and hands were coming alive.

Bit by bit the pain in his head began to recede and his vision cleared. Whatever had been in that syringe was like manna from heaven.

His tongue remained as thick as a slab of meat. A horrible coating that tasted of death by carpet. The drug did nothing for his hearing.

With hands that were easier to move, he lifted his right arm and went for his ear.

Kind Eyes started to take his hand away, but then a considering expression crossed his face. He moved closer and bent down, looking into Andres's ear.

More garbled words, but they were soft, reassuring in tone if not in context. He said something to the doctor, then left again.

The next few moments were spent in wet discomfort as Kind Eyes cleaned Andres's ears with what smelled of a medicinal lavage. It didn't precisely hurt, but it made him want to shake his head like an old dog.

When the procedure was complete, he could hear with greater clarity, but the words were still difficult. These men did not speak his mother tongue. Where was he?

He knew the language. Had spoken it before—knew it almost as well as his own.

Kind Eyes leaned closer. Andres's heart fluttered at his nearness. "Is that better?"

Andres nodded. His throat remained dry and made it hard to speak. He mimed his hand in the motion for something to drink. Anything on his parched throat was better than the scratchy dryness he had now. Even some of that medicinal Kind Eyes had shot into his ear.

"Henri, get him some water."

A light grew in Andres. Henri. Kind Eyes's name was Henri. It was lovely to hear the name with its French pronunciation. He didn't feel nearly as alone as before—the sound of the letters so familiar and right.

Henri returned to the bed and lifted Andres by the shoulders into a sitting position. His head spun. Whirled around like a cup on a stick. He held still for a moment, then gave a nod when he was ready to drink.

Andres tried to hold the cup when Henri brought it up. "No. Let me. You're still a bit shaky."

His throat was so raw even water didn't want to go down. Swallowing was difficult, painful.

"Take your time. There is no need to rush."

Andres locked gazes with Henri. He'd never known such compassion or gentleness from anyone—but he didn't remember why. Memories were distant things, having more in common with stars than thoughts.

He managed to finish most of the cup of water before he'd gotten his fill.

"Is that enough?"

Andres cleared his throat again, but his yes came out as a squeak of sound.

"Was that a 'yes'?"

Andres blinked—he couldn't manage to repeat the word.

Henri smiled. "Dr. Stanslovich, I believe his voice is returned."

Stanslovich. The name sounded Russian or Slavic. It explained the slightly slanted accent, though from what little Andres had heard, Stanslovich had a better grasp of the language.

Where had he—Andres—learned to speak English?

About the only thing he remembered with any clarity was music.

Stanslovich turned a stern gaze to Henri. "He will improve over time."

The confidence with which Stanslovich imparted that opinion was nice to hear, but Andres would rather know how he'd come to be in his current situation. Whatever had happened, he'd been grievously injured.

A well of uncertainty opened low in his gut. He was supposed to be somewhere. Not here. Why was it all so fuzzy and distant, as if his life happened to another?

He struggled to get the question out and never quite succeeded. Tired beyond all reason, he lay against the pillows and fell back to sleep.

Dreams stretched out before him, without rhyme or reason. Was this his life or that of the unconnected subjects that cropped up during sleep? Had his life been filled with so much darkness, hiding in every corner, under every bed, and behind every door?

He came awake with a start.

A soft glow of gaslight came from the corner of the room. Full night had turned what lay beyond the windows into an obsidian forever. He'd never liked looking out the windows once the sun went down, afraid that the darkness might recognize him.

A shadow moved across the wall. "You're awake."

Henri.

Andre's heart began to calm a bit at the knowledge. He pointed to the open drapes.

"You want them closed?"

Andres nodded.

Henri stalled by the window and looked up, leaning against the ledge. "I've always loved the moonlight. It's full tonight. Beautiful."

Henri hadn't been touched by the horrors that infected the night. His heart and mind were pure, unspoiled. He sent Andres a sly smile. "I've gotten some of my most inspired ideas on nights like this."

"Darkness is a lonely emotion." The words were low, garbled, barely recognizable.

Henri frowned. "Darkness of the heart maybe, but the night is made for possibilities."

Weren't they one and the same?

"I prefer sunshine and fresh air."

Henri snapped the drapes closed, then came over to sit by the bed. "Do you know your name?"

"Andres."

"Is that all?"

Andres thought about it for a moment. He had a name, but it was unimportant. From this moment on, he could be anyone he wanted. Maybe even hide from whatever lay beyond the window.

"Do *you* know who I am?"

Henri canted his head. "Of course, but my knowledge of your identity isn't the issue at the moment. We need to ascertain how much you remember."

Andres tried to push up from the bed, but his arms refused to support his weight. "So weak."

"That's to be expected. It's early days yet for your recovery. Though I will admit, you have made an amazing recovery so far."

"From what?"

Henri turned away. He stood. "That is not for me to say."

"Please do not let Stanslovich dictate your conscience. I can tell by your face you want to tell me."

Henri gave a bitter laugh. "He is my employer. If I do not follow his instructions, I'll be discharged."

Frantic to have the company, Andres held out his hand. "Stay. Please."

"For a little while, but you need to get some sleep."

At the moment, he had no want for sleep, afraid the scattered images might return.

He closed his eyes and held a vision of Henri until he fell asleep.

CHAPTER SIX

MIKHAIL WENT back over the notes compiled since taking on Valentine's case. All of the dictations, observations, and medications were recorded by his own hand or that of Dante or Henri. He trusted their attention to detail, and yet something had gone wrong.

Valentine had awakened too early and before all the dosages had been administered. Now Mikhail had only to discover why.

The only variable from the other subjects had been the compression machine of Henri's. Did the extra electrical impulses stimulate the serum and react with the resurrection fluid? A ripple effect must have occurred where the addition of the device spread tendrils outward. Unfortunately he had no way to know how that might affect the rest of Valentine's recovery.

Considering the lapse between time of death and submersion in the resurrection fluid, it was a miracle Valentine had even come back to the land of the living.

Mikhail ran a hand through his hair. His eyes burned from studying the script. Nothing jumped out to indicate a problem, nor did any of the information offer a solution.

There had to be one.

Scientific research hinged on the ability to reproduce results. How was he supposed to duplicate Valentine's miraculous recovery without even knowing how it had occurred?

The only answer had to include the compression device.

Shoes sounded across the floor, a soft tap that grew closer. Mikhail glanced over his shoulder, not surprised to see Dante.

"Have you found anything?" Dante crossed the room and took a seat near the window. Late morning sunshine fell across his face, highlighting deep red in his dark hair.

"Only the compression device, but I fail to see how that can speed up the reanimation process so drastically." He'd have to ask Henri to make smaller ones to try on the local fauna.

"There are other explanations you've failed to take into account."

Mikhail blew out a breath. "No. I haven't. I've gone over all the evidence as presented within these ledgers."

"What you're looking for isn't written in any ledger." Dante twirled the gold ring that encircled his little finger.

"Please do not revisit this argument."

Dante held up a hand. "I've come to inform you that I'll be leaving today. I have business that I can no longer neglect."

A feeling of being plunged into cold water threatened to drown him, take him under. "Dante, if it's because I fail to bend to your fanciful explanations, I urge you to not take the matter so personally. It was never meant as a slight to you."

Dante looked down at the table beside him, moving around a pen and letter opener, arranging them so they were perfectly parallel. "My reasons are my own and will remain so. Feel free to call on me if you encounter any problems and wish to confer."

Mikhail frowned. This behavior was not like Dante. Not at all.

"Something happened to you in Venice."

Dante glanced up sharply. He barked a laugh. "Yes! We brought a world-class musician back from his death, and the poor devil has no idea of his fame. Bastard doesn't even know his name."

"I'm confident it will come back in time. What I really want to know is why Herr Maestro pitched him out the window in the first place." The idea was enough to turn his stomach. Why had someone who'd brought such a talent up from the gutters thrown him into the canal? Because he'd decided to leave? Strike out on his own? Show some independence?

Dante gave a shrug. "Lovers' quarrel?"

The very thought that Valentine had a male lover caused Mikhail's heart to stutter, then begin to beat faster, harder.

Dante stared at Mikhail, his dark gaze going from speculation to pain. He gave a nod and stood. "I will see myself out."

Mikhail pushed to his feet. "You've already packed?"

"Yes, and I've taken the liberty of having the carriage waiting. I hope you don't mind."

"Mind? Of course I mind. You didn't come in here to inform me you were leaving. You came to say good-bye—a function you still haven't performed." Desperate and conflicted, Mikhail reached out to grab hold of Dante's arm. "Don't leave. Not yet."

"Why not? You have Valentine now. You don't need me. And you have Henri to help you. I'm impinging on your time."

"Damn it. This isn't like you."

Dante gave a humorless laugh. "For all you know me, you really don't at all."

With the cryptic remark hanging in the air, growing, seeding the study with negative atmosphere, Dante left. His head up and shoulders back, he wore his dignity like a cloak.

Mikhail stood there alone as a well opened in him, dark and endless. They'd been through so much together. Why had Dante walked away?

He wanted to cry foul for the unfairness. What did he mean that Mikhail didn't know him? Of course he did. They'd been so close. More than brothers.

"Is something wrong, Dr. Stanslovich?"

Mikhail still stood staring at the door when Henri descended the stairs from the upper rooms. He shook his head in response to Henri's question. "Only that Dr. Savoy has taken his leave."

Henri made a noncommittal noise in the back of his throat. "I need to pick up some supplies."

"You'll have to walk. Dr. Savoy has taken my carriage for his convenience." Not that he begrudged him the use when he'd been instrumental in helping them get Valentine to England.

Henri glanced outside. "Looks a nice day for a walk. I'm sure it will present no hardships for me."

"What is it you need?"

Henri made a face, his cheeks stained crimson. "Valentine refuses to say who he is this morning—but I think he knows. I tried last night and again just now, but he's scared to say. I figured a few pieces of sheet music might help to shake his reluctance loose."

An idea came to Mikhail, beautiful and inspired. "While you are out, purchase a violin and have the account sent to me."

Henri's eyes widened. "I know nothing about the purchase of a violin."

"It doesn't have to be the finest one in the shop, though it seems a shame to present Valentine with an inferior instrument." The thought alone was an insult. "Is there anything else you observed about him?"

Henri shrugged. "He's afraid of the dark."

A pit opened, threatening to pitch Mikhail over the edge and into the black void below. "Did he say why?"

"No. I tried to draw him out a bit last night, but he wasn't biting." Henri frowned. "Did I do wrong? Should I have forced an answer?"

Mikhail ran a shaky hand around his mouth. "No. We need to gain his trust and confidence."

Mikhail hated to admit it, but he feared Henri might have done that by simply being the one to save Valentine from the resurrection tank. That alone instilled a bond between the two that Mikhail planned to exploit. What he really wanted was to get Valentine to look at him the way he did Henri. Unfortunately, as the master and thus the authority of the household, Mikhail might find it harder to gain Valentine's trust. No telling how much the man remembered of his life before his drop from the window.

Noise on the stairs brought Mikhail's head up and his attention to the doorway. Valentine stood there in his nightshirt, feet bare and hand to his chest.

Mikhail hurried forward, eager to try to regain the ground he'd lost to Henri. "Why didn't you ring for someone? You shouldn't be wandering the halls in such a state."

Valentine looked down at his clothes. "I didn't know."

Mikhail tried to soften his voice. "Didn't know what?"

"Where to find any clothing."

Henri took a few steps forward. "Do you want me to take him back abovestairs?"

"No. Go about your errands. I can assist him."

Mikhail thought he heard Henri mumble something about the master playing valet, but he ignored it when he noticed how closely Valentine watched him. "Come, let's get you back upstairs and into some proper clothes."

Valentine allowed Mikhail to guide him back up the stairs to his room. "Sit down, and I'll select some clothing for you."

Valentine stood his ground. "May I select my own?"

Surprised, Mikhail only nodded. He opened the wardrobe and stood to the side. "There aren't many to choose from, but what is there is of good quality."

"I don't need many. I can only wear one pair of trousers and shirt at a time."

"That is true spoken." Mikhail smiled, amazed at the rate in which Valentine regained his faculties.

The human brain was a delicate and fascinating organ. Some patients with similar head injuries might never have regained consciousness let alone been able to stand, speak, and react with anything close to cognizance. Yet here stood Valentine, a symbol that not only reanimation but orientation to time and place and a sense of self were possible after the process—even one as delayed as he'd received.

Valentine looked through the shirts and selected a plain white one. He picked up a pair of trousers and set about stripping down and dressing without thought to modesty.

Mikhail tried not to stare, but it was difficult when the subject was as beautifully made as any Roman statue, but with a hell of a lot more virility. He let his gaze travel top to bottom and stopped at the mark on the back of Valentine's lower leg.

The jagged outline of teeth marks was visible in a fine white scar shaped in a perfect arc. There was no mark where a lower jaw rested. Why hadn't he noticed it on initial examination? Because he'd been so focused on Valentine's head injury and looking inside his peritoneal cavity that minor healed scars on the lower extremities weren't going to garner any attention.

Seeing the marks shifted the puzzle pieces of the night in Paris around in his mind. Before they fit and locked into place, Mikhail swatted them away like a pesky bug, refusing to dwell on that night.

"Ugly, aren't they?"

Mikhail forced himself not to startle at the sound of Valentine's voice. Heat threatened to creep up into his face at being caught staring. "I am a trained physician. The same man who placed an incision on your belly. I'm not likely to find old, healed scars repulsive. If anything, I wondered at the story behind them."

Valentine turned as he buttoned his shirt. He fumbled with the movements. It took longer than it should have. His fine motor skills were still not as good as they'd been. "I don't remember. I know I was a small child and there had been a lot of blood."

"Is that all?"

"I think my parents might have died that night. I'm not sure."

Mikhail sat down at the small writing desk, trying to play the confidant. "It's a good sign that you remember anything of your childhood. I feared it would be weeks or months before you even regained your ability to speak with any coherence. If at all."

Valentine frowned. He failed to tuck in the tails of his shirt. "As far as I know, I've always healed fast."

Another piece of the puzzle fell into place. Mikhail tried to smash it—not wishing to see the evidence before him. In a bid for self-preservation, he changed the subject. "Henri doesn't think you know your name."

Valentine's expression turned sour. Distrust filled his eyes. "Henri didn't say that."

A slight miscalculation in strategy. The bond between Valentine and his rescuer was already strong enough for him to defend Henri. "No. Not quite. But he did intimate that he felt you are holding back."

"If I am, then I have my reasons."

Mikhail tried for levity. "If it is any consolation, we already knew your identity when we took on your case."

"This is my chance to start fresh. Would you deny me the opportunity?"

Mikhail swallowed, looking deeply into those hazel eyes that seemed to see way too much. "I would deny you nothing."

The honest answer did not have quite the impact he hoped for. Valentine pulled back as if the words were abhorrent, but offered no rebuttal.

"That makes you uncomfortable?"

"I already owe you my life. What more do you wish from me?"

I want you to love me.

Mikhail kept the confession to himself. For now. There would be plenty of time to make Valentine return his feelings.

"Henri is going to bring you a surprise when he returns from his errands."

Valentine's expression warmed at the mention of Mikhail's assistant. "He doesn't have to do that."

"It might help you as you regain your strength and convalesce."

"My strength has improved significantly."

"And you had trouble buttoning your shirt."

Valentine gazed down at the placket. "I will admit my fingers are a little stiff, but they will regain movement and dexterity. Won't they?"

"That is my hope." He gave Valentine what he considered a reassuring smile. "I will devise some exercises to help in that area."

Silence descended on the room. Valentine began to hum the tune he'd played to open the Venice concert. Chills erupted on the back of Mikhail's neck.

"Where did you learn that tune?"

Valentine gave a shrug. "I've hummed it from the time I was a child. Played it on the street as a busker."

At least two decades had passed since Valentine had been plucked from the street by Herr Maestro. Mikhail knew the story, as did all who followed the beloved musician. Accounts of Valentine's rise to fame had been chronicled in newspapers all over the world.

"Do you remember where you first heard it?"

Valentine shrugged. "No."

Mikhail let the matter drop. He pushed up from the chair. "If you'll care to accompany me to the lab, I can give you a dowel to twirl."

"I'm not sure I know what that means." Valentine followed Mikhail from the room and back to the laboratory.

Mikhail went to the tool chest and found a long thin wooden stick. "I want you to twirl it like this." He demonstrated by flipping it from finger to finger, letting it roll through each digit. When it reached the end, he sent it back the other way. "Here. You try."

Valentine took the dowel, giving it a skeptical look. Where Mikhail managed a smooth transition over his hand, Valentine worked in stops and starts. His angelic face showed only intense concentration.

As Valentine worked on his dexterity, Mikhail returned to the ledgers, fearing the answers he sought were nowhere on the page.

WILHELM WALKED the streets of London. The address he searched for did not seem to exist. Where in the hell had that so-called physician taken Valentine? They left the boat in some godforsaken part of England and disappeared into the moors.

He narrowed his eyes.

The world took on a hazy view. All the evil leeched from out of people as they walked by him, touching that part of him that he hid from the world. He'd been touched as Valentine had been, but where Andres Valentine played music, the Maestro controlled it.

Music was *his* domain. He controlled those who should play on the world stage and those who were relegated to drawing rooms. Serendipity had nothing to do with finding Valentine on that street corner that fateful day.

Crowds moved by him, a sea of people rushing to meet the shore. He wished they'd all crash upon the rocks. The only thing they were good for was to pay the price for seats to watch his orchestra.

Anger surged to his head, threatening to blow out of the top. The Kering Orchestra no longer existed. Valentine had seen to that when he'd cut and run, forcing him to make a hasty decision.

How dare he turn to bite the hand that fed him?

It was a pure outrage to those forces that made him into the musician he'd become. Valentine would have been nothing without *him*. All that talent wasted on a street corner, being played for people who would have never truly appreciated it.

Not such as they were.

Wilhelm glanced around him. The faces of these savage Londoners morphed, changed before his eyes. Oh, yes, the dark fae were here in great numbers, and they were not pleased. He'd lost control of their greatest creation. A creation that had decided to rebel instead of work to please them.

He crossed the street and saw the dark-haired man from the Venetian villa come out of a shop. Wilhelm stepped back, hiding in the doorway of a business a few doors down.

They had made this happen. Their watchful gazes led him to this spot and this time in order to follow the man back to the residence of one Dr. Mikhail Stanslovich.

The man juggled a few boxes as he started off in the opposite direction. Wilhelm pushed off from the wall and hurried after him.

Never in his life had he seen a more circuitous route taken from one place to another. If he didn't know better, he'd swear the man knew he was followed. Why else would he travel from one side of London to another without any particular destination in mind?

If any of his subordinates wasted as much time doing nothing, Wilhelm would have kicked them straight out of the company. But then there didn't appear to be anything magical or mystical about this particular man, though he did have a certain quality Wilhelm couldn't quite place at the moment.

Finally the man caught a hackney and hurried from the area along the clogged city streets and away from Wilhelm.

Damn it. He'd lost him.

He tried to catch a carriage, but luck had turned against him. The sun began to set; darkness fell over the city, painting the alleys and side streets in shadow. He didn't mind. He rather liked the murky black that came alive with otherwordly beings when he glanced in their direction.

Most humans only felt the presence of the dark fae, sensing them as a feeling of skin crawling or unrelenting cold. Often they'd hurry away from an area of intense activity and never knew the reason why they fled. Sometimes the dark fae went in pursuit, sending their *wolfsine* to hunt for victims.

Suppose the dark-haired man was to meet with an unfortunate accident with a *wolfsine*. An incident was easily arranged. First Wilhelm had to know where to find him in order to send the fae in pursuit—or he needed a name.

Names were power.

Wilhelm patted his pocket. A square about the size of his palm felt solid against his hand under the fabric of his coat. Inside were the names of musicians, from the obscure to the famous. He had their names and controlled their destinies. Only he determined if they would be mediocre or adored. This was the charge given him by the dark fae. By Azgarth himself.

Heat, generated by the fae magic surrounding the book, seeped through the wool and into his hand. He was close to one whose name needed to be added—who had been kissed by the fae forces for their particular talents.

The search for the dark-haired man would have to wait.

Wilhelm turned in the direction of the vibrations he felt coming from the music store. He pushed open the door and entered to the sound of bells tinkling overhead to announce his arrival.

Several customers looked through sheet music and others perused the instruments. None of them struck Wilhelm as being anything out of the ordinary. He certainly didn't feel the essence of the fae on any of them.

A man came from the back room, walking with a young woman dressed in the height of fashion and elegance. The book heated. A scent of hot fabric wafted up to his nose.

There was another woman with them. Judging from the cut of her clothing and angle of her jaw, the women were related. Though the second one was quite a few years older. Her mother possibly.

Wilhelm moved closer, pretending to look over the music books.

"Juliana must have the very best teacher in order to cultivate her talent."

"Yes, Mrs. Alexandre. I will pass your name to Mr. Enbright."

"I simply will not have her taught by less than the best."

"Yes, ma'am."

Wilhelm took his book out of his pocket and wrote the name Juliana Alexandre into the ledger. The ink glowed a vivid red, burning down into the page, becoming one with the paper. Now her name was added to the rolls, she'd see her dreams manifest, but at a price.

They all paid a price.

Valentine had wanted to cut and run before he'd paid the debt in full.

Miss Juliana Alexandre started to finger the cameo at her throat. A frown marred her perfect brow. She turned a graceful neck to look around the shop and spotted Wilhelm. Her eyes rounded and mouth made a perfect bow.

She leaned into the woman Wilhelm assumed was her mother and whispered, keeping her gaze fixed on Wilhelm.

He gave a nod in greeting, touched his brow in a salute, then turned to leave the store. He might be working on the behest of the dark fae, but he could still be thrown into a mortal jail and hanged from a tree as any common criminal. Unfortunately he'd not been made immortal, only enjoyed greater longevity than most men, provided he managed to keep his neck out of a hangman's noose.

This time a hackney waited in the street. As he spoke to the driver to take him to his lodgings, the shop door opened.

"Sir? Sir?"

Against his better judgment, he turned around. "May I help you?"

"Excuse me for my forwardness, as we haven't been introduced, but are you Herr Maestro Kering?"

Wilhelm's heartbeat kicked up, pounding up into his neck and causing a pulse that made his vision jump. He gave them a smile and shook his head. "No. My apologies. You have mistaken me for a great man."

Mrs. Alexandre glanced around the street, then came closer. "I understand if you do not wish to have your identity known after that unfortunate incident in Venice."

Wilhelm pretended to have no idea of the incident in question. "You have me at a disadvantage, ma'am. I have never been to Venice."

This doting momma would clearly do anything to have her daughter taught by a maestro, but alas he wasn't in the market for a student and had no idea of her particular talent in the first place.

Mrs. Alexandre raised a brow and took a conspirator's stance. "The way I understand it, Valentine was brought to England for his convalescence. An unfortunate accident, but nothing to cry foul over."

If Wilhelm didn't himself possess such a mercenary spirit, he might have been shocked or horrified by her unrelenting quest.

"Again I have to admit my ignorance of such things. I have no notion of this Valentine. Is he an actor?"

"Violinist." The talent was said with a tone of annoyance.

"Ah." He nodded to the women. "If you will excuse me. I have business to attend to across town."

Juliana Alexandre placed her hand on her mother's sleeve. "Mama, it might be dangerous for him, even here in London. Leave him be. We'll wait to see if Mr. Enbright will contact us."

Wilhelm scratched at his chin. Inside his pocket, the book began to grow warm again. "Out of curiosity, what area of music do you need lessons?"

"She is a soprano."

"I see. I hope it all works to your advantage." With that he climbed into the carriage.

He'd never enjoyed singers. Each one was more pretentious than the last. He much preferred those who poured their heart and soul into creating sound through an instrument other than the vocal cords.

Let Mr. Enbright grow Juliana Alexandre to her full potential, but leave him out of the mix, with her overbearing mother.

He didn't worry they would go to the authorities claiming they saw him in London. What were they going to tell the constabulary?

That he denied being Wilhelm Kering and didn't know the infamous Valentine? The authorities would never take their tale seriously.

The carriage clattered over the cobbled roads. Clouds raced in from the north, covering the city in a dark gray. Winds kicked up, sending refuse scattering along the ground. Women held their hats as they hurried to find shelter before the rain hit.

He arrived at his hotel, frustrated and annoyed.

Shadows in the corner of his suite shifted, solidified. Azgarth grew from the darkness, taking on substance and form.

"You failed in your quest, Maestro."

The rebuke made him inwardly cringe. "The man got away, and I could not obtain a carriage."

Azgarth made a graceful swipe with his hand as if dismissing the problems of the mortal realm. "Not the agent in league with Valentine, but the soprano. She was sent to you for a reason, and you sent her away."

Wilhelm froze.

Azgarth folded his hands together. Black feline-like eyes rolled skyward in a dramatic fashion. "What are we to do with you? First you lose control of one of our favorites. Then you let a sweet soprano slip through your fingers."

The fae did not reward failure in their mortal agents. Wilhelm's breath came faster. His heart began to flutter in his neck. Sweat broke out in the small of his back.

"Well, what do you have to say for yourself?"

"It is a simple matter of not having the time to devote to a new pupil, much less a singer. That is not my area of expertise. Her talent might be better served with another master." The advice was the only solution he had at hand, and he hoped it did not anger Azgarth.

Dark lines oozed over the walls, bleeding in black rivulets that pooled on the ledge made by the wainscoting. Manifest anger even as Azgarth sat on his brittle throne showing no emotion.

"Unfortunately you do not deal in seeing the multitude of possibilities as we do. Your mortal insights give you limited vision."

Wilhelm did not know quite what was expected of him.

"The girl was to be your alibi while in this dark, dreary city. The least you could do was take the service as offered. We do not move events to amuse ourselves."

Wilhelm begged to differ. That was exactly the purpose of the dark fae—to create mayhem, stir passion, and instill fear in mankind.

If he spent his time teaching an empty-headed girl how to sing, he'd have little time to search for Valentine.

"If I agree, you need to make it easier to find Valentine."

The shadows grew and shifted. A cold breeze blew through the room, though no windows were open.

"You do not have the luxury to agree or disagree. You do as you are commanded. Make no mistake, as we have been good to you and given you a golden life, we can also take our gifts away."

Wilhelm's gut clenched. For the first time since falling into the service of the dark fae, he felt real fear.

"I will find the girl and offer my services."

"And we will reward you handsomely."

He'd believe that when and if it materialized.

Chapter Seven

HENRI ARRIVED back at the estate with a harsh, cool wind on his back. An unsettled feeling pooled in his belly. He'd heard of an ill wind blowing, but he'd never believed such fanciful notions until now.

Something hid in the breeze, and for the life of him, he didn't know what it could be. He knew the entire idea bordered on the insane. He dealt in the tangible world, not the mysticism that Dr. Savoy seemed to favor.

At the moment, though, he'd admit to wanting a bit of the good doctor's insight.

He came into the servants' entrance. This time of day, the area was full of cooks, assistants, and other servants. Call him a fool, but he really needed the fellowship of other humans at the moment.

Henri met Stanslovich as he came out of the laboratory into the main hall.

"You've returned." Stanslovich's smile faded, and he placed a hand on Henri's shoulder. "My God, man. Are you all right?"

"Fine." He handed the violin to Stanslovich. "One violin."

Stanslovich said nothing, but studied Henri for a long, silent moment before transferring his attention to the case. "I have him ensconced in the laboratory twirling a dowel between his fingers."

"I have the sheet music. I wonder if he can play the pianoforte."

"We can ask."

They started for the laboratory as Henri started to shed his overcoat but thought better of it. Cold centered in his being.

He held on to Stanslovich's arm to stop him before they reached the doorway. "Before you go inside, you need to know that Herr Maestro is here in London."

Stanslovich frowned. "I'm not surprised. Too much fanfare of our crossing in the papers. I'd be more surprised if he had fled to Paris or Berlin."

"What do you want to do?"

"Alert the constabulary that we've seen him in London, and trust they will do their jobs. Unless he shows his face here on the estate. Then we do what can to hold him."

Henri glanced to the laboratory. "I suggest we say nothing on the subject to Valentine."

"Agreed."

They entered the room to find Valentine not twirling the baton as instructed but skimming through the ledger of his recovery.

"You might have an easier time reading this." Henri reached into his pack and pulled out the sheet music he'd purchased. "It will make more sense."

Valentine glanced up, his gaze haunted. "Did I die?"

Stanslovich offered a friendly smile. "Death is so subjective."

"Not to most people." Valentine held out his hand for the sheet music. He walked away without saying another word. He hadn't even spared a glance for the violin case Stanslovich carried.

Henri turned and stared after him. How did Valentine ever manage to make sense of the notations in order to extrapolate his demise?

"Did you tell him?"

The accusation came so swift and severe Henri had no time to mount a defense other than to shake his head.

"Did you teach him how to read the ledger?"

Henri shot Stanslovich a glance to convey he cared not for the implication. "When would I have had time to teach him the nomenclature you insist we use?"

"Then how did he read it?"

"We can't be sure he did, unless we ask him and he admits to doing so. He might have remembered being tossed out of the window by Herr Maestro and opened the ledger to look for answers." As an explanation it made more sense than Valentine deciphering the odd symbols and numbers on his own.

Stanslovich ran a hand through his hair. "We will have to tell him that he was grievously injured, but his vital signs remained strong."

"Hard to call back your first response." What had Stanslovich been thinking? Valentine had already proved to be a curious, if evasive, man.

"I will not be required to amend my words. What did I say that isn't true? Death is subjective. An initial assessment that yields a slow or thready pulse might leave a caretaker to believe a patient has succumbed to his injuries. In the hands of a more experienced practitioner, that same thready pulse is a sign of life and a call to fight on."

"And that same information in the hands of a suspicious patient?"

"Can be explained in terms that will calm them without a second thought."

Perhaps, but Henri didn't think Valentine was the type to forget something so significant. Call it intuition, but this situation was going to cause them problems. As if they didn't have enough already with Herr Maestro being in England.

Henri rubbed a hand across his forehead. A headache started to pound from the base of his skull into the area behind his eyes. "Let me talk to him. He might open up if given a gentle nudge."

Stanslovich shot Henri a quelling look. "Give him some time. He'll talk when he is ready."

Henri felt the reason more along the lines that Stanslovich didn't want him to get any closer to Valentine. In order to do that, Henri had to let go of his compassion and humanity. Who could look at Valentine and not feel protective? A person he'd trusted, who had cared for him since childhood, had pitched him out a window. That had to damage the soul and crush the spirit.

Henri would not be party to that brand of cruelty. "If you have nothing further for me, I'll go and prepare for the coming terms' lectures."

"Ah, yes, they begin next week."

"Yes." He wanted to be able to finish this term and begin his practice, get out from under Stanslovich's thumb.

"I can't afford to have you away from the estate for long periods of time. You might have to forgo this terms' lectures and resume at some other date."

Henri froze.

He hadn't heard correctly. He wasn't about to place his life and vocation on hold again because of someone else's folly. "No."

Stanslovich's eyes narrowed in anger for having his order countermanded. "What did you say?"

"I said no. If you look at it logically, it makes more sense to have me continue my studies so the household appears normal. If I don't resume my classes, people are going to question why you need me here when Valentine is on the road to recovery."

Stanslovich rubbed his chin in thought. "A point well made, but what if I need you here?"

"I will return in the evenings. Lectures do not last all day." He tilted his head, looking at Stanslovich from a different angle. "Do you plan to take on more subjects while Valentine remains in the house?"

Stanslovich walked to the ledger where Valentine had abandoned it. "I'm not going to put my practice on hold for him. There is still so much to learn and explore. For one, how he woke before getting the full benefit of the resurrection fluid."

"We should take a sample of his blood and look at it under the microscope. The serum will still be in his system."

"I've considered that. However, I'm hesitant to ask him to allow me to draw a tube or two when he's still recovering."

"You won't need that much. A finger stick should give you enough blood to determine if there is anything else besides the serum involved." Henri crossed the room to the supply cabinet and began to search for a lancet. "I'll give him some time and then ask him about it during the course of the conversation."

"Do you have such confidence that he'll agree?"

"No. I don't. But asking him if I can stick his finger is going to go over a hell of a lot better than asking for two tubes of blood."

"And if we need more?"

Henri smiled. "We'll cross that bridge when we get there."

It never failed to surprise Henri how Stanslovich had no finesse or diplomacy when it came to the subjects he treated. Oftentimes his autocratic behavior bore poor results because subjects tended to resist if pushed too hard. In Henri's limited experience, he'd found better compliance if a potential patient was asked to participate in their care rather than told.

But then he thought that about most situations.

ANDRES STALKED through the estate, unable to focus or concentrate his thoughts long enough to make sense of his suspicions. How could he have been brought back from the dead? It wasn't possible. Even when he'd been attacked as a child, he'd been ill, his dreams fevered through infection and blood loss, but he'd never stood on the threshold of death.

Even now he wasn't certain the numbers he'd seen in the book meant what he'd believed they did. Why then did he ask the question? He had the thought and then his mouth opened and he saw the words coming out though he'd not given his brain permission to say them.

Dr. Stanslovich's answer unsettled Andres as no other words in his life ever had—with the exception of Herr Maestro. That man had the propensity to say things that disturbed on a soul-deep level.

He rubbed a hand over the back of his head. His scalp itched where the sutures remained. He'd hit his head very hard indeed to receive such an injury.

Andres took a turn and found a cavernous library. Books lined the shelves in the round. An articulated skeleton of a man stood in one corner wearing a top hat and tails. The clothing was unexpected and quirky in a house that did not appear at first blush to understand either concept.

He wandered to one of the shelves, pulled out a book at random, and began to leaf through the pages.

The door opened with a slight creak. "You won't find any books on that side of the library that aren't geared toward physicians or healing. Mostly medical texts, some of them obscure." Henri came farther into the room and stood behind a wing chair with his hand resting on the back.

Andres returned the book to the shelf. "Not my particular area of study, but I'm always willing to learn something new."

"That is a very admirable trait. Most people become set in their ways and never bother to learn another thing once they reach their maturity." Henri came around the side of the chair but did not sit.

An elusive quality shone from Henri, sent out a sensual allure that tempted Andres to want to learn more about the handsome assistant. He wanted so much to ask Henri to tell him the truth, but was afraid of the crushing blow should that result in a lie.

"Have you remembered anything else from your past?"

The question pricked Andres sure as any pin. "I don't want to remember. I want to forget and start again."

"Why? Your life wasn't so awful, was it?"

"Ha!" The bark of sound echoed in the room. "You try living and working for a man with moods as mercurial as the wind and see if you don't want to start fresh."

Henri looked over his shoulder to the open door. "I do and I am."

"What? Are you leaving?" Panic started as a small stone lodged low in his gut.

"I have to return to lectures. My dream is to start my own medical practice."

Andres ran his hand through his hair and took a seat in another chair that faced the one Henri stood beside. "I've only had one dream of my own: to go to America and live a quiet, comfortable life without demands or adoration. To simply be me. To find out what that means for the first time in my life."

The confession was the closest he'd get to admitting his identity, even if they already knew him, recognized him, and had followed his career.

Henri canted his head. "Why America?"

"Why not? It's a growing nation, making it easy to get lost and to begin a new life with a new identity. The past, a construct of fantasy and wishes. No one is going to know differently." At least not once he cut his hair and grew a beard and mustache. He would no longer look like his photographs.

Perhaps not even the darkness would find him.

He tried to suppress a shudder.

Henri started forward. "Have you taken a chill? Come let me help you to your room."

Andres put up his hand, silently refusing help. "I'm warm. It's only a bit of the shakes left over from my illness."

Henri narrowed his eyes, not fooled by the excuse. "You might have overdone your strength today. There's no shame in resting if that is what your body needs."

Hearing it from Henri's lips, it did not sound like a failing. "You are a very tenderhearted man."

An expression of regret shuttered Henri's face. "Not always. I can be quite mercenary when called upon to be so."

"But only when a loved one is in danger."

Now Henri looked up, piercing him with dark eyes that penetrated through Andres's skin. "I have no loved ones. I'm alone. The only connections I have are the ones residing in this house. I make my own way in the world and have only my hard work and determination to thank."

Andres let out a wistful sigh. That sounded like paradise to him. Beholden to no man or… entity… for his sustenance. No obligation to serve a dark master who had only their interests at heart.

"You are a fortunate man, then. No ties to bind you. No commitments to keep you rooted in an arrangement you no longer find satisfactory."

Henri folded his arms and crossed his feet at the ankles as he leaned against the chair. He raised a brow in consideration. "You mistake me. I have commitments aplenty. To my studies, to my chosen vocation, and to Dr. Stanslovich for this position. Without him, I'd not be able to afford to finish school."

"But if you wanted to, you could leave."

"Yes, and then I'd have to find another situation."

Frustrated, Andres shook his head. "You don't understand what I'm saying. You are free to choose. Either to stay or go. I wasn't so lucky. I dared to try and for that I was punished."

Henri nodded. "You never have to worry about that again. You are safe here."

"Will I be allowed to leave once I am fully healed?"

"I can't see the future, but I can tell you Dr. Stanslovich isn't a cruel man, only an arrogant one." Henri took a few steps, closing the space between them, sending Andres's senses whirling. "Concentrate on getting well, not what happens after you do."

Easier said than done. He needed to plan. Had obtained papers and identification in his alias. Where had those gone? Most of his funds were safe in America. He needed to get to them to start his new life.

"What will you do after you start your new life?"

Henri gave a shrug. "Do you mean after I finish at university?"

"Yes. Are you going to stay here in London?"

"I've not given it much thought. I might immigrate to Canada or return to France."

Andres kept his opinions of what Henri should do to himself for now. He didn't want to push. Didn't want to hope for something that might be one-sided. Still he'd never met another man who had captured his imagination so completely.

Chapter Eight

Strange energies enveloped the estate. Shadows filled corners and niches too dark for normal eyes to penetrate. Mikhail glanced at the mantle clock. Midnight.

He rolled his eyes. The passage of time on a clock and the way the day was broken up into minutes and hours was a man-made concept. Evil didn't tell time. It happened whenever it saw fit—in this instance, it was nothing more than a greater amount of static electricity in the air raised by a coming storm.

Pure imagination and a heightened sense of foreboding, all thanks to Dante putting ideas in his head. Mikhail rubbed his eyes. He'd still made no headway into understanding where the resurrection had gone wrong—why the compressed time in the chamber.

He stood and hurried to the tank. He climbed up the steps with a beaker in hand. Henri had not come through with Valentine's blood. He'd given his apologies along with an explanation that Valentine had seemed melancholy. In the interest of retaining trust, he'd not even asked for a sample. Now a missed opportunity might degrade any sample obtained.

Time was important when it came to experiments. It marched and marked and took its toll on the world around it. Once the heart started and normal function returned, the body eliminated the serum with quiet efficiency. The fluid in the tank stayed stagnant. If the analyzed results were normal, then the fault had to be in another parameter.

But was it a fault?

Granted, he wanted Valentine to live, but he'd also wanted to control the ascent back into consciousness, not have it taken from him at the microscopic level.

He dunked the beaker into the fluid and pulled out a large sample. Enough to run several experiments and not have to dip into the tank again.

Movement from the corner of his eye caught his attention. Shadows swept across the floor, spreading darkness in a pattern resembling spilled ink.

He glanced to the lamp on his desk. Oh heavens above, the damn wick had burned down, and the oil was near empty. No wonder the light had a hard time keeping the dark at bay.

Rational explanations accounted for everything in the known world and were responsible for those things attributed to the unknown. Mysteries were only facts as yet unexplored. Dante had done his best to make Mikhail suspicious, and he'd succeeded, the bastard.

Wind rattled the windows. Tree limbs danced in front of the panes as a storm blew outside.

Mikhail set the beaker down on the desk and found another wick and some oil to fill the lamp. He planned to work long into the night and didn't need to be caught in the middle of an experiment when the light finally sputtered and died.

The shadows continued their constant spread. A figure appeared in the center—the silhouette of a man, tall and lean, with long, pointed ears and elegant hands.

Mikhail stopped in his task and stared at the apparition. As he watched the image, he moved the lamp over a few inches to the right. The shadow followed, but was slow to react. He blinked a few times.

His eyes were tired. He'd been staring at the same ledger pages for hours, and as a result, his vision retained the script burned onto his retinas. It made him see things that weren't there.

This time he moved the lamp all the way over to the credenza. The shadow grew larger, taking on more ominous proportions. One of the appendages that looked like an arm rose and pointed straight at Mikhail. Accusation stirred the air.

Perhaps he needed to lie down for a while and start fresh in the morning. He turned the lamp down, tamping the flow of oil into the wick. Darkness filled the room, save for the glowing blue light from the resurrection tank.

Images danced around the room. A far-off waltz sounded in an echo of merriment from some forgotten dream. Along the sides of the tank, dancers kept time with the music. Laughter rose and glasses clinked together in a toast.

Now this was a little harder to explain away, other than through strain or a waking dream. Perhaps he'd fallen asleep at the desk and only believed he was still awake. It seemed as likely a scenario as any other available at the moment.

He left the laboratory and headed directly for his rooms. The climb up the stairs seemed to take forever. If memory served, there weren't this many stairs in the estate. For each step he took, two more appeared.

Music followed him—a haunting melody he'd heard only twice before.

Definitely a dream, fast turning into a nightmare.

For a brief moment, he thought to call for Henri, to wake him, but rejected the idea as shameful. Grown men did not call others because they feared shadows in the night or ran from disquieting dreams. Responsible men went to their beds—even their dream beds—and lay down to sleep so they could wake up in a more natural state.

No matter how bloody long it took to climb the damn staircase.

Dawn broke through the upper story windows as Mikhail made the landing. He turned to go to his room. Shadows waited for him at the end of the hall.

His leg began to ache where the bites had been, as if they'd only happened yesterday.

He opened the door to his room and fell onto the bed still wearing his clothes. He closed his eyes and prayed for true and restful sleep to claim him.

When next he woke, sun streamed in through the windows, chasing all the shadows away. Judging from the position, it was well past midmorning. He shook the remains of his odd dream from his head and ran a hand through his hair as he sat on the edge of the bed.

So many tasks to accomplish and he had lain in bed like a drunk after a night of heavy imbibing. Truth of the matter, his head pounded and his tongue felt thick, as if after a full night of chasing the green fairy.

He pushed up from the bed and did not bother to ring for his valet. The less the servants knew about him falling into bed in his clothing, the better. They already believed him an eccentric, no need to reinforce their opinions.

After he washed in the basin, shaved, and put on fresh clothing, he went downstairs to the breakfast room, where he found no food waiting for him.

He stood in consternation, glaring at the empty sideboard as if doing so might produce the required sustenance.

Henri entered the room. "I thought I heard you come down. Late night?"

"Yes, but not in the way you may think." Mikhail looked around again. "Please go to the kitchen and have Cook put together a meal for me. I'll take it in the laboratory."

Henri nodded and left the room.

Mikhail hadn't heard or seen Valentine as yet that morning. He made a detour for the music room before heading for the laboratory. Valentine was nowhere to be found—at least not in the places Mikhail thought to find him.

The laboratory looked so different in the daylight. High windows that ran from the wainscoting to near the ceiling let in plenty of light. The beaker he'd placed on the desk was gone.

Henri might have thought he'd forgotten to put it away last night and did so this morning. Mikhail crossed the room to the instrument cabinet and pulled another beaker down. It was then he noticed the full one teetered on the top of the case.

A cold chill swam down his spine a second before he rejected the implication.

"Henri!"

A few minutes later he heard shoes over marble flooring.

"Did you call for me, sir?"

Mikhail simply pointed to the beaker. His eyes hot with anger.

Henri cocked his head. "How did that get up there?"

"Do not stand there and deny you put it there for some mischief. I do not have the time nor inclination for such childish games."

Red flags appeared on Henri's cheeks. His nostrils flared in umbrage. "I assure you I had nothing to do with placing that beaker up on the cabinet."

Mikhail narrowed his eyes. "If I discover you've had anything to do with this, you will be discharged."

"And I will take all my devices with me. I'm sure I can sell them to physicians and hospitals who can make use of them." Henri's hands were clenched at his sides. "If you have nothing further to accuse me of, I shall take my leave."

Henri turned on his heel and marched away. The silence was punctuated by the steady tread of his shoes across the floor as he moved away from the laboratory and toward the front door. A brief pause, and then the door slammed.

"Damn it!"

Music filtered through the manor. A violin played the dying strains of a melancholy tune. Ah, Valentine had found the violin and hadn't been able to resist the temptation to play. Mikhail abandoned the laboratory to search for the violinist. Desire mixed with anticipation swam through his veins. An odd euphoria came over him. The urge to run through the manor yelling at the top of his lungs bubbled up into his throat.

Instead of the music getting louder as he approached the music room, it faded as if carried away on the wind. He peeked inside the room, thinking perhaps Valentine had let the last chord die of its own, but the room was empty. The violin case sat untouched near the music stand.

Mikhail frowned and started away, listening closely for the music. The melody began again, but this time it sounded as if played beyond the windows in the garden. A quick look revealed Valentine hadn't gone out there to play in the elements either.

One by one, he checked each of the rooms but found them empty, save for a few servants who were busy with their tasks. There were no gramophones playing.

Finally he came to the library to find Valentine sitting in a chair reading a book.

Mikhail stopped and stared. "How long have you been in here?"

Valentine glanced up. He blinked a few times, giving the appearance of trying to gather his thoughts. He glanced to the windows. "Since a little after sunrise. I couldn't sleep. I hope you don't mind."

When Valentine started to get up to put the book away, Mikhail waved him back down. "I can think of no better occupation than reading to pass the day while you heal."

Gentle as a summer breeze, the tune filtered through the library once more. Distant. Faint. Mikhail studied Valentine for reaction. A slight tightening on the book caused Valentine's knuckles to turn white; however, his expression betrayed nothing.

"You can hear that too?"

Valentine nodded. Hope shone in his eyes. "A recording?"

Mikhail shook his head. "No."

"He's found you."

A chill shot down to Mikhail's gut, tightening it. "Who?"

"Azgarth."

Mikhail had no idea who it was that Valentine spoke of, but he did not care for the way the name made his skin crawl. Recognition fluttered as a vague memory in his brain, yet he had no notion of how or why the name sounded familiar.

"Who is Azgarth?"

Valentine locked gazes with Mikhail. "No one you want to cross."

WILHELM WOKE tied to the bedpost. Little rivers of blood had run down his body and pooled at his feet. The now dried offering had turned to a crust that itched something fierce. Damn Azgarth for taking his pound of flesh.

Punishment for failing to acknowledge the Alexandre whore.

How was he going to get himself free? To wait for the maid to untie him was unthinkable. This, he knew, was part of the punishment. Humiliation. Azgarth gave, and he most certainly took away, if crossed. Living under his grace was beautiful, colorful, and festive. Once his ire was piqued, the world faded of color. Light and music turned from graceful waltzes to dark dirges.

He worked his hands around, trying to stretch the rope. The heavy fibers and coarse grain chafed at his wrists.

The bedpost was smooth polished wood. He'd find no assistance from that quarter.

Damn Valentine!

This was all his fault.

If Valentine had never thought to leave the fold, Wilhelm would not now be strapped to the bed, wearing nothing but his skin and shame.

The fall had been steep.

From Herr Maestro to one of the most celebrated orchestras in the world, to being tied to a bedpost, bloody, angry, and vengeful.

Oh, he'd contact Miss Juliana Alexandre all right, and when he did, he'd make her sing until her vocal cords bled. Until the very idea of singing filled her with fear.

Over on the bedside table, his pocketknife gleamed in the light coming from the window. Even if he spread out his leg, he was still too far away to grab it with his toe.

He closed his eyes, hoping inspiration might strike.

Keys rattled in the door.

"Go away!"

The lock turned.

"I said go away! Leave me the hell alone!"

The jangling became more frantic.

"Jesus Christ." He hung his head, resigned to the fact he was going to be discovered in the most embarrassing of circumstances.

The door burst open, and the hotel concierge entered. "Oh dear heavens, Mr. Kane."

The manager hurried over and started on the ties securing Wilhelm's hands. At least he'd used an alias when he'd checked into the hotel, and no one would associate this incident with Herr Maestro.

"We had a report that there were inhuman wails coming from this room, as if a murder were being committed," the concierge explained.

"Then I wonder at you coming in here without a constable."

The manager shook his head, an action Wilhelm felt more than saw. "Our guests require we keep the utmost standards. Seeing constables in the halls might create a panic."

Or cancelled reservations.

Wilhelm kept the thoughts to himself. At least it was a man and not one of the maids, who probably would have seen the state of Wilhelm's body and run shrieking from the room. Still, who had reported wailing? There had been none. Azgarth had not broken him during the lashing. He'd never even cried out, though the skin of his back and shoulders was rent.

"Will you require a physician, sir?"

Wilhelm's hands came free. "No. Only a bath."

He rubbed his wrists, trying to get some feeling back into his hands. The skin was red, raw, but otherwise undamaged. A small saving grace for a punishment that could have continued on through the afternoon.

The concierge helped Wilhelm to his feet, never asking what had happened or who had tied him to the bed. Discretion was an admirable virtue.

"Will there be anything else, sir?"

"No. Thank you."

The concierge gave a nod and left the room.

By rights Wilhelm should have been angry that the concierge had not listened to the instruction to leave, but in retrospect, it had been the best scenario.

Alone now and thankful for the privacy, Wilhelm went into the bath and studied his reflection. He'd awoken to worse punishments and more pronounced injuries since he'd been overcome by Azgarth. A little soap and water, a bit of salve, and he'd be good as new.

But first.

He crossed the suite to the liquor cabinet and poured a liberal amount of liquid anesthetic in the form of whiskey into a glass and shot it back, then repeated the process a few more times until a gentle curtain of euphoria settled over him.

Past experiences had taught him that cleansing the wounds wasn't at all pleasurable. He went back into the bath and doused a hand towel with both soap and water. When it was good and sudsy, he stuck a washcloth in his mouth, picked up the hand towel and wiped it across his back, holding it at both ends. The rough nap of the fabric in concert with the brushing back and forth over the marks brought a shout of pain to his throat. The washcloth muffled the sound of his agony.

Tears ran down his cheeks, products of the pain. This was one aspect of the position he'd never quite liked—but he'd always found it necessary to visit on his protégées what Azgarth had done to him. After all, it was their fault he got punished. It was only fair they should reap the same.

Vigorous scraping knocked off a few of the scabs and fresh blood ran down his back. If he smeared enough of the thick salve on it, he might be able to staunch the bleeding. Not that the flow was life threatening, but he wanted to get dressed and not bleed through his shirt.

He went back to his bag and grabbed the large pot of salve he'd acquired for just such a pass. The expense was worth every coin he'd spent, though he'd much rather have sneaked back into the opera house and retrieved the one in the dressing room. The damn thing hadn't even been opened yet, but when he'd fled, he'd left all his belongings behind.

Azgarth should have seen to his safety, but he hadn't. The master of the dark side of the arts had not been available when Wilhelm had called out to him. Or he'd simply not answered the summons.

Wilhelm took another towel, then rolled it, and smeared the salve along the center. He then repeated the actions he'd taken when he washed to get the medication onto his back. Not the best method of application, but he had very little choice at the moment.

He waited a few minutes for the salve to be partially absorbed before he dressed, starting with a heavy undershirt. When he was pleased with his appearance, he went to the book of names and opened it to the last page.

Now to find Miss Juliana Alexandre's direction.

CHAPTER
NINE

DR. SAVOY gave Henri an indulgent smile. "Now, what do you suppose your master might say if he discovered that I'd hired you to assist me? He'd be furious with both of us."

"He's not my *master.* He is my employer. No man has mastery over me." Henri pushed up from the chair and went to the window.

They were ensconced in Dr. Savoy's home office in a fashionable section of the city. Henri had been so angry upon leaving Stanslovich's estate that he'd walked for hours until he'd come to find himself in front of Dr. Savoy's home. With nothing to lose, he'd acted on impulse to ask Dr. Savoy to take him on as an assistant.

Dr. Savoy canted his head. His expression softened. "Of what did he accuse you?"

Henri waved the charge away.

"Come now, if you want me to even consider taking you on, or referring you to another who might be willing to pay an assistant, I would at least like to know why you'd been angry enough to walk away this time."

This time.

Dr. Savoy was right. A long history of crude comments and curt behavior had peppered his relationship with Dr. Stanslovich, and yet Henri had stayed on, knowing he worked toward a goal.

"It was stupid, really. Something no rational man would ever suggest."

Dr. Savoy raised a brow. "Do tell. You'll find no more rational man than Mikhail Stanslovich."

Henri's cheeks heated, either through shame or anger, he wasn't quite sure at the moment. "He accused me of placing a filled beaker atop the equipment cabinet to play some bit of mischief. When I assured him I did not, he threatened to discharge me if he found out that I had lied."

Dr. Savoy came forward in his seat. His face registered mild shock. "All this over a misplaced beaker?"

"Yes." Henri gave a shrug. "I may have threatened to leave and take all my inventions."

To this, Dr. Savoy began to laugh. "I wish I'd have been there to see his face."

Henri nodded. A smile lifted the corner of his mouth. "It was extraordinary."

"That alone is enough to make it worth all the trouble."

There was an odd bitterness to Dr. Savoy's tone. Henri decided not to ask what might prove to be an imposing question. If the doctors had had a falling-out, he really didn't want to know.

"He's not been the same since he took on Valentine's case," Henri offered.

Dr. Savoy rolled his eyes. "Do not remind me. I'm as much to blame on that score as anyone. I, who encouraged the infatuation when I should have done the opposite. I knew it would not come to a good end."

Henri frowned. "It's not over yet. Valentine is improving by the day, though he's determined to hide his identity from us."

"Kind of hard to do when the whole of England knows who he is and that he's staying with Stanslovich." Dr. Savoy leaned back and lifted the lid of a humidor. He took out an expensive cigar and snipped the end. "How are they getting along?"

A catch in Henri's lower gut took him by surprise. He'd not thought he'd feel that way simply by admitting to himself he didn't like Stanslovich getting closer to Valentine. "Valentine is rather secretive and standoffish. He opens up to me, but I don't feel he trusts Dr. Stanslovich. At least not completely, though it might be a matter of trying to feel out the situation."

Dr. Savoy raised a brow. He lit his cigar and puffed to get a burn started. White smoke rose into the air, rich and fragrant. When he finished, he took out the cigar and held it away from his face, inspecting the end. "Does he remember anything of the night he was… killed?"

"Not that he's admitted." Henri slid his hands down into his pockets. "The situation has grown rather delicate. Herr Maestro is here in London."

Dr. Savoy's eyes opened wide. His jaw went slack. "The hell you say."

"I scarcely believed it myself; however, I'd not forget his face so soon. He followed me around Venice, and I have no qualms he'd follow me through London."

"No. I don't doubt your word, Henri." Dr. Savoy stood and paced the room. "Is the man mad?"

"I would have to assume so, sir." The words were said with only a hint of irony. "I fear it may be much simpler than that even."

Dr. Savoy had his hands on his hips. His coattails spread out like a bird's wings when he turned. "To finish what he started."

Henri touched his nose.

There had always been a better, easier rapport with Dr. Savoy than with Stanslovich. Why that was true, Henri had no idea, but he valued Dr. Savoy's opinions and conversations.

"Good God," Dr. Savoy said under his breath. "Mikhail is up there in that big rambling house with only himself, a few servants, and one walking corpse."

"Valentine is much more than that." Henri crossed his arms. Anger bubbled at the slight. Consternation filled his gut. Unwilling to offend an ally, he changed the subject. "I haven't left Dr. Stanslovich's employ yet."

"No, of course not." Dr. Savoy took a few more turns around the room. "Perhaps I should move back into the estate until Kering is caught. An extra set of eyes, ears, and dueling pistols might come in handy."

Henri studied his hand for a moment, not sure whether to broach a very delicate subject. However, he did feel a responsibility to at least warn Dr. Savoy before he returned to the estate—if he decided to do so.

Dr. Savoy caught on to Henri's hesitation and stalled in his pacing. "You're holding something back. You've come this far, Henri, you might as well enlighten me to the rest."

Judging from Dr. Savoy's level of agitation it might not be the best policy at the moment. "No. There's nothing. I'm only worried for Valentine's safety. We risked ourselves to bring him here without discovery of his… condition. He seems to be healing well, and I'd hate for that to be in vain. Dr. Stanslovich's breakthroughs could revolutionize medicine, and I'd hate for anything to taint those discoveries."

Not the complete truth, but not a total lie either. Henri was concerned over that aspect of the case, but he was more worried about Dr. Savoy setting his sights on his best friend and getting his heart broken for the effort. Though he had mentioned he knew of Dr. Stanslovich's fascination with Valentine and had rather indulged it. To what end, Henri hadn't a clue and had no intention of asking. The relationship between the doctors was none of his business.

Henri straightened away from the windowsill. "I've taken up too much of your time. Thank you for seeing me."

Dr. Savoy waved him away with an absent gesture.

Dismissed, and glad to be so, Henri walked the streets for several more hours, trying to keep soul and body together. If he left his current situation, he'd be hard pressed to find another one before the lectures started. He had enough money saved to pay for his studies, but nothing much to live on. His room and board were included in his employment with Dr. Stanslovich. He ate with the servants, unless otherwise invited to dine with the doctor.

Henri's was a very odd position within the household. Neither servant nor family. He'd never really had much of a family to call his own. His parents had both died by the time he was twelve, and the rest of his life he'd lived either on the streets or doing odd jobs for locals.

Loneliness didn't bother him—much. On most days he had too many tasks to complete to really ever notice he was alone in the world. Then there were other days, like this one, when he'd have killed, maimed, and stolen to have someone care enough about him to give a damn.

Odd music filled the streets. Haunting. Beautiful. Where had he heard that song before? The melody sounded so familiar, and yet he couldn't place it.

His footsteps echoed against the uneven cobbles. An unseasonably cool wind blew through the streets. Henri pulled his collar closer to his neck.

A low growl came from the shadows.

He glanced over his shoulder but saw nothing there.

Music continued to follow him long after it should have faded from his awareness. Even with the aid of the wind, the human ear could not hear that far without amplification.

The feeling of being watched and followed raised the hair on the back of his neck. An odd, restless energy filled the streets.

He increased his pace.

Ridiculous!

He wasn't being followed or watched. If indeed anyone did, it had to be in the form of Herr Maestro.

Henri tucked down a side street, standing flush against a wall to wait.

Foot traffic had slowed to a trickle. If he didn't know better, he'd swear London had been placed under curfew.

Hard, heavy breath came from his mouth. He snapped it closed to reduce the noise he made. His heart hammered so loud he was afraid that might be heard by anyone passing by. Unfortunately there wasn't much he could do to slow that down but take deep breaths and hope for calm.

The music grew softer as a sniffing noise came nearer his hiding spot. He remained still as a long, wide snout came into view.

The creature looked like no dog he'd ever seen. Large yellow eyes hunted with keen intelligence. A long sinewy body moved with a grace more suited to a cat than a canine.

It sniffed the air, coming ever closer.

Normally he feared no animals. He'd had no experience with animals to draw from, though he did remember reading somewhere that wild animals did not like sudden moves. If he remained completely still, perhaps the creature would realize he meant no harm and move on by his hiding place.

If that thing attacked, he had nothing to use as a weapon. Slowly, quiet as possible, he started to back up, falling deeper into the shadows.

Finally the thing swung its huge head around to face him fully. Henri stifled his reaction. Revulsion brought bile up to his throat, and at the same time, overwhelming pity for this malformed species tugged at his heart.

It came at him at a slow gait. Shoulders rolled with power, muscles bulged beneath what at first appeared to be fur, but in the gaslight coming from the end of the alley, shone like scales. Oh, if he didn't fear for his life, he'd love to study this horrific beauty of a beast.

It opened its wide maw. Row upon row of razor-sharp teeth glinted with deadly intent. A long tongue, forked in the same manner as a serpent's, flicked the air as if tasting it for the presence of human flesh.

A loud whistle sounded in the distance. The beast turned its head in the direction of the sound. It did not, however, leave the alley.

One, two more steps forward.

The shining golden gaze met his. Oh, yes there were mysteries as well as intelligence aplenty in those eyes.

Exposed was the only word to describe the encounter. That odd creature stripped him to the bone and laid his wildest dreams bare.

An overwhelming compulsion to touch its head, to feel the scaly skin nearly had him reaching out. Good way to lose an arm.

The whistle sounded again. Two sharp trills.

It lunged forward, going up on its hind feet. Standing that way, it was taller than Henri. He started to fall away when its huge paws landed on his shoulders.

It licked his face.

Henri gave in to the sensation to stroke the creature. The skin was smooth, warm to the touch. Muscles rippled under the surface. Tense. Energetic.

Then as suddenly as it had lunged for him, it turned and fled, bounding off into the night.

Henri stood there in amazement, wondering if he had experienced a hallucination or dream.

ANDRES PUT down the book to look out at the night. Where was Henri? He'd not seen him all day, nor had he heard his voice echoing through the manor.

Fear that Azgarth had gotten the assistant beat a staccato along his nerves.

Wind began to beat against the windows. Trees danced in macabre choreography. Their barren silhouettes resembled the figures of the fae court.

He shuddered.

Beauty often hid a darker side, and nowhere was that more apparent than the realm of the dark fae.

The book in his lap no longer held his interest. Not that he understood most of the medical text to begin with, but it kept his mind occupied while he waited for Henri to return.

Where had he gone?

"Dinner is served, sir."

Andres glanced at the door, where the dour-faced servant stood. "Have you seen Henri?"

"Mr. Vauss is off the estate at present, sir."

Andres looked to the darkening sky. He'd been gone all day and was even now outside in the wind and…. Azgarth was near. Even Dr. Stanslovich had heard the eerie music playing earlier in the day.

"Should I tell the master you will not be joining him in the dining room?" The servant raised a brow and folded his hands together, awaiting instruction.

Andres had the distinct impression there was only one acceptable answer. Truth of the matter was, he had no appetite at the moment. All his thoughts and energies were focused on his worry for Henri.

"When do you expect him back?"

"He left no itinerary, sir."

With one last look to the windows, Andres rose from the wing chair and made his way slowly to the dining room. He'd not changed for dinner. Saw no need to observe the formalities. He was neither nobleman nor guest. He'd been brought here under odd circumstances and had no idea of either his place or function within the household.

From the time Herr Maestro had plucked him off that street in Vienna, Andres had been forced into a role he neither wanted nor cherished. Some might call him ungrateful for his good fortune, but they'd never understand the hellish conditions beneath the opulent veneer of the music world. They'd call him mad if they knew of a being such as Azgarth and his minion, Wilhelm Kering.

Dr. Stanslovich stood when Andres entered the room. The doctor was impeccably dressed in his evening attire. A frown spoiled the polished effect.

"Hopkins can hold dinner if you'd like time to dress?"

Valentine walked purposefully to the table. "Will the clothes I wear change the flavor of the meal or prevent me from eating it?"

Dr. Stanslovich reared back a bit. "No. Why do you ask?"

"Because I don't see the purpose of holding dinner on the excuse that I am not dressed appropriately for the occasion. It is only the two of us here in the dining room." Valentine glanced at the footmen. "Besides the servants, and I doubt they care what I wear."

Dr. Stanslovich gave a low laugh. "Then you know nothing of English domestics."

"I have been served by domestics the world over, and I believe they enjoy a little gossip to take belowstairs. Am I right?" The last of the statement was directed at a footman who seemed startled by the question.

The footman shot an unsure glance to his master, as if looking for a way to extricate himself from answering.

Dr. Stanslovich shook his head, letting the footman off the hook. "Henri is not arrived home as yet."

"I fail to see what that has to do with dressing appropriately for dinner or the state of domestics."

Andres sat and placed his napkin in his lap. "Even if you are not worried for your assistant, I am. He's been gone all day."

A pinched expression tightened Dr. Stanslovich's mouth. His nostrils flared in anger. "Henri can take care of himself and has been for more years than he's worked for me."

"That doesn't mean he should have to."

Dr. Stanslovich canted his head. "You are very decided in your opinion."

"Because I know what it's like to live on the streets and I know what it's like to have that freedom taken away."

Fascination filled Dr. Stanslovich's eyes. "From that statement it sounds as if you enjoyed the life of a vagabond to that of a celebrated musician."

Andres lifted a shoulder. "Both have their advantages. I would have better liked the security of my life in the orchestra married to the freedom to come and go as I pleased and to build relationships with those who interested me without having to gain the approval of Herr Maestro first."

Desire flared in Dr. Stanslovich's eyes.

A warning shot fired in Andres's blood at the same time a door slammed somewhere in the house. Air stirred in the great hall as if the bluster from outside had breached the windows.

Andres rose and hurried to locate the noise and found Henri running through to the servants' quarters. "Henri! Where have you been?"

Henri turned. He held his hand out for Andres. "Come, I want to tell you something fantastical that I have a hard time believing happened."

Andres placed his hand into Henri's, and his heart knew a steady beat for the first time since waking in the chemical bath. Maybe ever. He squeezed his hand around Henri's, not wanting to let go. "Dr. Stanslovich will be looking for me. He's already offered to hold dinner while I changed."

Henri looked up and down the hallway, then opened the door to his room and slid inside, taking Andres with him. Once inside he closed the door and leaned against it to barricade them inside. "I'll let you return to him, but only if you promise me you'll come back here. I'm near to bursting with the experience, and I want to share it."

Andres took a deep breath. Words clogged in his throat. Was it possible Henri wanted to share something with him that he'd tell no other? What began as a small seed of love began to grow, spreading outward, trying to reach the sun. "And you can't tell the doctor?"

Henri shook his head. "He'll have me committed to Bedlam."

"And you believe I'll understand?"

"Yes." Henri swallowed. His dark eyes filled with a pleading look. "At least I think you might."

A violent knock shook the door at Henri's back. "Henri! Are you in there?"

Dr. Stanslovich, and he didn't sound too pleased.

Henri put his finger up in front of his mouth, urging for quiet. "Henri!"

Henri fluttered his hand for Valentine to hide.

Confused over the need for secrecy, Valentine hurried to a small wardrobe and opened it. Shelves prevented him from stepping inside and closing the door. Finally he decided to fold himself under the small desk and pull the chair to. It wasn't the best of hiding places, but it was better than being caught by the doctor.

Henri dove for the bed, pretending to be asleep. The knob turned.

The door opened. Dr. Stanslovich stalked to the bed. "Have you lost your hearing as well as your senses?" He shook Henri's shoulder.

Henri feigned a startled reaction. He sat up. "What? What?"

Dr. Stanslovich put his hands on his hips. "You are in danger of overplaying your hand, Henri. Where in the bloody hell have you been all day?"

Henri rubbed his face. "You didn't expect me to stay here after you accused me of so infantile a prank even after I professed my innocence. I thought we both could use a break."

Dr. Stanslovich let out a harsh breath and paced away from the bed. "Yes. Well. I still have my doubts on who placed the beaker on the shelf, but it's too late in my research to train another assistant I can trust."

Henri let out an offended laugh. "That's quite the concession."

Andres huddled in the cramped space under the desk, watching the exchange as his heart bled for Henri. He was so brilliant, so beautiful, so kind, he should never have to endure such ill treatment from an employer. No wonder he wanted to finish his training and become his own man.

In that they were perfectly matched.

"Will you stay?"

"Yes, but you are going to have to agree to pay for my tuition. Anything less is not worth my time when I could go elsewhere and make money on my inventions."

Dr. Stanslovich stood very still. From the way he faced, his expression was lost to the shadows, but Andres bet he had thunder on his brow.

"Very well. It's a small consideration for all you've done."

Henri stood and held out his hand. "I'd have a gentleman's agreement."

Dr. Stanslovich was slow to react but shook Henri's offered hand. "Welcome back."

Chapter Ten

Henri motioned for Valentine to stay put long after he heard Dr. Stanslovich's footsteps recede from the servants' quarters. When he felt they were no longer in danger of discovery, he pulled the chair away from the desk and helped Valentine from the cramped space.

"I'm sorry to put you through that, but it wouldn't have been worth his ire to have you found here."

Valentine frowned. "He doesn't own me. I am my own man."

Henri decided against telling him the truth about Stanslovich's interest.

"I've said that a few times myself during my employ." He clapped Valentine on the upper arm in commiseration. "I think it best if you use the servants' stairs and go up to your room, then take the front staircase down to the dining hall. That way if he should see you again, you won't be seen coming from this direction."

The frown deepened. "I'm not afraid to get caught coming to see you."

Heat scorched Henri's insides. "Be that as it may, it will save us both considerable trouble if you are not."

Valentine started for the door, then stopped. "Aren't you going to tell me about your experience today?"

"Later. You go and finish dinner with the doctor. I'll wander down to the servants' hall and eat. Meet me in the library later."

"When?"

"When he thinks you've gone to bed for the night."

Valentine nodded and left, but not before touching Henri's hand in a gentle caress. "Until later."

The door closed and Henri shut his eyes and leaned his forehead against the wood. His heart was fair to bursting—not from his experience earlier in the evening—but from the tenderness Valentine was able to convey in a single touch.

Henri tightened his fist to hold on to the feeling. Life had shown him very little tenderness. It would be a shame to let the moment pass without noting its significance. Who knew when he'd experience it again?

After a few minutes in silence, he sneaked to the pantry to steal a couple pieces of hard cheese and bread. It wasn't enough to make a full meal, but it would keep him from starving. Also, Cook probably wouldn't miss it too much.

He cut through the servants' quarters and wended through the warrens of the manor that took him straight to the library to wait. Flashes of his experience with the odd creature continued to plague him, caught between the lines of fantasy and dreamscapes. The longer the time away from the incident, the more trouble he had believing it happened.

The day had been stressful, but he'd not thought he'd gone around the bend into the throes of insanity. He sat facing the window, staring out at the night. Wind continued to batter the panes. Naked tree branches danced before the window, their limbs extended like skeletal hands frantic in their message of warning.

Fanciful thoughts that he couldn't quite shake filled his head.

What had the creature wanted? It stalked him as if it already knew his scent but only meant to play with him a bit before making its move. And yet....

The library door opened, and Valentine slipped inside. He hurried across the carpeted floor and took the chair across from Henri, facing away from the window. "I told him I was exhausted and excused myself from dinner early."

"He will probably go up to check on you in a bit, so we'll make this quick." Henri held up his hand in caution. "Now I will profess, I don't rightly know what I saw or what it was, I can only describe it as it looked to me."

Valentine's eyes grew wide, and he leaned forward. "What?"

"As I walked home this evening, darkness descended quickly as the storm moved in. I sensed something following me, aside from the music that permeated the city."

"Music?" Valentine rose and went to his knees in front of Henri, taking his hand between both of his. Calloused fingertips from years of playing the violin gave his hands an erotic texture. "Oh, Henri. You must promise me you will be careful."

Henri tried to drag Valentine from his supplicant position, but he'd not budge. The man was heavier than he appeared. "I will, but you haven't even heard what tracked me."

Valentine shook his head. Golden hair glowed radiantly in the gaslight. "I don't need to. I've seen them before. Long sinewy bodies, graceful movements, teeth to rip and shred a man whole. Scales that appear obsidian in the dark."

Henri swallowed. "You have seen it?"

Valentine gave a solemn nod. "A *wolfsine*."

"I've never heard of it before." An exhibit escaped from the zoo, perhaps?

Valentine pushed up from the floor and moved to stand near the bookcase. "You won't find them in the zoo, or in books, or even in this world most of the time. They travel between this realm and that of the fae. Hunters. They search for those with special talents, and when they find them, they bite them, changing the victim's very essence until they are no longer themselves."

Henri started to laugh, but at the sincere expression in Valentine's eyes, he checked his reaction. Nerves bubbled up from his gut. His hand shook. Someone had told Valentine this tale when he was a child and he'd never learned the truth. That the *wolfsine* was an animal like any other, though perhaps very rare indeed.

"It didn't bite me. I thought it might, but when it lunged, it placed its paws on my shoulders and licked my chin."

Valentine went still.

"What?"

"I don't know. I've never heard of one reacting that way before. They either bite to turn or are sent to kill. There are no other outcomes for an encounter with a *wolfsine*."

Henri stood and indicated his body, whole and unscathed. "Apparently there is. As you see, I am unharmed."

Valentine's gaze traveled over Henri, searching, intimate. "Yes, but why?"

Heat crept through Henri's veins. He shifted in place. "I have no idea. Until today I'd never seen nor heard of such a creature. I'd be a poor candidate to tell you how they react or why." A memory came then, sharp and defined. "I believe it might have been controlled by a handler. I heard a whistle. Short blows. Commands, I think."

"Did you see anyone?"

"No. That was the oddest thing. The streets seemed to be deserted. Not right for that time of evening in that particular section of the city."

Valentine turned away and hid his face in the bookcase.

Henri closed the distance between them, then placed his hands on Valentine's shoulders. "You know something more?"

Valentine turned. Their faces so close Henri could see the tiny flecks of gold in Valentine's eyes. He swallowed down desire so raw it burned his throat.

"Tell me."

"You were between worlds. That of humans and that of the fae."

Henri hung his head for a moment, gathering strength for his argument. Valentine was not only a great talent, but he was trusting, and that made him vulnerable. Protectiveness rose up and clamped around Henri's heart. God in heaven, he didn't want to hurt him, or cause him embarrassment for believing in something that was too fanciful to be true.

But then, what was truth?

Until he'd seen the odd creature he'd have never believed it existed, but he'd felt its weight as it rested its paws on his shoulders. Felt the silky texture of its scaly hide. Its tongue had been rough and wet where it licked his chin. The sensations were real. The physical being of the creature—the *wolfsine*—was real. That had not been fabrication or imagination, but reality.

Instead of condemning Valentine for believing in the inexplicable, Henri took another route. With gentle persuasion, he brought Valentine back over to the chairs and sat him down.

Taking one across from Valentine, Henri said, "Tell me what you know of the fae."

Valentine glanced off into the room, his gaze not focused on the library or books, but some distant point only he saw in his mind. "They are every bit as tricky and spiteful as the legends claim. Azgarth even more so. He bears gifts you believe are roses, to wake and find only the thorns remain."

"And Herr Maestro?"

Valentine snorted in derision and stared into Henri's eyes. Hate, anger, and shame were palpable on the air. "I was a mere child when he took me from that street corner. I had no idea of what going with him that day meant or the price I'd have to pay. He is mortal, same as you and I, and yet he acts as if he is above the laws that govern men."

Henri reached out and took one of Valentines hands. "Was he very cruel to you?"

"More so than anyone I've ever known."

"Then I'm sorry for it, but glad you are away from him." He gave Valentine's hand a squeeze. "What else can you tell me about the realm in particular?"

Valentine let out a sigh. "It's like walking through a dream, spattered with rain. It's hard to see anything in great detail. Lines shift and move. Fluid. The fae like it that way. Mortals' eyes cannot capture them as they are, only as they want to appear."

Cold rolled over Henri's skin. He chafed at his arms. "Are you able to move between worlds?"

"No. Not alone. I get pulled in every now and then to play for Azgarth's court."

The way Valentine spoke, the candid way he discussed the fae lent credence to his words, if for no other reason than *he* believed it.

"How do you think they get into this world if they live in a parallel dimension?"

Valentine shrugged. "I can't even begin to guess. It might be inherent in their race, a trait not possessed by humans."

Or it could be that Valentine had been conditioned over the years to believe what he'd seen as truth by the use of illicit drugs to control him. That, however, still did not explain away the *wolfsine* in the alley.

Keeping an open mind for alternative explanations made for greater possibilities. It did not make it easier to digest. The side of his brain that craved hard evidence and facts pushed the fanciful notion of an alternate realm away. The other side that had seen, smelled, felt, the physical being of a thing not of his experience wanted very much to lay blame for all this at the feet of the fae master Azgarth. And why not? It was as easy as blaming God or the devil for bad luck. No one was sent to Bedlam for blaming those two particular entities for their destruction. Pull out a fae master and wave him around and people tend to look at one askance.

"You don't believe me," Valentine accused.

Henri gave Valentine another reassuring squeeze. "I am trying to gather as much information as I can. Once we get all the pieces together, then we'll make a plan and proceed to find a way to extricate you from Herr Maestro and Azgarth's hold."

This promise seemed to relax Valentine. He nodded and leaned back into the chair, letting go of Henri's hand.

"When I opened my eyes and saw you standing over me, trying to help, I knew you were a good man."

A lump formed in Henri's throat that he tried to swallow down. He only hoped he'd prove worthy of Valentine's trust.

WILHELM KNEW the *wolfsine* hunted tonight. He'd heard the unmistakable golden whistle call of Azgarth, bringing them to heel. He'd just returned from a late supper when the high, clear notes had pierced the otherwise quiet evening. No one else on the street had reacted. Only Wilhelm.

And he'd shivered.

He might want to use the creatures against Valentine, but he'd not wish to see them used on others. They were vicious and bloodthirsty. Azgarth only called them out when he wanted to track down a human to add to his collection or remove a mortal obstacle from his path. Wilhelm wondered which category this particular victim fell into, but it wasn't his concern.

Right now his only concern was in finding the direction of Miss Juliana Alexandre and securing her talent for the master. Perhaps Azgarth had sent the *wolfsine* after her. But no. He'd wait until she was already deep in her studies before he'd give her the bite.

Every movement of his back and shoulders reminded him of the consequences should he fail to find her. Being on the receiving end of Azgarth's wrath was not a pleasant way to spend an evening, though Wilhelm would bet gold bullion that the dark fae master wrung perverse pleasure from the act.

A knock sounded on his door. The desire to tell whoever it was to go away filled his mouth, but he answered anyway, afraid there might be a repeat from the morning that brought the manager.

When he opened the door, the only thing there was an envelope on the floor. He bent down and picked it up. The stationary was of good quality, but not from the hotel.

He ripped the seal, and inside was a gift from God—or at least the fae. Miss Juliana Alexandre's address was scrawled across the single sheet without benefit of greeting or salutation.

Sometimes working for the fae realm was a blessing.

He would make it a point of calling around in the morning.

For now he had to concentrate on finding the whereabouts of Valentine. There had been no reports of him spotted in the city, other than his obvious residence at the home of one Dr. Mikhail Stanslovich. However, a prominent physician would be easy to locate in a city the size of London, especially if the man in question was well known.

Wilhelm had not yet seen the good doctor. He'd only so far managed to see his assistant. Did Dr. Stanslovich not venture outside of his dwellings?

What was he doing with Valentine?

CHAPTER ELEVEN

MIKHAIL COULDN'T shake the odd dream that continued to plague him throughout the night. Even as he tried to steady the slide under the microscope lens, his hands shook from the disquieting thoughts and lack of rest.

He'd woken several times to see shadows dancing along his walls. People dressed in finery, twirling to music that came on the gusts of wind that battered the windows. If he didn't know better, he'd swear he was sinking slowly into madness since he'd taken on Valentine's care.

Surely not.

Valentine, for all his world-weary experience, seemed a pure soul, if not a fanciful one.

All the talk of the fae Azgarth the day before had followed Mikhail when he climbed the stairs and went to bed. That was all. Nothing more, nothing less. Subconscious residue from a conversation that occurred earlier in the day.

A glance out the window proved the day promised no better. The storm remained over the area, dropping rain and lashing wind on the estate. Normally he didn't take much note of the weather, but today it seemed to restrict and confine him. Made him restless. An impulse to pace the laboratory rode him hard, but he stayed to his chair, determined to find the answer as to why Valentine woke without the proper sequence of events.

He balled his hands into fists, then released them, trying to pump good blood flow into his fingers. Proper circulation meant better control and function.

He gripped the slide and put it under the lens. A look through the eyepiece didn't reveal anything remarkable about the resurrection fluid—not in the sense that it wasn't as he'd created it. The only thing left to do was stain a couple of samples and see if any organisms were identifiable in a colored medium. Oftentimes it was harder to see the smaller working parts of a substance, or to discover bacteria unless dyes were used to color the cell walls in order to better appreciate their presence. If he found any traces of bacteria in the fluid, he'd be forced to dump the entire tank and start from scratch.

Dyes were kept in the cupboard he used as a carrying case. He didn't use them that often and, as such, they stayed packed away.

Footsteps sounded behind him. As he absently adjusted the focus on the microscope, he waved a hand in the general direction of the case.

"Henri, please bring me the bacteria stains."

"Well, I'm not Henri, but I believe I'm capable of retrieving a few small vials for you."

At the sound of Dante's voice, Mikhail turned and looked at him in a mixture of annoyance and relief. "You've returned."

Dante found the case and opened the small latches with quiet clicks. "So it would appear."

"I had the distinct impression you were angry with me."

Dante pulled two small vials out and closed the case. "When it came to me that Herr Maestro has been spotted in London, I decided I would rather be annoyed with you at close range where I can be of assistance, than to be across London worrying that you might need me."

Mikhail smiled and took the dyes Dante held out for him. "I'm not pleased with the turn of events, but did either of us believe any less of the Maestro? If Valentine angered him enough to push him from a window, he's mad enough to follow him from Italy."

"Yes, but why? That's the question I keep turning over in my mind. He's been accused of trying to kill Valentine once. If something happens to him now, Kering will still be blamed. Not you." Dante pulled up a chair and placed it near Mikhail's. "What are you working on?"

Mikhail took another sample of the resurrection fluid and placed it on a slide, then added the merest dot of stain. "Looking for a reason that Valentine woke earlier than expected."

Dante made a sound in the back of his throat. "You really do like to control your experiments."

"I like to know which variables cause certain reactions. Any dedicated researcher worth his weight would do the same. Are you saying you aren't curious as to the cause?"

"When dealing with the human variable, that's reason enough to expect unplanned results. Perhaps he lived but vital signs were undetectable, have you considered that?"

Mikhail's gaze snapped to Dante's. "You can't be serious? We're both trained physicians and so is Henri. One of us would have detected some small element to suggest life."

Dante put up his hands in mock defeat. "I only made the suggestion so you don't succumb to self-flagellation over one man's superior will to live. He's awake and doing well—or so I'm told—does it matter how it happened? I think the salient point is that it did."

"You of all people should know the importance of being able to repeat and verify results. I might have use of this in the future." Mikhail slid the slide under the lens. "If there is a method that is shorter, with less lasting deficits, then it needs to be explored."

"I agree, but I don't think you are going to find the answer under a microscope."

"For a physician, you do not place a whole lot of faith in science."

Dante laughed, the sound rich and full. "You put faith and science in the same sentence. How truly telling that is of you, Mikhail."

An unexpected punch to Mikhail's gut stalled his breath for a half a heartbeat before it once again flowed with ease.

"Science is my religion, Dante. There's never been room for anything else."

"Well, perhaps you should make room."

Instead of falling into the same old argument, Mikhail smiled. "I'm glad you've come back."

Dante merely sighed. There were times Mikhail felt the physical presence of secrets between them—a barrier—and he didn't much care for it in the least. If Dante kept secrets, Mikhail had no idea what they might be, but then every man had one or two hidden away.

He hunched over to look into the microscope, only to see that the stain had dispersed, but not stuck to any cells. A low growl of frustration came from his throat.

"Nothing?" Dante lifted a brow, waiting for an answer.

"No. Nothing of note. No presence of bacteria, but that doesn't mean there wasn't some other organism in the fluid that changed the results."

"True." Dante crossed his arms. "Or it might be there is nothing external to find. Have you taken any samples directly from Valentine?"

"Henri was supposed to, but I think he might have forgotten." Mikhail couldn't stop the corners of his mouth from pulling down when he thought of Henri's recent behavior. "I don't know what's wrong with the man these days."

"Don't you?" Dante's tone suggested Mikhail knew well and good the reason for Henri's attitude change.

"Has he talked to you lately?"

Dante looked down at his hands before meeting Mikhail's gaze. "He was very upset yesterday morning and came to see me. If you are not careful, you are going to lose the most brilliant and loyal assistant money can buy."

Mikhail let out a crack of laughter. "I doubt he will be going anywhere. He has gotten me to finish paying for his schooling."

The news brought a smile to Dante's face that lit his eyes, along with another punch to the gut that Mikhail could not explain.

"Good for you. Both of you." Dante slapped Mikhail on the back a few times. "It's about time you appreciated that young man for the genius he is. One day he's going to set the world on fire with his inventions. The fact he's studying medicine has always seemed a secondary vocation to me, but one that will provide well for him."

Mikhail narrowed his eyes. "If you were so supportive of his future, why haven't you stepped forward to help pay his tuition?"

Dante dipped a shoulder. "Do you want me to? I'll gladly split the cost with you if it means seeing him graduate at the top of his class."

Mikhail searched Dante's face for any sign he made the offer in jest, but detected none. "You're serious."

"When it comes to education—always."

"Are you sure you're not offering so you can steal him away?"

"If I had wanted to employ him, he'd already be working for me." Dante's smile grew considerably, making Mikhail very nervous. "I do not poach domestics or assistants from my friends. It's bad form."

Mikhail narrowed his eyes, considering his friend for a moment longer before turning back to his work.

"Where is Henri this morning?"

"I don't know. I haven't seen him yet."

"Has Valentine shown himself or does he stay mostly in his room?"

Mikhail set to work preparing another slide. This time he used blue stain on the sample. "Valentine spends most of the day in the library reading obscure medical texts."

"An odd pastime for a world-renowned musician. Has he forgotten how to play?"

Music from the day before flooded Mikhail's mind. "He hasn't said one way or the other. I had Henri buy him a violin. He has yet to take it out of the case."

"Perhaps when he quit the orchestra, he meant to quit playing as well."

Mikhail shook his head. "No. Music is as intrinsic to him as science is to me. Neither of us could live with the loss."

"I don't know. If Herr Maestro was a harsh taskmaster, he might have made playing painful for Valentine. There was very little joy in his last concert."

"Maybe not the entire set, but his last song was gilded in triumph."

"And then he was pushed out a window."

Mikhail ignored the comment. Dante was downright melancholy at times. If Valentine had known he'd be attacked for his actions, he might have slipped away in the dark of night and not told anyone of his plans to leave. So why did he choose to make so public a display?

He'd have to make it a point to ask at dinner. For now, he found it best to leave Valentine to his own devices, to gain trust through infrequent conversations and to let him realize the estate was a safe haven and that Mikhail made no demands.

Even as he told himself he didn't want to pressure Valentine, Mikhail lied to himself. The entire goal of having Valentine close at hand was to feed his obsession for the man. To make Valentine see him as a hero, a savior, a potential lover.

But things must proceed delicately or he'd frighten Valentine away.

More footsteps in the hall. Mikhail turned to see Henri enter the laboratory. Dark circles shadowed his eyes. His hair looked finger combed, and he had yet to shave.

"You look terrible."

"The storm kept me awake." Henri rubbed his hand across his forehead. "I stayed in bed later than I wanted. I apologize."

Mikhail watched him walk to the desk and pick up the ledger from the experiments. "You should probably still be there."

Henri waved away the suggestion as he sat down and opened the ledger. "What is the itinerary for today?"

"I've managed to conclude that the resurrection fluid has not been contaminated by either gram positive or negative bacteria."

Henri canted his head. "What would make you think that it had been exposed?"

For the first time since following his theory, Mikhail had a small twinge of fear he might appear foolish in his investigation. "I want to know why Valentine woke early. I won't rest until I know the answer."

"I reported my theory." Henri turned the ledger pages. "You chose not to take it under consideration."

"I haven't discounted it, Henri. I'm merely looking at other possibilities."

Dante glanced up at Henri. "What was your theory?"

"The small electric discharge from the compression device I placed on Valentine's chest accelerated and excited the fluid in the tank." Henri looked at Dante as if waiting for approval for his postulate.

Dante did not disappoint. "Sounds perfectly feasible to me."

Mikhail shot Dante a look meant to discourage him from feeding into Henri's ideas. The effort was wasted.

Henri turned back to the ledger, letting the matter drop.

It did give Mikhail an idea. So far he hadn't found any bacteria to account for the early awakening, but perhaps he might test the water for high electromagnetic conductivity. If the levels were higher than normal, he might suppose the properties had been changed by the device—proof that Henri's supposition was correct.

And wouldn't that just sting his pride.

Mikhail collected an amp meter and a few other items he needed to test the fluid. Before climbing up to the tank, he tested the area around the base, the lights, stairs, and finally the tank itself. Nothing of note registered; however, he did get a small spike when he waved the wand over the fluid's surface.

Music began to lilt through the room. Not played on an instrument, but hummed low and deep. The voice had a good sense of tone and quality—the tune hauntingly familiar.

Mikhail turned. Icy fingers walked down his spine. He glanced around and noticed Dante too heard the humming and stared at Henri with keen interest.

"Where did you hear that song, Henri?" Dante came up out of his chair and stalked to the desk where Henri worked.

Henri glanced up. "What song?"

"The one you were humming."

Mikhail came down the stairs, listening intently to the exchange.

"Was I humming? I didn't realize."

Mikhail stepped off onto the floor. How did Henri know that song? "You were. Where did you hear that particular tune?"

Henri closed the ledger with a sharp snap. "How can I possibly answer that if I didn't even realize I hummed?"

The air of the laboratory became charged with tension. Mikhail waited for an answer that was not forthcoming. He'd not expected it to. Henri had made a valid point—if he had no knowledge that he hummed, how could he possibly know the tune? Still it seemed that tune haunted Mikhail over several countries. What did it mean? What was its purpose if not to torment?

Henri stood, picking up the ledger. "I'll go to the library to work. That way if there is any more humming, it will not disturb you or Dr. Savoy."

Mikhail waved his hand in front of his face. "Please don't be ridiculous."

"Not ridiculous—accommodating."

Music once again filled the room, but this time it sounded real, substantial, and came from another part of the house. Mikhail turned away from Henri and Dante and followed the sound, hoping that this time it was real.

ANDRES SWAYED as he pulled the music from the instrument. It wasn't as fine as the one he'd left behind in Italy, but it was adequate for creating a tune. Some violins were made to fill the soul, a bridge from the musician to the audience. Others were pieced together by magic. He'd once played on a violin so fine it was said to have been crafted from wood found only in the fae realm. Azgarth had given it to him on one of his many trips to this world.

That violin, though beautiful beyond compare and with sound so sweet it made angels weep, was cursed. Nothing Azgarth gave to his chosen came without a price, including instruments. He was more about extracting payment than giving gifts.

This violin was different.

It was mortal, crafted by the hands of a human, without thought to anything beyond creating music. The instrument felt natural in his hands. His fingers had itched to play for days, but he'd refused until the need had overridden his common sense.

A distinct feeling of being watched crawled along the back of his neck. Ignoring it, he continued to play.

Wasn't that what Dr. Stanslovich brought him here for? To entertain and amuse? If so, then Andres had every intention of fulfilling that obligation in hopes for his freedom in exchange.

With the last note of the song dying on the air, he turned to his audience, only to find Drs. Stanslovich and Savoy in the doorway along with Henri. It was Henri's smile that warmed him. His approval meant the world to Andres.

They all clapped, and Andres gave them a stiff bow.

"How do you find the instrument? Does it suit you?" The expectant look on Dr. Stanlovich's face stuck like a bur on a bare foot.

Andres studied the violin, stroking the lines with his fingertips. "It is a worthy instrument. I like its simplicity and clean lines. There is a fair resonance to the notes."

Dr. Stanslovich came forward. "So you approve of it?"

Naked desire flared in the depths of his eyes.

Andres did not want to disappoint while he was under the doctor's care, but he had no love for giving false hope to an admirer where he did not return the affection. "As I said, it is a worthy instrument."

"Will you play us something else?"

Andres cut his glance to Henri, who still stood in the doorway. "Only if Henri chooses the song."

Henri tried to hide the expression on his face from the others, but Andres saw it and his heart soared. "Play whatever you wish. Never let anyone tell you what to play ever again."

Dr. Stanslovich faced Henri. "Very diplomatic, Henri."

When Dr. Stanslovich turned back, the anger remained in the blue depths of his eyes.

"What can I say? He's spent his professional life playing for others. He's earned the right to play for his enjoyment."

Andres wished Henri would not poke the snake—in this case Dr. Stanslovich. At the moment, they were at peace, but no telling when war might break out between them. Henri was not the type of man to take orders lightly. He was too brilliant, too passionate to ever be truly subservient to a master.

Andres lifted the violin and ran the bow across the strings. A melody sweet and seductive began to pour from the instrument. If Henri wanted to give Andres a choice, he'd choose Henri. With heart and soul bleeding into the air, he played for only Henri, to show him what he'd been unable to say so far. The words were there as notes, caressing, penetrating every part of the body.

His fingers still felt stiff from his ordeal, but they loosened a bit as he played, giving himself over to his talent. Behind closed lids he saw nothing of what happened in the room around him, but heard the movement of his small audience as they took seats in the conservatory.

A jolt of pure pleasure centered directly in his heart when Henri passed by. Andres cracked an eye open to watch him sit away from the other two men.

The man was simply breathtaking, and he had no idea of his appeal. No notion that he had captured Andres's imagination. That Andres dreamed that Henri might accompany him to America to start a new life together.

But it was too soon to ask such a question. To make such plans. They had only known each other a few days, and Henri's feelings might be ones of desire and affection, but not love. It took more than the want of a willing bed partner to cross an ocean with someone.

The music changed—Andres heard it but had no more control over what came from his heart and hands than if he'd been a marionette manipulated by a depressed puppeteer.

This was not the song he wanted to play. He'd let his emotions roll too close to the surface.

A change of chord here, an increase in tempo there, and he managed to salvage the tune. He didn't want his audience to think him saddened they had saved his life when nothing was further from the truth. No, he loved the fact he still breathed—though by what means that miracle occurred he had no idea, only suspicions and no way to confirm.

Waking up to Henri's face….

The mere thought brought desire raging through his blood.

Seeing that handsome face, filled with concern and compassion, inches from his own was akin to waking in the sweetest dream he'd ever had. No one had ever cared for him, for the act of caring alone. All his admirers had wanted him because he was *Valentine*. Their concern was for his fame, not his person. Until Henri.

He held out the last note, milking the moment when he'd awakened and looked into eyes that made his heart beat truly for the first time in longer than he remembered. The story told through the notes and given to the man he wanted to love.

The three of them clapped in appreciation. Andres gave a quick bow and set the violin back in the case. "It feels good to play again."

Dr. Stanslovich held up his hand. "I wonder if you will enlighten me on a song I keep hearing in my head. The one you said Azgarth plays."

Andres stilled with his hand on the violin. "What about it?"

"I wish to know the story behind the music."

A chill swept over Andres. He closed the case lid and chafed at his arms. "Story?"

Dr. Stanslovich raised a brow. "Come now, I am a patron of the arts. I know for a fact all music has some story behind it. If it didn't, it wouldn't be worth listening to."

Andres nodded, considering the words. "True."

"And the story behind Azgarth's tune?"

Andres lifted a shoulder. "Is not my story to tell."

"Yet you played the song in your Venice concert."

Andres smiled at the memory. He walked around the side of the piano and sat at the bench. Though the violin was his first instrument, he had considerable skill at the keyboard. He lifted the lid off the keys and plucked out a few notes of the song in question. "I played it as a farewell."

"Leave him alone, Mikhail," Dr. Savoy intervened. "You can see he doesn't wish to discuss the song. Even if Henri was humming it only this morning."

Andres stopped playing, and his gaze snapped to Henri's. "You've heard the tune?"

Henri shook his head. "I have no idea what song they are referring to, since I didn't realize I'd been humming that or any other song."

Andres rose. "It's insidious. You must not hum it or even think it."

Henri's eyes widened. "How can a song be insidious?"

"Trust me. You don't ever want to find out."

Chapter Twelve

The Alexandre house was located in a fashionable section of London not far from Grosvenor Square. Wilhelm presented at the door, holding out a card and telling the rather staunch-faced butler that Mrs. Alexandre had inquired for a music instructor for her daughter.

"Servants' entrance is in the back."

The butler started to close the door when Wilhelm slapped his hand on the wood, preventing it. "I am *not* a servant. I am Herr Maestro, and you will tell Mrs. Alexandre and Miss Alexandre I am arrived."

With that, Wilhelm pushed his way into the house and began to prowl the space. "Tell her I will await them in the music room."

The butler stood there for a moment, blinking until his powers of speech returned. "Very well, sir."

Wilhelm nodded in a dismissing manner and plowed on to find the music room. Most grand residences had one. It was only a matter of finding it among all the salons, parlors, and other rooms.

He found it tucked away in the back of the house, as far away from civilized society as possible. It did not bode well for the "talent" of Miss Alexandre.

Wilhelm threw off his coat and stalked to the pianoforte, then lifted the lid. Such a small instrument for such a large home. The sound emitted from one wasn't as good of quality as that from a larger instrument. When one chose a piano, size mattered, as far as he was concerned. However, the piano was in tune, and that was the salient point at the moment.

Mrs. Alexandre and the timid and lovely Miss Juliana Alexandre entered the music room with a servant hot on their heels.

Mrs. Alexandre had her hand on her chest, enormous breast heaving with what appeared to be hyperventilation. "Herr Maestro, it is indeed an honor to have you in our home."

He gave a nod. "Yes. It is. And I must swear you to secrecy that I do this for you, to teach your daughter to be a celebrated soprano."

Not willing to give up the chance to have her daughter taught by such a great man, Mrs. Alexandre quickly nodded. "Yes. Of course. Anything you ask."

Wilhelm gave a twist of his mouth to pass as a smile. "Good. I may ask much of you and your daughter over the course of her training. It is not an easy road she travels, nor is it for the faint of heart. The road to greatness is paved with many hours of work, determination, and dedication to excellence. I will accept nothing less. Is that understood?"

Mrs. Alexandre nodded. Juliana, however, looked a bit white around the lips.

Wilhelm moved away from the pianoforte and stood before Juliana. "Is that understood? Do you wish to be the most celebrated soprano in all the world?"

"Yes." The single word came out very low and unsure.

Wilhelm cocked his head. "Is that you speaking or your mama? I want to know your opinion, and I want the truth." When Mrs. Alexandre started to interrupt, he held up his hand to shush her. "I will need her full cooperation, not yours. She will be the one spending long days singing to perfect her craft. Not you."

Mrs. Alexandre's eyes widened in shock, but she wisely did not open her mouth.

He absently gestured to a low settee in the back of the room. "Please sit over there. We want to keep this proper but without interference."

A smile hid in the corner of Juliana's mouth. So she appreciated the fact Wilhelm put her old bat of a mama in her place. He could build on that. As a matter of fact, it was important to his duty to Azgarth to cleave his chosen from their families—if they had any.

"We will start with easy scales. The voice, as any instrument, must be tuned before playing it. Singing the scales gives your voice a chance to warm. You see?"

Juliana nodded.

"Now, step to the piano."

Wilhelm took a place at the keyboard. "Stand up tall. Shoulders back. No slouching."

He played a few notes, going up the scale. "Sing with the notes I play. And begin."

The voice that came out was soft, ethereal, but too breathy to be a force or even heard unless one stood next to her.

"No. No. No." He banged on the top of the pianoforte, punctuating his dissatisfaction. "Has no one taught you to breathe properly?"

She glanced back at her mother, then to Wilhelm. "Breathe properly?"

Azgarth had exacted a punishment more cruel than any whippings he'd ever lashed out. The child knew nothing. Not even the first thing about her craft. At least she hit the note on the first try.

Wilhelm stood from the bench and came around to where Juliana stood. "Do not breathe from your throat, from the diaphragm." He touched the corresponding body part on himself. "From here. Let the air move from here and out."

He sat back down. "We try again."

He played a note and she repeated it, complete with breathiness.

"No. No. No." He slapped his palm against the piano keys, creating a cacophony of disharmony. "When you talk, do you speak like this?" He demonstrated. "No. You do not. You speak clear. For now I want you to speak the words until you understand. Again."

With each correction, a sense of vengeance soared through his blood. What he'd failed to extract from Valentine, he'd more than make up for in this slight girl who had no idea where her talent came from or what to do with it once it manifested.

"And again."

HENRI SNEAKED away from reviewing the ledger to find Valentine. Though he knew he shouldn't allow himself the pleasure of being in the musician's company alone again, a burning desire to see Valentine consumed him.

A tricky road of denial, deceit, and danger awaited him. He'd seen the look on Dr. Stanslovich's face. Had heard the speculation mixed with jealousy and anger in his voice when Valentine made the offer to let Henri choose the song. This growing attachment Henri felt for Valentine was going to end in heartache and pain for several of those he cared about.

A trip to the library found Valentine going through the book stacks. Henri watched for several minutes as Valentine picked up a book, read the first few paragraphs, and placed the volume back on the shelf.

"Is there anything in particular you're looking for?"

Valentine turned, his body stiff until he saw Henri's face, and then a gentle smile lifted the corners of his sensuous mouth. "Henri."

"I had some work to finish before I came to find you." Henri stepped into the room, pointing at the weighty medical text in Valentine's hand. "I think you might find that one a bit pedantic."

Valentine slid the book on the shelf. "I haven't found the answers to any of my questions in here, and I doubt I will."

"What questions are those?"

Valentine raised a brow. "Will you tell me the truth, I wonder? Or will your loyalty to Herr Doctor make you choose a more diplomatic response."

Henri smiled. His gaze drifted downward, landing on Valentine's mouth. "Depends on the questions."

"I want to know if I died, and if so, how did you bring me back?"

Henri looked away. He'd not be able to look into Valentine's eyes and lie. Not to a man who had tried to warn him about the *wolfsine*, even if that story seemed nothing more than a fairytale. "Dr. Stanslovich will not thank me for this, but you already know the truth. I see no harm in verifying it."

Valentine let out a shaky breath. "Herr Maestro pushed me from the window. I know that much. The last thing I felt before the darkness came was the rush of wind against my face and the sense of weightlessness."

Henri placed his hand on Valentine's arm. "You need never think of that again. We will not let anything happen to you. *I* will never let anything happen to you."

Valentine's gaze dropped to Henri's mouth. It was more than any mortal could take. Henri leaned forward, hesitantly at first, then brushed his lips ever so gently against Valentine's.

"Henri." The name came out soft and low as Valentine pulled Henri close, taking the kiss from a brief taste to a full banquet.

The book crushed between them dropped to the floor with a thud. Henri backed him up to the shelves and dove in, sampling more of the unique flavor Valentine offered.

Finally Henri broke away and leaned his forehead against Valentine's. "We have to be careful."

"Yes."

"Dr. Stanslovich wants you for himself."

"I know."

Their breath came hard, mingling in the space between them. Henri moaned, then kissed Valentine again. Desperation brought the kiss to the very brink of uncontrolled passion.

This time when Henri pulled away, he smiled against Valentine's lips. He let his gaze stray upward, trying to gaze into those beautiful hazel eyes. Valentine's lids were still closed, his mouth wet and swollen from Henri's kisses.

"Let me take you someplace special."

Valentine's eyes opened. "Where?"

"You'll see." Henri stepped back, putting space between them. "Get a coat and hat."

Excitement filled Valentine's face. "You're going to take me out in public?"

"Of course."

"I get to leave?"

"Only for a short while." Henri put his finger across his lips. "We have to be quiet if we want to sneak out without getting caught."

A line appeared between Valentine's brows. "Are you not allowed to leave either?"

"I come and go as I please. It's your presence here that will be missed."

Valentine stalled. "Am I a prisoner?"

Henri didn't want to deny the fact that Dr. Stanslovich might not let Valentine go so easily when he was fully healed, but at the same time, he didn't want to cause panic either. A good possibility existed that he'd not allow Valentine to leave, though Stanslovich had never seemed the type to keep someone against their will.

"Meet me in the garden in twenty minutes."

Valentine nodded, then leaned forward and kissed Henri hard and quick.

Henri left the library and hurried through the back passages to his room. If Valentine wanted to read esoteric works having nothing to do with science, then Henri knew just the place to find such treasures.

After donning a hat and coat, he slipped out the back doors and to the garden.

He found Valentine hunched under a tree, behind an arbor. A hat hid the long fall of his hair, creatively tucked up underneath.

"Hurry, while the doctors are ensconced in a debate in the laboratory."

Henri brought Valentine out the back of the property and to a cross street. They took a circular route until they came out in a small string of shops in one of the business districts.

J. D. Haven Booksellers was a two-story building with books for every taste and pleasure. If the book was worth finding, it was found at Haven's.

They entered the door to a soft tinkling of bells.

Henri removed his hat and headed for the back of the store. Valentine followed close behind.

"What kind of book were you searching for?"

Valentine turned in the stacks, looking up to the top story. "Nothing medical."

Henri laughed. "Spiritual, then? Metaphysical? Occult?"

"Mythological." Valentine began to read the spines as he walked along the aisles.

"Ah. Those would be on the next aisle over." Henri directed him to the next row. "Is there a particular mythos you are looking for?"

Valentine walked deeper into the aisle. "I'll know when I see it." He took a few more steps, then turned. "Do they sell old books here? Or only new ones?"

Henri pointed upward. "Older editions are upstairs."

Valentine walked to the circular iron staircase and began to climb.

A clerk bustled over, his hands clasped in front of him. "Is sir looking for anything in particular?"

Henri watched as Valentine disappeared into the upper floor. "Sir says he'll know when he sees it."

"If I can be of any assistance."

"I'll let you know."

When the clerk had moved away, Henri started up the stairs after Valentine. The books in this section weren't nearly as orderly or organized as on the first floor. Some were still in crates where they had been acquired from estate sales and other means.

Valentine looked over at Henri with an expression that conveyed an abundance of joy. "This is amazing."

"If I had known you liked books this much, I'd have brought you here sooner." Though with Valentine's condition, it hadn't been possible until now.

"Books were denied to me after I went to live with Herr Maestro. I don't know if he thought reading might make me more willful to leave or if I'd realize how to break Azgarth's influence."

Henri frowned and took a few steps closer to Valentine. "It doesn't matter which, I suppose. I hate hearing of anyone denied the pleasure of reading. It makes me hate Herr Maestro even more."

Valentine's gaze went molten. He reached out a hand and touched Henri tenderly before letting it drop. "He never knew I sneaked newspapers from all over the world. I read articles and advertisements with insatiable greed. What I was denied in books, I more than made up for in the culture of other people."

"You must have found something in one of those papers to break Azgarth's hold." Not that Henri believed the tale of Azgarth being of the fae, but that wasn't saying he wasn't a real man of great influence. He might very well be a wealthy backer who owned the orchestra to which Wilhelm Kering gave his name.

"A slight loophole in the contract that I exploited for my own benefit. Nothing more substantial than that. However, I don't believe for one moment that Azgarth has let his hold diminish. How else was I to live through my ordeal?"

Henri looked around in case someone might overhear their conversation. "I can explain that much of your story, but not here."

Valentine's gaze dropped to Henri's mouth once more, reigniting the earlier heat. "You said that before, but I became distracted by a kiss."

"I will tell you on our way back to the estate."

Valentine gave a nod of agreement. He'd hold Henri to the bargain, of that he had no doubt.

He watched as Valentine perused the shelves and dug in crates. The time grew later and day slowly slid into early evening. The sun had sunk behind the buildings on the opposite side of the street casting the upper story of the shop into dimness.

"We should be getting back. Stanslovich is going to discharge me yet."

Valentine didn't look up from his quest but pulled a book from the bottom of a dusty pile. He blew along the spine, sending up a cloud of debris from the side. He coughed.

"Find something interesting?"

"I may have." Valentine opened the cover and glanced at the pages. "It's handwritten, not done with a printing press. Old."

Henri stepped closer, looking down on the yellowed pages and faded script. "That looks like Gaelic."

"Does it? I've never seen Gaelic." He turned a few more pages. "This is Latin. And the hand is different."

Henri slid his hands down into his trouser pockets. "It's interesting if nothing else."

"This passage is written in French." Valentine glanced up, his eyes alight with the growing mystery. "Can we purchase it?"

"I don't see why not. It was lying in an old crate, forgotten."

Valentine stood and a page fell out from the back of the book. He bent down to pick it up. "Mercy."

"What is it?"

Valentine turned the page over to show Henri, and there, rendered in pen and ink, was a drawing of a *wolfsine*.

Chapter Thirteen

Mikhail paced around the manor, hands on hips and anger on his brow. Dante watched with an expression of amusement playing around his lips.

"I fail to see the humor in this?"

"Then that is to your detriment." Dante lounged in a chair by the window. He turned and glanced out into the garden. "I believe this is your errant assistant and the object of your obsession now."

Mikhail crossed the room to look out the window over Dante's shoulder. "Damn them both," he said under his breath, but a little too loud.

"Wait. Mikhail. Do not go barging off to scold either one of them or you'll wake one morning to find Valentine missing and Henri on board a ship for America. Calmly ask them where they've been and if they enjoyed themselves. It will go a long way to gaining Valentine's trust if you act more like a friend and less of his jailer."

Mikhail gave Dante a stern look to the back of his head. Sense and compassion seemed to fly out the window when he thought of Valentine.

Beautiful, passionate Valentine.

His heart gave a painful thud watching Valentine and Henri walking together through the garden, their mouths moving in an intense conversation. What could they possibly be discussing that was so important?

"I suppose I should be thankful they returned and did not run off to the wilds of America or, God forbid, Belgium."

Dante gave a throaty laugh. "Do you see Belgium as equally wild and untamed as the American West?"

Mikhail raised a brow. "Depends on the neighborhood."

Valentine and Henri angled away from the windows, coming up to the back of the house. Sneaked out and back in the servants' entrance. They had not wanted to be seen by him at all.

He hurried from the room and crossed the house to intercept them as they came down the hallway to the library. Thinking of Dante's advice, Mikhail tried for a smile as he spoke. "Enjoy your outing?"

Henri gave a shrug. "We only went to a bookseller. Never left this part of the city."

Valentine glanced at Henri before directing his attention to Mikhail. That same small stab of desire hit him as it did every time Valentine looked at him. "I needed something else to amuse me during my stay. Henri was kind enough to show me his favorite store. I am obliged to him."

What could Mikhail say to that? Anything that came to mind at the moment was going to sound sour and cross. "Henri has always gone above and beyond his duties."

There. Not even Dante could find fault with so diplomatic an answer.

Henri's expression was more than a bit uncomfortable, but he wore the emotion with dignity.

It struck Mikhail then that Henri had started to come into his own. Wild and angry when he'd come to work for Mikhail, in recent months he'd begun to settle and show signs of greater maturity.

He'd also started keeping secrets.

"I see you found something to excite your interest." Mikhail gave a passing nod to the books in Valentine's hands. "Anything of particular note?"

Valentine lifted the books a bit. "A journal written in several languages and a couple of language books to aid in deciphering."

Mikhail canted his head. "I didn't know you had an interest in languages."

"I thought it might be a good way to keep my mind agile."

"That it will." Mikhail locked gazes with Henri. "Did you have the account sent here?"

"Of course." Henri leaned against the wall, too casual for the way his shoulders tensed. "I rather thought you wouldn't have begrudged him a few books."

"Never." He gave a nod to the staircase. "It is almost time for dinner. Why don't you go change?"

Valentine gave a low assent, then turned to go to his room. Henri stood for a few moments simply looking at Mikhail, as if waiting for an invitation. None would be forthcoming tonight. He had already spent enough time with Valentine today, and Mikhail wanted a chance to spend time with him without interference.

Henri straightened away from the wall and gave a small salute before walking away.

Everything in Mikhail went tight as he watched the dejected way Henri moved to the back hallway the servants used.

"Mikhail." Dante placed a hand on Mikhail's shoulder. "Tread softly."

"I have the oddest feeling that there is a subtext here I'm missing." It didn't sit right with him either.

"How far will you go to discover the truth?"

Mikhail frowned and turned to Dante. "As far as I can."

"And if you don't like what you discover?"

Mikhail feared he'd go out of his mind with madness. Ever since the first time he'd heard Valentine play, he'd been seduced by sound and presence, knowing the music spoke to him alone. His heart had been surrendered in that moment and there had been no room for anyone else. To think Valentine might share intimacies with Henri, a man without culture or connections, it was not to be borne.

If there were some indiscretions, Mikhail knew they would all be on Henri's part. He'd have to speak with him about importuning Valentine. Perhaps he'd have to lay down a new rule about even interacting with Valentine. Now that Valentine was mostly, and miraculously, healed from his injuries, Henri needed to work on other projects.

"Come, let us share a drink while we wait for Valentine to come down."

From the look in Dante's eyes, he hadn't missed the fact Mikhail failed to answer the question. Truth of the matter, no simple answer existed. He doubted he'd throw Henri to the street, though it burned in his soul to do just that. The man's inventions were too precious to lose, even if the man himself was not.

They entered a small parlor near the dining room. Dante moved to the drinks table and poured them both two fingers of aged Scotch.

When Mikhail reached for his drink, Dante held it slightly out of reach. "Guard your heart, Mikhail. I fear it's in for a sound breaking."

"Warning heard and appreciated." Mikhail took the glass and stared down at the liquid. Shadows moved against the fluid, reflections from the gaslights. "However, no amount of caution is going to alter the way I feel."

"Then be the better man. Let Valentine go if it's what he wishes. You can't hold him here forever against his will."

"So you've said on numerous occasions."

"Because I worry for my friend." Dante put his hand on Mikhail's shoulder, squeezing tightly. "I hope you know I'd walk through a lake of fire to save you from folly."

Mikhail gave his dearest friend a sad smile. "You have my word as a gentleman, that shall never come to pass."

Dante made a noise in his throat, whether doubt or agreement, Mikhail wasn't certain.

The butler came into the room to announce dinner was served and Valentine awaited them.

"He changes quickly." Dante set his empty glass on the table and followed Mikhail into the dining room.

Valentine stood behind a chair, but had as yet to sit. His head was bowed in a prayer stance. When Mikhail walked by, Valentine glanced up. The expression was anything but serene; instead it was mutinous.

Mikhail took his place at the head of the table. Dante sat halfway down the table, leaving Valentine to sit at the opposite end, facing Mikhail.

"Do you have something you want to say, Mr. Valentine?"

Valentine placed his hands on the back of the chair, but did not sit down. He stood staring down the length of the table as if at a reckoning. "I have quite a few things, as it happens."

A charged silence followed the proclamation.

"Well. Tell us," Mikhail encouraged with an edge to his tone that conveyed the anger boiling in his gut.

Valentine reached into his coat pocket and pulled out an old yellowed piece of paper. He passed it to Dante, who glanced at the picture. His face went white and his eyes closed.

"You've seen it before?"

Mikhail held out his hand. "Give it here."

Dante handed the paper to him. On it was a drawing—a rather dated one. A creature, caught between a wolf and a serpent, stared out of the page at him. Confused, he looked up at Dante. "Where have you seen this?"

Dante picked up his wine and shot back nearly the entire glass. "Paris."

ANDRES STUDIED Dr. Savoy. Judging from the way his color drained, he did know the *wolfsine,* up close and personal. His unexpected answer jolted Valentine. "Paris? Yes, they have been noted to congregate in centers of great artistic achievement."

Dr. Stanslovich stared at the drawing. "I don't understand. Where is this leading? Why have you shown us this picture and upset Dr. Savoy?"

"Because it is important to know your house is under attack."

Dr. Stanslovich narrowed his eyes. "By this… this… creature?"

Andres felt the verbal blow as if it were a well-aimed fist. "You know who targets you. We've discussed it."

"We've discussed your vivid fantasies and paranoia." Dr. Stanslovich directed the servant to pour him more wine. "I am starting to believe you did suffer some form of brain injury in the fall."

Air stalled in Andres's throat. He gave a slight cough to get things working again. "You can't deny the proof."

"Proof? What I see is a picture of a heretofore unknown creature that may or may not have attacked Dr. Savoy and I in Paris. If so, it is a material being. Not something from the ethereal world." Dr. Stanslovich made a gesture. "Sit down, Valentine. Please."

How was he to make Dr. Stanslovich understand the peril he and the entire household stood? He shook his head. "You can insult me and question my sanity at every turn, but I know the truth. I've lived it since Herr Maestro pulled me off that street corner."

"I will say one more thing, and then I must insist we change the topic and save it for a more appropriate time and place." Dr. Stanslovich leaned forward. His direct gaze skewered through Andres with an arrow's precision. "The mind, when exposed to trauma and emotional upset, can and will play tricks. Your experiences are nothing more than your mind trying to make sense of an insensible world. Nothing more. Nothing less. Now, let us eat. Williams, if you will please serve."

Cut to the quick and having lost all sense of appetite, Andres stalked to the head of the table and plucked the drawing of the *wolfsine* from beside Dr. Stanslovich's place. He left the dining room without a backward glance.

Henri had been correct. Dr. Stanslovich's mind gave no room for speculation on the unexplained. Not even those things he'd seen and heard inside the walls of his own home.

On the walk back from the bookseller, they had discussed the situation at length. With the proof of the *wolfsine's* existence in his hand, Andres believed the drawing gave his story credence. How could they look at the drawing and not see it was true? Andres stopped on his way to the servant's quarters.

The scars on his leg.

Dr. Stanslovich had seen them when Andres had dressed on one of his first nights after waking. The jagged tooth marks on the scar matched the rendering of the *wolfsine's* mouth.

If it was material proof Dr. Stanslovich wanted, then that's what he'd get.

Andres started walking again. He found Henri in his room with a tray, eating at a small desk with papers spread out in front of him. At the intrusion, Henri looked up.

"I thought you went to the dining room?"

Andres shook his head. "You were right. He doesn't want to hear it. Even after our talk the other day, he refuses to believe there are forces he can't see or explain with science."

Henri took his hand and kissed the back of it. "Sit. I have enough food for both of us."

Warmth raced to Andres's core. Tenderness shone in Henri's dark eyes. Love swelled with all the finesse of a symphony.

Another chair, this one upholstered, sat in the corner. Odd pieces of clothing were thrown over the back. Henri's color pinked as he rose to bring the chair over to the desk.

"It helps when you have a place to sit."

"I could have sat on the bed." Andres watched and waited for a reaction. The world of music had taught him that lovers were fleeting. Relationships were often superficial, a balm to curb sexual appetite. The connection with Henri sank deeper than surface emotions. It penetrated and spread like the deep roots of a mighty tree.

Henri let out a low growl. "Is that wise?"

"Depends how you feel about having me there."

Henri gave a small self-deprecating laugh. "I want you there. You have to know how much. I just think we need to be extremely careful."

Lights burst to life in the bottom of Andres's soul, shooting multicolored sparks out along the channels of his talent. Oh, for the love of God and all that was holy, he wanted his hands on his violin to pour out these feelings that were so quick to consume.

Henri sat back at the desk and began to divide the food, using one of the smaller serving plates to place Andres's meal. "I hope you don't mind the rustic service."

"Sweet Henri, this meal is more a banquet for its sincere offering and loving company."

Color once again stole up Henri's cheeks. "You're a bit of the poet as well as musician."

Andres shook his head in denial. "No. I'm only saying what is in my heart."

"Then you have the heart of a romantic." Henri's smile suggested he didn't mind that knowledge in the least.

Andres took the plate and nodded thanks. "Most musicians do, I suppose, or our music does not ring true. There is a vast difference between being technically perfect with the execution of a song and pouring your soul into the composition."

Henri made a thoughtful grunt in the back of his throat. "It's the same with science. A man can be educated and know what he is doing, but if there is no passion behind it, success is not forthcoming."

"You wish for success?"

"I wish for a lot of things." He picked up a piece of bread and tore a hunk off. "I wish the man who sponsored me into university hadn't died before I finished school. I wish my parents had lived longer. I wish…." He broke off and gave a shrug. "No. I can't wish any of it different. If my life had unfolded on a divergent path, I'd not be sitting here now, sharing a meal with a man I've come to care for a great deal."

Andres raised a brow. A bit of a prod in the direction of truth might be just what Henri needed at the moment. "Enough to tell me the truth about my injuries?"

"Do you want to hear it over a meal?" Henri's mouth turned down. He pushed his plate aside.

"If you are ready to tell me, the hour of the telling doesn't matter much."

Henri's gaze captured Andres's. "My part in your healing began once you were brought to the villa. I was not present at the scene."

"Is your lack of presence at the scene significant?"

"Only if you want a true view of the events I witnessed."

Andres nodded. He nibbled a bit more on his food, then set the plate aside. "Go on."

"By the time Drs. Stanslovich and Savoy arrived home, there was no life left in you."

Everything in Andres went tight. He'd known all along the dark void he'd fallen into after being pushed from the window was death, but how had he been pulled from the abyss? Azgarth's influence only went so far. If Andres had died, Azgarth would have taken control of his soul, hiding it forever in the fae realm.

"How is it that I'm here?"

"Dr. Stanslovich, and Dr. Savoy to some extent, have created a procedure to bring the dead back to life. A resurrection, or as they call it, a reanimation. When you arrived at the villa, you were given a serum to arrest cell decay. You were kept in stasis by artificial means until we could get you back here to the resurrection tank."

Andres stood and started to pace the room. He had to get his mind around the events and why Azgarth hadn't been able to pull him from the material.

"Look, I am sorry. I know hearing of your own demise is difficult."

Andres crossed the room to Henri. He cradled Henri's face in his hands. "Do not be sorry. You've given me a second chance at life. One where I might yet break the bonds placed on me by Azgarth. For that I thank you." He brushed his lips across Henri's. At the moment he wanted so much more, but contented himself with the knowledge he could kiss Henri whenever he wanted.

Their feelings were mutual.

He'd never had anyone love him for himself. Not once in his entire life. Oh, they might have pretended, even been enamored, but not real, honest love—the kind he saw shining from the depths of Henri's dark eyes.

Andres ran his thumb over Henri's bottom lip. "I owe Stanslovich and Savoy for saving my life, and for that I will continue to try and get through to him."

"Unless or until he comes face-to-face with a *wolfsine*, he won't believe they exist."

Andres took a step back. "The key is to convince Dr. Savoy. He recognized the picture. Knew the *wolfsine*."

Henri made a considering look. "Then that will be our in. Dr. Savoy shares a particularly close relationship with Dr. Stanslovich. I'll try to cultivate his support."

Andres let out a slow, even breath. "When we've done all we can to protect him and I'm free of Azgarth, I want you to come to America with me to start a new life."

Henri stood. "Are you in earnest?"

"Complete."

"Then I accept."

Chapter Fourteen

WILHELM WOKE with a start. He wasn't alone.

Azgarth watched him, sitting on an obsidian throne up in the corner of the bedroom. The fae master lounged sideways in the seat, one leg draped over the arm. He raised a silver goblet of wine to Wilhelm.

"The Alexandre woman is coming along?"

"No. The Alexandre woman is a disaster in the making. She fails to listen to direction and refuses to do anything unless her mother approves."

Azgarth pursed his lips. "Perhaps I can intervene with the mother."

Wilhelm knew what Azgarth's version of intervening meant and doubted Miss Juliana would ever see her mother again. But what did he care? As long as she was out of his way and he could mold the impossible child to fit the image of a diva.

"Work harder. I have arranged for her to sing at the Malmount on Friday."

The Malmount? Azgarth said that as if the name bore significance.

"She will not be ready."

Azgarth straightened, then leaned down, his face morphing into a menacing mask. "You will make her ready or this time I'll leave no skin on your back."

Wilhelm shuddered.

MUSIC POURED down the hallway of the Alexandre home. Voices mixed in melodious delight. One high and slightly breathy—though not as bad as before. The other a clear, rich tenor that showed immense talent and promise. He hurried to the music room to find the owner of such exquisite tones.

A handsome man with dark golden hair and rakish eyes sat playing the pianoforte while he and Miss Alexandre sang.

The man cut off playing when he saw Wilhelm and stood from the bench. Miss Alexandre turned. "Herr Maestro. This is my brother Niko… Nicholas."

Wilhelm bowed. "You have a lovely tone, Mr. Alexandre. A pure tenor."

A sly smile came to Nicholas's face. He raised a tawny brow and crossed to the back of the room. "If you will excuse me, I have work to do."

Confused by the look on Nicholas Alexandre's face, Wilhelm turned to his student. "We have a lot of work ahead of us the next few days. You are booked to sing at the Malmount on Friday evening."

Miss Alexandre clasped her hands in front of her chest. Her eyes danced in excitement. "Nicholas! Did you hear that? I'm going to sing at the Malmount."

"I did indeed." Nicholas flipped his jacket tails out of his way as he sat at the desk. "I shall encourage all my friends to attend."

Wilhelm took the piano bench, then turned to face Mr. Alexandre. "How would you feel about singing alongside your sister?"

Nicholas laughed, the sound rich and throaty. "My public talents lie elsewhere."

What did that mean?

Enigmatic and mysterious, Nicholas Alexandre reminded Wilhelm a great deal of Valentine.

"I assure you, Mr. Alexandre, you have enough talent to be the most celebrated tenor of your generation."

Nicholas's laugh took on a cruel edge. "Oh, yes. I can see the marquee now." He put up his hand and waved it in a grand gesture. "The Singing Alexandres. Tonight only."

"You scoff, but it can bring the world to bow at your feet."

"Like it did Valentine before you pushed him out of a window?" Nicholas rose.

"Nicholas!" Miss Juliana hid her face in shame.

"Leave the fame and fortune to my sister—if you dare?"

Nicholas Alexandre walked out of the room. A few moments later, a servant entered and took up a place near the back of the room.

"Is your mother not in residence this morning?"

"No. She was called away unexpectedly."

Azgarth worked quickly.

Wilhelm set his fingers to keys and started the painful act of putting Miss Juliana through her scales.

HENRI WOKE feeling as if he'd drunk more than he should without benefit of having a good time. Pain pounded behind his eyes with such ferocity he swore blood dripped across his pupils. What in the hell had happened? The last thing he remembered, he'd been talking with Valentine; the next he'd fallen into a hellish dreamscape.

He rose from bed and went to the washbasin to splash cold water on his face. Though it refreshed, it did nothing to truly revive him. Sun broke through the edges of the curtains on his window. His was the only room in the servants' quarters equipped with one, other than the butler's apartment and parlor. The tiny concession made his life in Dr. Stanslovich's household at least appear a bit more pleasant. Truly he was given great latitude when performing his duties, something not every employer would allow.

After dressing and a quick breakfast in the servants' dining room, Henri hurried to the laboratory, intent on working all day on the ledger and to run tests on electric current within the tank.

Dr. Savoy was already at work. He sat at the table looking into the microscope. Henri sat adjacent to him and opened the ledger to the last page he'd studied. First glance at the notes and already frustration built. Nothing stood out as remarkable or indicative of a malfunction of the unit. Temperatures in the fluid and tank were steady and within normal limits. Increases as they slowly warmed Valentine were all inside the expected and predicted parameters.

Yet, Valentine knew he'd died.

Did some cerebral function remain when the serum was administered? To Henri's knowledge, Dr. Stanslovich had never explored that idea. If there was a low level of electrical impulses coming from the brain, was it possible Valentine had willed himself awake to stay out of the clutches of Azgarth?

Even if there was conduction, that did not necessarily follow he enjoyed any cognitive function while in stasis.

"You are working very quietly over there, Henri." Dr. Savoy's voice cut through the silence of the room.

"Contemplating brain function while a subject is in stasis."

"A very heavy topic, indeed."

Henri turned, considering Dr. Savoy. "Valentine relayed to me that he knew the moment he died. If he knew that, is it possible he retained some electrical brain function in order to bring himself up from stasis quicker than Dr. Stanslovich intended?"

Dr. Savoy frowned. "Did he report anything during the time he was deceased?"

"No."

"It is hard to say where the brain function ends and when the subject, once awakened, fills in the gaps of what he thinks should be there. Frankly, given Valentine's head injury, I'm surprised he even knew that much, let alone his last performance."

Henri's initial assessment had been similar, but that's not what he'd found. Not since Valentine woke with the fear and pain in his eyes. He'd looked as if he'd been running for his life—and maybe he had. Perhaps it had been Herr Maestro he'd attempted to get away from and not Azgarth.

Henri ran a hand down his face as high, sweet music began to move through the house. Dr. Savoy's expression grew tight.

"You know that tune as you knew the *wolfsine*."

Dr. Savoy stood. "Is Valentine playing that song?"

"I doubt it."

Dr. Savoy shot a look of anger. "Why do you doubt?"

"Because it has bad memories for him."

"And yet he led off with it at his farewell concert. Why play it then if he hated it?" Dr. Savoy seemed to enjoy playing the part of provocateur.

Henri shrugged. "As a final sword thrust to Herr Maestro. Because Valentine does not set the program. If we ask Valentine, we'll have the answer to that question."

"You are probably correct. I doubt the infamous Maestro has ever given up enough control to let his musicians decide the program."

The haunting melody continued to lilt through the laboratory. Shadows danced along the walls, echoes of waltzes long since faded. Henri turned first one way, then the other, not trusting his eyes.

"It's not the fault of strain or poor lighting. Oh, they are very much there."

Henri stared at Dr. Savoy. "You've seen them before?"

"Yes, and so has Mikhail, though he'd never admit such to himself, let alone the rest of us."

The music faded, shadows dimmed. No, not dimmed—moved. Henri rose and went to the door and looked out. Figures twirled in concentric circles getting closer to each other. When they were in as tight a space as could be, a tall column of dimness stayed fixed on the spot. The music had changed. Gone higher in pitch. Flatter. The notes incongruous, chords sinister.

Henri felt the heat of Dr. Savoy's body at his back. "What do you think that is?"

Valentine came running into the great hall from the opposite direction. He skidded to a halt, his arms out to catch himself at the archway, eyes wide and frightened. "Henri, come away from there!"

"You know this phenomenon?"

"It's how Azgarth enters from the fae realm."

Dr. Stanslovich came from another hall. He glanced at Valentine's unlikely explanation. "Don't be ridiculous, man. It's caused from chemical bleed over from the laboratory mixed with dust motes and sunlight."

A deep laugh filled the room, echoing from the walls and causing the column to quiver.

"Mikhail, this is no chemical bleed over. We've used none this morning." Dr. Savoy skirted around the perimeter of the room, keeping away from the well of shadows.

"Then it has collected as the house has been closed. Get these windows open and drive it outside instead of standing here like frightened old women."

Dr. Savoy managed to make it to the windows, flipped the lashes, and threw open the panes. The column remained in place, as if defying Dr. Stanlovich's reason.

Dr. Stanslovich fanned his arms in a vain attempt to get the thing to move. It continued to spin in place, gaining speed. "Bring me the fireplace bellows."

Henri ran back into the laboratory to grab the ones located there. He slid them over the floor to Dr. Stanslovich, who stood facing the window and thus had a better vantage to fan the column in the desired direction.

Dr. Stanslovich picked up the bellows and worked them with all the vigor of a demon stoking an unholy fire. Sweat dripped from his brow, wetting the fringe of hair around his face. Again the column most stubbornly remained in place. "Damn! I've never seen anything like this. Henri, you don't have any electric devices running in the laboratory do you?"

"No. I've only opened the ledger."

"Go and power down the tank."

Henri stood in shocked silence for a moment. As long as he'd worked for Dr. Stanslovich, the tank had never been powered down.

"Go!"

The same haunting laugh followed Henri to the tank controls.

From the great hall, he heard Valentine protest that all the electricity of a thunderstorm could not alter the truth.

Circuits popped and sparked, sending the stench of burnt ozone into the air.

"Henri...."

His name was an echo on the wind.

"Henri Vauss...."

He blocked the sound. No way in hell was he going to answer the summons from some dark master. He reached down, going for the tank's control panel. Lights flickered in the water, showing the power was neither steady nor reliable. It seemed whatever strange phenomenon had invaded the manor had decided against Dr. Stanslovich maintaining control of his own equipment. This was not the way Henri would have chosen to confront the strange energy, but it was not his call.

No matter what happened to the tank, Henri could fix it—make it better. He disconnected the control box from the circuit. Power ceased. The tank went still, dark. The laboratory sounded eerily quiet without the constant burble of the fluids contained within. Tiny bubbles rose to the surface. They burst and popped with great efficiency.

Interesting.

Henri grabbed a beaker from the cabinet and climbed to the top of the stairs. He'd assume the bubbles were caused by the release of oxygen molecules in the liquid, but the mixture had since settled. Reactions of this magnitude and ferocity should have been spent long ago.

Raised voices came from the great hall. The argument escalated. Angry words peppered the air, followed by what sounded like someone spitting. Valentine was in rare form.

He tried to block out the events unfolding beyond the laboratory and concentrate on the tank.

"Henri! Is the power down?"

"Yes!" Henri lay on his belly and scooped some fluid out of the chamber. Movement stirred the bottom of the liquid. He jumped back, scrambling down the stairs.

A side view of the tank didn't reveal anything of note.

He took a deep breath and let it out slowly.

Just his imagination. He'd seen nothing. Only his imagination playing tricks.

"Are you sure you've disconnected the power source?" Dr. Stanslovich's voice was closer this time.

Henri turned from staring at the tank, waiting for a life-form to spring from the depths. "Yes."

Dr. Stanslovich frowned. He tapped his lip in thought. "It had no effect on the column. It's still there."

"Maybe you should listen to Valentine. He seems to be the only one who knows what is going on." Henri pointed to the tank. "I've lost perspective and a bit of my mind. I'm even seeing—"

"Henri! Watch out!"

The warning came a moment too late. Something hard, heavy, and wet crashed down on him from the rim of the tank. He fell to the floor, fighting his scaly opponent. The *wolfsine* bit and snarled. He grabbed its head between his hands, trying to keep the sharp teeth from sinking into his flesh.

The head swung around, connecting with the underside of Henri's chin. His head jerked back. Stars exploded behind his eyes, and he bit his tongue. Blood filled his mouth.

Another sleek body crashed into the first *wolfsine*. The two creatures rolled end over end, giving Henri enough time to crawl away.

His heart beat up into his throat. His breath came hard and fast.

He recognized the second *wolfsine* as the one from the alley. Had it come to save him from its brother?

His protector grabbed the attacker by the base of the tail and swung him up into the tank. Resurrection fluid splashed over the sides, drenching Henri in the deluge. Protector approached Henri and nuzzled his chin before bounding up the steps to disappear into the tank.

Henri sat perfectly still, careful to avoid Dr. Stanslovich's gaze.

The silence was oppressive. Confining.

If Henri was asked to describe the events that had taken place, he'd have no words to adequately convey the scene. Had it been hallucination or imagination? How had they gotten into the tank in the first place?

The silence was broken by the steady tap of Dr. Stanslovich's shoes across the floor as he approached the tank. "Up, Henri. We need to dump this now. Now!"

For once, Henri didn't even think to argue.

He sprang from the floor and hurried to the cabinet where the vacuum pump was located. With the size and capacity of the tank, it was going to take hours to drain it down to the bottom, even with the modifications Henri had made to the system. For all the good it would do. If the *wolfsine* wanted to find a way into the manor, they didn't need to use fluid or shadow columns or any other means. They'd come if they were summoned by their master to do so.

Henri connected the pump to the hose. Last time they'd had to dump the tank due to a contaminant, Henri had converted the old hand crank to a steam-powered engine.

Dr. Stanslovich opened the window to pull the drainage hose outside to spill the runoff into the garden.

"Where are Dr. Savoy and Valentine?" Henri straightened from his task and wiped his forehead with his sleeve. His hands continued to shake from the *wolfsine* attack.

"Dr. Savoy is tackling the phenomenon in the hall. Valentine has stormed off to only God knows where." Anger and annoyance dripped from Dr. Stanslovich's words.

"He's passionate about what he believes in."

Dr. Stanslovich raised a haughty brow as if about to pass judgment. He opened his mouth to say something when he shook his head. "I'll admit I'm—we're—out of our depth here, but I'm not about to agree that it is anything more than illusion."

"Valentine is a musician, not a magician." Disgusted, Henri turned from the tank and started for the hall.

"Where are you going?" Dr. Stanslovich called after him.

"To see where Valentine has gone to sulk."

Chapter Fifteen

Andres had come to the manor with nothing and intended to leave with only the clothes on his back and the violin with which he'd been presented. He'd not even leave with that much if he could get away with it, but he had no way to make enough money without the instrument. He knew no other vocation than playing for someone's pleasure.

He'd been a busker when Herr Maestro discovered him. Life might have taken him in a different path and shown him riches beyond his imaginings, but he hadn't risen so high that he forgot how to play for his supper. Or in this case, passage to America.

Andres glanced up, feeling someone watching him. Henri stood in the doorway.

"Where are you going?"

"To find a street corner."

Henri came forward and put his hand on Andres's arm. "Don't leave."

Heat curled up from his belly to spill along his insides. The words clenched at his heart. He swallowed. A lump formed in his throat. "I won't stay where I'm not believed even in the face of overwhelming proof."

"What you see as proof, he sees as another mystery to solve."

If Henri meant to absolve Dr. Stanslovich, he'd used a poor example.

"I don't care what he calls it." Andres picked up the violin. "May I take this, or will I be called a thief?"

Henri shook his head. "It was a gift from Dr. Stanslovich. You may keep it."

Andres planned to, but he'd as soon ask as get accused of taking things that did not rightfully belong to him. "May I contact you here?"

Henri crossed his arms and leaned against the wardrobe. "As you wish, but I'd rather you stay here until I'm in more of a position to leave with you."

That stopped Andres as nothing else. "I can't stay in this house another night. You saw the rift. Azgarth is coming, and there is nothing we can do to stop him."

Henri pushed off from where he leaned and crossed the room to take Andres's arms in a firm grasp. "If that is true—and no, I'm not questioning you—but if Azgarth has the power to rip the fabric of alternate dimensions, then running to America isn't going to do you a damn bit of good. You need to stay and confront him. Find out what he wants."

A well of fear and sorrow opened in Andres. "I already know what he wants. He wants my soul. My life. He wants me to play for eternity in his palace. Don't you understand? Once he's chosen you, you are nothing but his property, able to only do what he wills and at his pleasure."

"And yet you tried to run. Is that why you announced you were leaving the orchestra? Because you no longer wished to be in his service? Or thought you might be able to outdistance him?"

"I left because I could no longer bear Herr Maestro's torture." Andres watched as Henri slowly sat down on the bed. "What?"

Henri shook his head and held his curled hand to his mouth. "Nothing."

"It's something, or you wouldn't look like you've eaten something that didn't agree."

"How did Herr Maestro become an agent for a dark fae?"

Whatever Andres supposed Henri might say, that question was not it. "I have no idea."

"I wonder. Is there a talisman or relic? Anything that signifies him as an agent for Azgarth? If so, perhaps if we were to steal the relic, we could release you."

"I don't remember any relic. Nothing that appeared a symbol of power." If he saw one, would he have recognized it as such?

"Think on it. You might have been unaware of it at the time because you weren't looking for it."

Andres fingered the violin case. "I would love to find such an item. To destroy it and gain my freedom once and for all. To know I will no longer have to live under Azgarth's thumb or fear Herr Maestro."

Henri's jaw tightened. Unable to stand the expression a moment longer, Andres leaned over Henri, caging him with his arms. "You know something about Herr Maestro. What is it?"

Henri's gaze slammed into Andres's, only to slide down to his mouth. Heat rose and flamed out of control. Andres lowered his mouth, attacking Henri as if brutal passion might loosen his tongue.

Henri's hands settled on Andres's back, pulling on his shirt to get to the skin underneath.

Andres broke off the kiss. "Yes. Touch me, Henri."

Henri complied, running his fingertips down the center of Andres's spine. Andres bucked his hips, grinding his rising erection into Henri's groin.

He'd never wanted a man so much in all his life as he did Henri Vauss.

"I want to make love to you." Andres spoke against Henri's lips before taking another taste.

"Are you sure? You've been—"

Andres didn't let Henri finish his sentence, afraid the words might be denial or postponement. Instead he began to seduce, entice with teeth and tongue. Gentle persuasion was often more successful than brute force. Not that he'd ever force Henri to capitulate. No, he much preferred his bed partners willing and eager.

He broke off the kiss and stared into Henri's dark eyes. "Will you really go to America with me?"

"If you want, but not as a follower. You've had enough of those during your career."

Andres ran a hand down Henri's face. "Ones I've never asked for."

"Then why me?"

"Do you have to ask?" At a loss, he ran a thumb beside Henri's eye. "Because you've the most loving and compassionate soul I've ever seen. You are gentle and kind when I've known very little of that emotion—at least from those who want nothing from me."

"Why should I treat you any other way? You've done me no harm, or offered offense."

Happiness raced through Andres's body. He laughed despite his earlier anger at Dr. Stanslovich. "You prove my point. You cannot imagine being any other way. You are simply the most decent man I've ever met."

Color splashed across Henri's cheeks. "A decent man wouldn't be thinking about all the ways he wants to pleasure you so soon after you've been revived."

Heat speared Andres. He leaned forward, his mouth barely grazing Henri's skin. Stubble grated against his lips, sending erotic sensation down to lodge in his groin.

He'd always loved the texture of a masculine face. The subtle feel of a day's growth of beard just breaking the surface. He wanted to see and feel the rest of Henri. To know him in every sense of the word.

Andres ran his lips along Henri's jaw to whisper in his ear. "Why think when you can act?"

Henri turned his head and pulled Andres into another heated kiss. Then there were no more words, simply passion and emotion. The only thing that mattered in this moment was the fact they were together. Alive. The rest would sort itself out in time.

Andres lifted the hem of Henri's shirt and skimmed his fingertips up the warm muscles and smooth skin underneath. Elegant strength was evident in every movement of Henri's body. "Let me see you."

Henri took a step back and unbuttoned his shirt, then shed it quickly. He let it fall with a careless release of his fingers. Andres drank in the sight. A dark dusting of hair covered Henri's chest, narrowing to a thin line that disappeared under the waistband of his trousers. The rigid outline of his erection tented the soft wool fabric.

Andres said nothing as he gently unbuttoned the placket and shimmied the garment off Henri's hips. He went to his knees and took Henri into his mouth. A shuddery moan filled the room as Henri submitted, wending his fingers through Andres's hair. Little sounds urged Andres to work him as he would a musical instrument, coaxing a song that built to crescendo until the exciting finale.

Henri's grip tightened on Andres's head. "Stop."

Andres released Henri's cock and gazed up at his lover.

Henri reached down and pulled Andres to his feet, then backed him up to the bed. "Lie down."

Andres did as told, keeping his gaze trained to Henri. Naked, Henri crawled up Andres, taking time to undress him as he did. Andres put up no defense, but fell into sensation as Henri began to lick and kiss each new uncovered patch of skin. He proved compassionate not just as a healer, but in every aspect of his lovemaking.

Scars—Andres had many—were left bare for Henri to see. Shame at how many he had put a lump in Andres's throat. He'd never want Henri to see him as weak for having failed to fend off Herr Maestro's punishments. Lash marks covered his upper arms, back, and thighs in silver lines. Henri gently nudged Andres over onto his belly where he began the slow act of kissing the remembered pain away from each mark left behind in a lifetime of torture.

This was the healing and acceptance Andres needed—what he knew he'd find in Henri's arms from the moment he'd woken in the resurrection tank. A new life had been granted him. Not quite the answer to the prayers he'd made, but then so much more than he'd ever expected.

Andres closed his eyes as Henri made his way down to the small of Andres's back. He opened his mouth on a moan. Then Henri turned him over and started on the front.

Andres held his hard length away from his body, offering it up to Henri.

Henri moved over him, wrapping his hand around Andres's cock at the base. Then he was there, taking long pulls that took Andres down into a sweet oblivion.

This lovemaking was all things beautiful. Nothing that came before could even compare. He felt the moment his balls tightened, readying him for orgasm. He tried to hold back the inevitable, but it was as sure as the tide. Henri slid his hand under Andres's bottom and lifted, taking more into his mouth.

When Henri began a sweet pressure against Andres's anus, the fight to hold back came to a stunning and incredible end. Finally Henri released him and stared up into his eyes.

Andres's breath caught and held at what he saw there. "I wanted to make love to you."

"Who said you can't?"

Andres felt the smile that curled one side of his mouth. He pushed up onto his elbows, looking down at the top of Henri's head, who had gone back to licking and sucking. He lifted his hips in offering. Even now, when the first blush of passion had yet to dim, when the sweat had not yet dried on his skin, he was growing hard again, ready to continue this lovemaking. Henri was a practiced lover. Perhaps his knowledge of the human body made him well versed in how to please a partner. Who was to say? Only that Andres had never felt more loved and cherished. This was how it should be between lovers. A give-and-take of exquisite care. Unrushed and unruled by the outside world.

Rolling up, Andres reached for Henri and pulled him along his body until their lips met. "Let me love you. Return to you all you've given me."

Andres felt rather than saw Henri smile against his lips. "Is it what you want?"

"More than anything in the world." He put action to deed and reached down to circle Henri's cock with a firm grip.

Henri let out a low moan. "I love the feel of your hands on my skin."

The soft words were all the encouragement Andres needed before turning Henri onto his back and moving over him in reciprocation. This time instead of taking the hardness of Henri's erection into his mouth, Andres moved his cock over Henri's length, rubbing them together.

Henri reached down between them, massaging them both. Andres joined in as they rolled their hips, brushing their cocks together.

His hair fell like a curtain between them. He couldn't see Henri's face and wanted so much to watch the expression of pleasure that moved over his beloved features. How could any one man become so important to his life so quickly? The emotions defied logic and sense, and yet here he was lying on a bed, entwined in Henri's arms, giving and receiving incredible pleasure as if a gift from the heavens.

"Kiss me." Henri brushed his lips against Andres's. Passion put heat behind the words.

Denying Henri hadn't entered into Andres's mind. He opened his mouth, running his tongue along the seam of Henri's lips, tasting the saltiness of his earlier orgasm there. A moan rose from his throat.

Henri bucked his hips harder, grinding into Andres. "I'm going to come."

Hearing the words shifted something elemental inside Andres, where he'd never be the same again. He tightened his grip on Henri, bringing him to an explosive finish.

They stayed that way for a few moments, kissing and touching. Then Andres rolled over, immediately missing Henri's warmth.

Andres placed a hand under his head and stared up at the ceiling. Beside him, Henri lay in a similar position. Their breath still had not come under control.

Into the quiet that followed their lovemaking, Henri turned to him. "Don't leave."

Leave? How could he even think to leave now he'd been loved by a man like Henri? His heart was filled with emotions too large to contain in a mortal vessel.

"I won't go far, but I can't stay here in this house. You know I can't. Each day brings a new way Dr. Stanslovich offends me." Andres turned, resting his head on a bent arm. "Do not misunderstand me. I am grateful he intervened and saved me, but I'll not be his whipping boy."

Henri ran a tender hand down Andres's face. His eyes closed of their own volition. "I'll not let him treat you that way, but I will say that Herr Maestro is in London. Going out alone or planning to live outside these protective walls is not in your best interest."

Andres blew out a breath and rolled away to stare at the ceiling again. "All right. I'll bow to your wisdom in this, but I won't allow Dr. Stanslovich to address me as he would a naughty or ignorant child."

"Then tell him that. You are his equal and so much more. Don't let him use you to wipe his feet."

Andres raised a brow and sneaked a look at Henri. "You should take your own advice."

"I'm an employee, not a guest. The same rules do not apply to me as they do to you."

They fell into silence once again. It stretched out. The only sounds in the room were those coming from the rest of the manor. When Andres could stand the silence no longer he turned to Henri.

"What do you want to do?"

Henri glanced at Andres. "About Herr Maestro?"

"And Azgarth. Do you have any ideas?"

"Other than finding a talisman, no." Henri sat up, turning to Andres. The sheet bunched around his waist. "I wonder if your book has any ideas. It did have a picture of a *wolfsine*."

Excitement flooded Andres's veins. He stood and began a mad search for his clothes. "Then come on, let's get dressed and go to the library."

Henri wasn't as quick to rise. He set about looking for his clothes as if drawing out the moment.

Andres paused in dressing. "You don't think that is a good idea?"

Henri gave a laugh. "In earnest, it's a fine idea. I just don't want to leave this room and let the problems and personalities intrude."

Love spilled in a warm rush through Andres's veins. "Me either, but the sooner we can figure out a way to break the chains Azgarth has placed on me, the sooner we can live our lives without fear."

Henri glanced up as he stepped into his trousers. "I fear nothing, Andres."

"Not even the *wolfsine*?"

Henri opened his mouth as if to say something, then closed it again. "What?"

Henri shrugged off the question and picked up his shirt from the floor.

"Henri, love, please tell me."

Henri shot his arms through the sleeves. His expression remained tight, closed.

"Are you not going to tell me?"

"It's not a matter of not wanting to tell you, more of not knowing quite how to put my thoughts into words."

Andres relaxed a bit. "Then perhaps once we begin work on the translation you might find the words."

Henri gave a laugh. "Though I doubt they'll be in English."

THE PAPER was brittle, thin as dry leaves of seasons past. Henri copied a passage onto a separate sheet, then sat with the appropriate language text to translate. He knew French, of course, and Latin as it pertained to Mass and medicine, but German and the Scandinavian languages were a different matter altogether. Some of the passages were written in Italian and Portuguese. The journal appeared to have been passed around the continent, with each country electing one or two people to write their accounts of the tale. Whatever that might prove to be.

Andres worked across from him, able to translate whole passages as he read.

They'd divided the entries into who read what language fluently. For the ones neither of them spoke or read, they'd have to work their way through slowly, methodically, as Henri did now.

So far the entries revealed nothing but what they had already witnessed. *Wolfsines* shifted easily between dimensions. Henri had no idea how it had gotten into the tank if not simply appearing from some place unknown by mortal man.

"Are you ever going to return to the laboratory today?" Dr. Stanslovich stood in the doorway with his arms crossed and anger on his brow.

Henri tapped his pen against the paper. "I'm doing research at the moment. Looking for something that might explain the phenomenon we encountered. Not all answers can be found in a laboratory, sir."

Dr. Stanslovich pushed off from the door and came into the room to look over Henri's shoulder at the papers strewn across the table. Andres had looked up from his work, his face tight with anger and distrust.

"This looks like it might take a while. Can't you create a device to analyze the anomaly?"

Henri folded his arms across his work and looked up, locking gazes with Dr. Stanslovich. "In order to devise an apparatus, I must first know what it is I'm looking for; otherwise, how will I know it is working?"

"And you believe you're going to find what you're looking for in an old book?"

"An old book of observations from experiences such as we had," Henri corrected. He didn't bother to enlighten Dr. Stanslovich that he stretched the truth a bit. What would be the point in that? Enough, though, leeched from the pages to seed Henri's argument with a kernel of truth.

Dr. Stanslovich made a sound at the back of his throat, not quite a clearing, but enough to sound skeptical. "I will give you some latitude here, because we have no idea what we're dealing with, but I warn you, I will not entertain the esoteric."

Andres put down his pen, anger having reached critical mass. He began to light the room with angry German phrases. He stood, continuing the diatribe that neither Henri nor Dr. Stanslovich understood. The angered musician began to pace, strut, gesture, and smolder.

Dr. Stanslovich put up his hands. "Please calm down, Valentine. I don't wish for you to overset yourself."

"Then open your eyes to the world around you!" Andres switched to English, broken though it sounded. "There is more in the universe than you can devise in your laboratory."

"What is going on in here?" Dr. Savoy entered the room, hands on hips and giving each of them a stern look. "You're like a nursery full of noisy children arguing over a toy."

Dr. Stanslovich spared Dr. Savoy a heated expression. "I only came in here to inquire when my assistant might be disposed to do the work for which he's being paid."

"Henri doesn't speak German." Sarcasm dripped from Dr. Savoy's words, with quite a bit of quiet anger.

Andres gave a huff. His hands hooked low on his hips. "I let Dr. Stanslovich know what I think about how he treats Henri. How he treats me."

Dr. Stanslovich's expression never changed—his eyes, however, showed an abundance of hurt. "It was never my intent to treat you unfairly, Valentine. I hope you know that."

"But Henri?"

"Is paid to do a job. He's not a guest here, but an employee. The rules that govern him are not the same that govern you."

Andres folded his arms over his chest. "I did not ask to be a guest. I have no idea why you chose to pluck me from the canal and put me back together as you did, but I do know this is as close as I've ever been to freedom since Herr Maestro took me from the street corner, and I will let nothing get between me and my dream of going to America."

"Wait until you have fully recovered, and I will take you to America myself."

Andres rolled his eyes. "For a brilliant man, you know nothing of the human heart."

With that he sat back down and stared at the text.

For once, Henri felt a bit sorry for Dr. Stanslovich. Looking at him, Andres's words had put Dr. Stanslovich at a complete loss.

Henri stood. "It's been a very trying day. We have all drifted out of our element. Let me see if I can find anything to point me in the right direction for dispersing the phenomenon. Before the commotion in the laboratory, I pulled some fluid from the tank. Maybe you'll find something of note in there."

Dr. Stanslovich frowned. "What did you hope to find?"

"I wanted to see if the water held a current of its own or had become magnetized in some way."

Dr. Stanslovich's expression changed to one of awe and possibilities. "Oh, Henri. Your mind never ceases to amaze me. You and Valentine stay here. Dante and I will begin the experiments on the water."

Henri nodded and retook his seat.

When the others were gone, Andres turned to him. "You manage him very well, my love."

"I told him the truth. I was going to look for that when the anomaly appeared. If he wants to work on a scientific explanation, let him."

"Still, it was clever."

"And it illustrated that I am in agreement with his theories or at least gave the appearance."

"As I said before, you know how to manage him."

Henri smiled and went back to work.

Hours later, his eyes hurt, the script blurred, and his head had the makings of a terrible ache. Henri put down his pen and rubbed his eyes. "I need to get up and move."

Andres continued to read, his brow knit in concentration. "I might have found something, though it's hard to tell. The author of the entry has a unique style that rambles and takes impossible tangents. I have doubts of how helpful it will be."

Henri leaned over and looked at the script. German. "Read me only the most interesting part."

Andres cleared his throat. *"And the darkness swirled around him with unbearable emptiness—a tall column of shadow that emitted the sounds of a party just beyond its dim borders. I felt sucked into the vortex, birthed into a new existence with no way to return home. What were these people before me, their shapes and movements so foreign to my own? I watched them as if through rain-soaked glass, never quite seeing them clearly enough to make an identification."*

Henri rubbed his chin. Stubble scratched and caught at his palm. "Sounds vaguely like what appeared in the foyer."

"Wait, listen to this part." Andres jumped down a few lines. *"I came before the dark being sitting high on the air. Do not mistake me. He did sit in the air as if upon a golden throne, but there was nothing to support him save the immense power. He told me I'd be made as new. I asked what form this newness should take, and he mentioned only my talent for architecture. He said I should build monuments in his name. When I asked him what name I should call him, he gave me nothing but a wicked laugh."*

"An odd account, if nothing else." Henri studied Andres's face. "Have you seen this too?"

Andres ran a hand through his hair. "I have. Herr Maestro had many an opportunity to send me before Azgarth. Usually when his discipline failed to take."

Henri winced. "I can't imagine what you must have suffered."

"He sometimes called it motivation."

"I'm sorry." Henri placed his hand on Andres's. "It's unfathomable how anyone could ever hurt you."

"Or toss me from a window?"

"That goes without saying."

Andres's gaze moved to the door. Henri turned to see if they were being watched, but no one stood there.

"I see a lot of Herr Maestro's qualities in your Dr. Stanslovich."

Henri gave a nervous laugh. "I assure you, he might be abrupt at times, but he's never hurt me physically. I think he knows better than to lay hands on me. It would not go well."

Quiet filled the room, unfettered by inadequate words. None of the normal phrases used to convey sympathy or compassion covered the act of being disciplined by a being not of human experience.

Instead, Henri let his speculations speak for him. "I wonder if Azgarth has a particular goal in mind. Does he want to fill the earth with those who will build monuments in his honor?"

Andres shook his head. "I don't know what he wants to do other than create another world in the image of the fae dimension. He doesn't quite grasp the concept that humans need money and industry to survive. I think he sees us as a race with little humor who fail to wrest enjoyment from the world."

"We do enjoy the arts, though not many of us have time to do nothing more than pursue pleasure."

Andres frowned. "I worked at my art. Anyone who tells you creating art is not working has never done so for a living."

"Fair enough." Henri tapped the page. "What else does it say?"

"Let me read a bit ahead and see."

Henri looked back down at his own work, but it still swam before his eyes. He doubted he'd get much more done on that passage. Not today.

Thunder rumbled in the distance. Another storm was rolling in. Henri rose and moved to the window, allowing Andres to read alone without being watched or interrupted.

Clouds covered the sky. The sun hid behind a large bank of dark gray. Lightning zigzagged across the horizon. In the flash, a large column, darker than the surrounding cloud, rose up through the center of the formation like an ominous monolith. He blinked a few times, but he could no longer see the strange pattern.

Another streak of lightning illuminated the clouds. The column now appeared as an open doorway.

He closed the curtains with a quick jerk.

Andres turned around. "Is something the matter?"

"Another storm blowing in."

"England is full of storms."

"Not always, but I have noticed more storms this season than is usual." Hair rose on the back of Henri's neck. He rubbed a hand across the area to help calm the tingles.

The air grew close, oppressive. This storm was going to be a big one. An angry one. All the vengeance of heaven and Earth collaborated in the sky to put on a show. An angry king shaking his fist at the world.

What had the world done to deserve such venom?

If anything the world already held its share of harsh lessons and needed no outside influences from weather. People born without fortune or connections were subjected to the harshest of conditions from the cradle to the grave. Imagining a being who came into this world and foisted his own means of torture on unsuspecting humans whose only crime was to possess some talent for music, art, or science was not to be borne. It had to stop.

But how did one go about banishing a member of a fae race from coming into this world? Humans had not the power of God. They did not possess the ability to open or close rifts in dimensions. As far as Henri knew, there was no way to do that on a scientific level.

Thunder crashed. Closer now.

The flashes from the lightning were directly overhead.

Electricity.

Many experiments had been conducted lately using that most powerful of nature's weapons. He'd seen the destructive forces up close, back in his youth. If he could only find a way to harness that power and send it straight into one of those dark columns, would it close them for good?

A foolhardy and spectacular idea to be sure. But how would one even go about doing such a thing and not bring the house down around them or kill them in the process?

Chapter Sixteen

THE ONLY thing Wilhelm wanted after his long, trying day was a large glass of strong spirits. The bitch Juliana Alexandre was going to be the death of him. He'd have to devise a way for the audience to follow her every note without growing bored. Perhaps he'd have to change the presentation. Even in this age of modesty and morals, men were in want of a glimpse of creamy skin and a comely face. Those things Juliana Alexandre had in abundance.

As for the brother.

Wilhelm shivered in memory of that handsome face, wide shoulders, and knowing glint in his eyes. Nicholas hid something from the world, and he wanted no part of revealing it to a stranger. At least not an infamous one.

He walked to the drink table and poured a generous amount of whiskey into a glass. A quick shot to belt back the harsh liquor and his eyes watered from the bite. The fortifying sip did nothing to quell the emotions roiling up into his chest. Taking Miss Alexandre under his wing was an exercise in futility, and it was going to cost him dearly.

Noises came from the bedroom. Voices lifted high in merriment. He rolled his eyes heavenward. Why did Azgarth only show himself at the most inopportune times? The last thing Wilhelm wanted at the moment was to travel into the fae realm to entertain his dark master.

Perhaps he'd remain in the parlor and pretend he didn't hear the party coming from the portal in the other room.

He unbuttoned his coat and sat down and closed his eyes.

The music grew louder. Scents of wildflowers and bonfires drifted in to tickle Wilhelm's nose.

Azgarth used every trick he knew to try to seduce Wilhelm to join the party.

Not tonight. Not tonight.

"I do not show you favor in order for you to ignore my pleasure."

Wilhelm opened one eye and stared at Azgarth, resplendent in court dress from a bygone era. He was beautiful, sinister, and haunting. As with each time Azgarth came into Wilhelm's presence, he felt his breath hitch. No one on earth—save perhaps Valentine—was as beautiful as a dark fae. Seconded only by Nicholas Alexandre.

Even as Azgarth stood before Wilhelm, his form shifted and changed, making it hard to discern his features. So it was when he wished for concealment.

"I did not ignore your pleasure. I merely wished a moment of quiet from the wailing I've had to endure this day."

Azgarth slapped a hand down on the drink table. Bottles scattered, falling to the floor with a crash. "You will attend me!"

Wilhelm stood. Shaking overcame him, undermining his will to stand strong against this ungodly being.

"How does the Alexandre woman come along?"

"Not well. She has a good ear, but no strength in her voice. She will be an embarrassment to your court."

A faint flash of a smile showed through the shifting scene. "No."

"I beg your indulgence, but you haven't heard her, my lord."

"I don't have to hear her. I know she will prevail."

Wilhelm sincerely doubted it, but he wasn't going to say so. Disagreement would only upset Azgarth and get Wilhelm more scars laced across his back.

"And the brother?"

At this, Wilhelm glanced up. "A fine tenor. Better than I've ever heard in my life. He refuses to sing with his sister. I invited him to share the stage with her, but he was unimpressed with the offer."

Azgarth flicked his fingers. "His talents are many, but he loves only one. Leave him be for now. His time will come."

Wilhelm bent his head in supplication. The master had made his wishes known on that front. It did make him wonder what exactly Nicholas

Alexandre loved more than music and the avenue of his true talent. Who might be the one who brought him into the fold if not Wilhelm?

"Come now." Azgarth lifted his hand in a calling motion. "I have need of you at my gathering."

With a heavy heart and aching head, Wilhelm followed his master into the bedroom and the heart of the fae world.

MIKHAIL TESTED the fluid several times and came up with the same conclusion with each pass—the resurrection tank had somehow magnetized the liquid. Some of the chemicals contained within could indeed create magnetism, but to his knowledge, it had never happened until now. Had the compression device Henri constructed altered the fluid enough to excite the properties already inherent in the compounds? Stranger things had happened.

He turned to Dante. "Do you think the tank's generator is large enough to produce a magnetic field?"

Dante slid the goggles he wore onto the top of his head. He gave the generator a considering look. A frown knit his brows together. "It's possible, I suppose."

Excited by the prospect he pursued, Mikhail stood and went to the tank. "For a moment I want you to suspend disbelief and consider that moving through worlds—dimensions—is possible."

"All right." Dante turned. His dark gaze remained on Mikhail with the look of a man who dared hope his best friend's thinking had fundamentally changed.

"Imagine this tank, the magnetic fluid inside, used in conjunction with a magnetic field are powerful enough to open a rift between worlds."

Dante's expression never changed. "What did you see, Mikhail?"

And just like that, Dante nailed him to the wall.

They had not been friends for so long without learning a thing or two about each other. Dante knew Mikhail had to experience a life-changing phenomenon before he'd even consider the scientific properties that might bring it about.

Mikhail closed his eyes. A shudder moved through his body when images of the *wolfsine* attacking Henri surfaced. Lucky for Henri there had been a champion in another of the strange beasts.

"I've never seen anything like it, Dante." His hands visibly shook. He rubbed a hand around his mouth, trying to think of something intelligent to say, but all of his words seemed to dissipate under the enormity of what he'd witnessed.

The most unsettling aspect was the tickle at the back of his brain that acknowledged this was not his first encounter with such horrible things, despite telling Dante the contrary.

"Henri could have died. Murdered before me by one of those… those… things. I would have been powerless to stop it."

Dante rose. He flung the goggles off his head. They missed the desk and tumbled off to hit the ground, shattering the lenses. "Are you telling me that there was a *wolfsine* here, in this manor, and I'm only learning about it now?"

In all the years he'd known Dante, Mikhail had never seen his temper so ignited.

"How could you be so irresponsible to not let me know? To not warn Valentine?" Dante raked a hand through his hair. "How did Henri survive?"

"Another of the creatures came to rescue him, dragged the first one into the tank and they disappeared."

Dante's shocked gaze landed on the resurrection tank. "Is that why you had it drained?"

Mikhail nodded.

"My God. You are so concerned with appearing to have the answers to everything, you put us all in danger." Disgust twisted Dante's face into a caricature of angry emotions.

"Please, Dante. We need to find the way that rift opened in here and shut it for good."

Dante stood before him. His chest huffed in and out with each breath, looking for all the world as if he'd run for his life. Finally he gave a curt nod of agreement. "You made a good start. If the fluid in the chamber acted as a conduit, then emptying the contents at least shut the door some. Unfortunately it might not lock it."

Mikhail raised a brow. "You don't think it's enough?"

"No. The *wolfsine* are able to cross at will. At least it appears that way. There was no resurrection tank in Paris, on the city street, and yet we saw them."

Mikhail shifted, uncomfortable under Dante's scrutiny. "I don't remember them clearly. Only a vague notion of them."

"Look at your leg; you'll remember it clearly."

Mikhail flushed. Yes, his leg still carried the scars of that night. Yes, he'd been searching for years for a match to the bite marks. All the pieces fit together in a complex puzzle that shared no rhyme or reason with the material world. To even make the suggestion that the *wolfsine* existed or that traveling between dimensions was more than the work of writers and dreamers like H.G. Wells or Jules Verne was absolutely ridiculous. However, there was a fine line between the fantastic and reality. Thin as a hair and twice as fragile. He'd denied the existence of other realms for so long he'd forgotten that perhaps if conditions were favorable, a state might exist that showed a portal into another world.

"My mind wants to reject what I've seen in here today. The part of my brain that looks for logic in everything I see, hear, taste, and feel wants a better explanation than it came from a sister dimension where fae kings rule over their lands with bloodthirsty monsters."

Dante's expression softened. He reached out and clamped a hand on Mikhail's shoulder. "It isn't always easy leaving our preconceived notions behind or throwing out convention to search a new avenue of explanation. This is not the easiest belief to hold. It not only goes against science but all we were taught of religion."

Mikhail put his hand on Dante's arm, needing something to steady him in a world without rudder. "Not only has the rug been pulled out beneath my feet, but the very bricks that make up the foundation on which I stand."

"So you build a new one, stronger than before, infused with new understanding and greater information."

Those dark eyes met Mikhail's and everything shifted inside. Changed. He swallowed down the emotion and fear—overwhelming fear that he'd one day lose his best friend—and stepped away.

Mikhail cleared his throat. "All right, so if we go on the theory that the resurrection tank worked as a gateway into another realm, what can we do in the future to safeguard it so magnetization doesn't occur again?"

Dante studied him for a moment in silence, and then he turned to the tank. "What factors were different this time than in previous reanimations?"

"I've gone over that so many times since Valentine woke early. I keep coming back to the same factors."

"Henri's device," Dante guessed. "All speculations keep coming back to that."

"It's a very clever construct."

"But is it enough to cause a reaction of such magnitude?" Dante made a circuit of the room, looking in corners and hidey-holes.

Mikhail began to open cabinets and search for the device in question. "It's always been my observation that some of the smallest organisms can wreak the greatest havoc."

Dante pointed at Mikhail. "True."

Viruses were some of the tiniest predators in the food chain. No one refuted their power to fell entire civilizations or leave them devastated.

But this wasn't about viruses; it had to do with magnetism.

"Where did Henri put that damn device?" Mikhail heaved under his breath. He tore things from cabinets and drawers. Pulled items from shelves until they were bare and still he was no closer to finding that damn device.

Dante bent over next to the tank and held up the silver plates, about the same width as his palm. "I believe I've found it."

Mikhail held out his hand. Dante climbed down from the tank platform and placed the device on Mikhail's palm. He wasted no time in determining if the output from the current might have excited the compounds in the fluid.

"I don't believe this is the culprit. There is an electric discharge, but not enough to do more than register on the ampere." Mikhail set the device down on the desk harder than necessary. "I really hoped that was our answer."

"Maybe when used in proximity to the tank generator," Dante suggested.

"I'm not convinced."

Dante rubbed a hand over his brow. He looked wearier than Mikhail had ever seen him. "It's time to set science aside and think in a different direction, no matter how hard you might want to resist."

"No. It's here. We just haven't found it yet."

"Then let's cleanse the tank down to the molecular level and refill and see if we can find the answer."

Mikhail put a hand on Dante's shoulder and gave it a squeeze.

Thunder erupted overhead. The violent percussion shook the house from foundation to roof.

Mikhail looked at the ceiling, certain it might come down around them. "That was close."

"The storms have been unforgiving the past few nights." Dante went to the chemical cabinet and began to pull out the constituents necessary to create the resurrection fluid.

Yes, Dante had been with him so many times when he'd mixed the solution necessary to restore life the man knew what to use and the amounts required. Probably not the best policy for keeping his secrets safe, but he'd like to believe Dante would never betray him. No matter how far apart their core beliefs might be.

Dante might see the esoteric at work in everything, but at his heart he was a decent man and good scientist.

Mikhail came over to the workbench as thunder continued to shake angry fists overhead. "We were going to cleanse the tank first."

"I haven't forgotten." Dante held up a glass jar marked with the word ammonia. "Do we use something strong enough to strip away all remaining residue?"

"I'm willing to go that route. Also some ultraviolet light might not go amiss." Mikhail placed a ladder beside the tank and began to climb along the edge to remove the watertight seals where the glass plates came together.

A deadly silence fell over the manor.

A chill of warning lifted the hair on Mikhail's neck. A roar, not unlike that of a massive train, grew closer.

"Dante! Get down!"

The warning came as the windows imploded, showering the entire laboratory with glass. Mikhail lost his grip on the ladder. He fell to the floor, covering his face with his arms as he hit the ground.

Fierce winds swirled around the room, a tempest in a cauldron. The resurrection tank rumbled and shook. Mikhail looked on in frozen horror as the entire platform began to lift into the air. Odd how he remained pressed against the floor, as if the pressure from the downdraft kept him anchored to the earth.

He tried to wrench his neck around and find Dante, but saw nothing, even when he dared open his eyes against the flying debris.

With a deafening crash, the tank hit the far wall and shattered, bringing the shelves down. Instruments fell to the floor. Mikhail held his hands tighter over his head, hoping when the raging storm ended there might be something left of his laboratory to salvage—including he and Dante.

Quiet came as sudden as the storm. Those items sucked into the vortex landed with a clatter once no longer supported by the drafts. Sheets from a notebook fluttered down, like so many leaves ripped from their respective trees.

Breath, heavy and painful, sawed in and out of his lungs. Mikhail lifted his head and once again searched for Dante.

"Mikhail!"

Mikhail turned in the direction of his name. Dante scrambled over the ground to him. Blood ran from numerous cuts along his arms, cheeks and hands. Nothing serious or life-threatening.

Valentine and Henri arrived at the laboratory door in a run.

"My God! What happened?"

Dante helped Mikhail to his feet. Concern filled his deep brown eyes. He lifted a hand and gently brushed glass from Mikhail's clothes.

His heart continued to hammer, a result of fear and… something else. He shook his head and gazed at Henri. "We've been hit by a cyclone."

Gingerly, they both stepped into the room and surveyed the damage.

Dante still had his hands on Mikhail. "I suppose this negates the need to clean the tank."

It negated a lot of things, but not the need to clean and assess what might be salvaged and what was damaged beyond repair.

Mikhail waved an absent gesture at Henri. "Call the servants in. We can at least get all this broken glass cleaned up." He turned to Dante. "Go tend to your cuts. We can start while you're away."

Dante shook his head. His lips were compressed into a grim line. "I'll stay all the same."

Slowly, and with heart heavy, Mikhail turned away and began the process of sweeping up the shards of his life's work.

Chapter Seventeen

THEY'D WORKED long into the night, trying to set the laboratory to rights. A pile of broken equipment littered one corner. Most of the ruined instruments might provide much needed parts for other items, which was why they hadn't been taken out with the mountain of broken glass.

Henri surveyed the devastation and wanted to weep with the unfairness of it all. He'd kept his thoughts on the cause to himself.

This had been no cyclone.

Oh, it might have had all the hallmarks, but he'd seen the black column in the sky over the house and knew it for what it had been—another rip between the worlds. But why would Azgarth destroy the laboratory? What offense had he found in the experiments? If he'd gifted Dr. Stanslovich with the power to resurrect people from the dead, why destroy the means of bestowing that gift on those deserving of a second chance at life?

Had Azgarth decided his patronage was unneeded or unappreciated, since Dr. Stanslovich repeatedly claimed such beings could not possibly exist? This might have been an example of a complete break, or a show of the awesome power of a being not of this world.

The attack was too specific to the laboratory to be explained away by a cyclone. None of the other rooms had been affected, nor had the outside of the manor. All other areas remained intact. Not even the garden showed the slightest damage.

Not to say it could not have happened that way, it was just highly improbable. Even if the laboratory had somehow been the nexus for destruction by a cyclone, it did not explain why the grounds, fascia, and other parts of the house showed no signs of the disturbance.

Frustrated and concerned for his friends, Henri turned away from his musings and headed for the door.

"Henri? Where are you going?" Valentine stood in the great hall watching him. A look of concern clouded his hazel eyes.

"Out looking for Herr Maestro. I want some answers, and I'm determined to get them."

Valentine hurried to him. "I'm coming with you."

"No. I won't let you put yourself into danger that way. No telling what he might do if he sees you."

"I'll stay well out of his line of sight."

"That might not be possible. Please. Stay here and continue translating the books." Henri ran his hand through the fall of golden hair that escaped the band Valentine wore to keep it off his face.

"And if something happens to you?" Valentine shook his head. "No. I don't want some constable to come here telling us you've been killed."

Henri let out a resigned sigh. "You are a hard man to say no to, even if it is for your own good."

Valentine smiled when he realized Henri had relented. "Let me get my coat."

Henri waited patiently as he listened to the soft *shush* of Valentine's shoes as he went to collect his coat.

Dr. Savoy came from the area of the library, reading the spine of a book as he walked. Deep cuts had created angry scabs along his cheeks and hairline. When he noticed Henri, he stopped and looked up from his book. "Going out?"

"For a bit."

"What shall I tell Mikhail if he asks where you've gone?" Dr. Savoy held the book up in front of him. The volume was so old the letters had been rubbed off the front of the leather.

"Tell him I've gone to find Herr Maestro." Henri stepped closer to Dr. Savoy and lowered his voice. "That was no cyclone that struck last night. Right before it struck, I saw the same column we'd seen in the great hall. This is a calculated attack, not a weather system."

Dr. Savoy turned to look over his shoulder, as if afraid Dr. Stanslovich might come in and overhear the conversation. "Anyone who saw the way the resurrection tank was lifted and flung across the room would believe you.”

Henri shook his head. “Not Dr. Stanslovich. He still believes it’s merely a case of bad weather.”

Dr. Savoy capped Henri’s shoulder with a firm hand. “Not entirely. I think he may be fairly close to capitulating on that point.”

Henri tried not to hold his breath on that score. He’d believe it when Dr. Stanslovich said it out loud and drafted a written proclamation to that effect.

Valentine came down the hall, dressed with an overcoat and hat. He’d stuffed his long golden hair under the covering then pulled his collar up. A few days’ worth of beard growth changed the landscape of his face, filling out the hollow cheeks and hiding the square jaw. As far as a quick disguise, it wasn’t bad by half. No one seeing him on the street would guess he was the world-beloved violinist.

Dr. Savoy raised a brow at Valentine. “Are you sure it’s safe for you to go hunting the man who tried to kill you?”

“If it’s not, I’ll know soon enough.” With that, he pulled the brim of his hat a little lower and headed for the door. “Are you coming, Henri?”

Henri nodded in farewell to Dr. Savoy and hurried after Valentine.

Looking at the morning sky, no one would guess there had been a violent storm the night before. Not that it was all that unusual to have a rainy night in England, but the day was so bright and pristine it was as if the world had been made new.

“Where should we search first?” Valentine walked with his hands down in his coat pockets, head bowed.

“The last time I saw him was on the morning I bought your violin. He was in the commerce district.” Henri stopped them at a cross street. “I think we should start there and see if he makes an appearance. An agent of Azgarth might hang around there looking for more victims.”

Valentine narrowed his eyes. “Especially if he is looking for musicians.”

“What about vocalists?”

Valentine shook his head. “He often complained of vocalists. I doubt he would take on one.”

“All right, then, we look to the music shops and see if he’s skulking around, hoping to take on a student. He has to earn money somehow.”

Valentine shot a look to Henri conveying how naive he found his lover. "No. *I* have to find money to live; Herr Maestro will be provided for by Azgarth as long as he continues to cull talent for his master."

Henri had a hard time wrapping his mind around the fact a fae master gave money to keep Herr Maestro on the lam. Where did Azgarth get the money? Did he use local currency or pay in pure gold? Bank notes or sterling? Did it even matter? No. Probably not. He had to stop becoming bogged down in the minutia of the unimportant. What difference did it make how Herr Maestro was supported while in London—only that he was here and knew more about Azgarth than any of them.

Valentine placed a restraining hand on Henri's arm. "Do not underestimate him. He might be a mere agent of Azgarth, but he is still a dangerous man."

"I saw how you looked when Dr. Stanslovich and Dr. Savoy brought you to the villa. Underestimating Herr Maestro is the last thing I'm going to do."

They crossed the outskirts of London and into the city proper, back to the district where the music store stood, bringing lyrical beauty to the masses—or at least those who could afford the price of sheet music or a penny whistle. Henri knew enough about poverty to know that even penny whistles were sometimes considered luxuries if placed in a poor palm.

The shop had few customers for the time of morning. A young man with fine clothing and a rather impressive walking stick—for affectation—stood at a display of sheet music, looking through the offerings. Two young women slid their dainty hands along the keys of a pianoforte. Another man—middle-aged with the beginnings of a receding hairline and generous paunch—picked up a silver piccolo and inspected it as one might a treasured heirloom.

Valentine leaned in and whispered. "Are we to look for anything specific?"

At the moment, Henri didn't have any idea. This had been a good as place as any to start looking for a man who had devoted his life to honing the talents of virtuosos such as Valentine.

"You know more about music than I do. Look around. We are only biding our time until we see if Herr Maestro frequents this establishment."

Valentine made a face. "All right. When the gentleman leaves, we will browse the sheet music."

Fair enough. In the meantime, Henri perused a small cabinet that held pitch pipes, tuning forks, and a host of other small items to keep instruments functioning properly.

"May I help you, sir?"

"Do you have anything to tune a violin?"

The clerk looked at Henri as if he'd grown a rather shocking and grotesque head beside the one he spoke from. "It depends upon if you like to tune to a fork or a pipe."

Henri glanced up to find Valentine fingering a beautiful lute. He dared not call out to him and draw attention. Too many people had been made aware of Valentine's arrival in London. Seeing him in a small music store might overcome the clerk.

Valentine began to pick out a tune, both haunting and familiar. The same one Henri had heard in the street the first night he'd seen the *wolfsine*. The tune sounded softer, less menacing on a lute.

The clerk smiled and clapped his hands together in pure joy. "You have a gift, sir."

Valentine put his hand over the strings to quiet the vibration. "So I have been told."

Before the clerk said too much or began asking questions, Henri butted into the conversation. "Do you prefer a pitch pipe or fork to tune your violin?"

Valentine lifted an elegant shoulder as if it didn't matter to him. "I use neither. I tune by ear."

The clerk gave a startled gasp. Recognition dawned in his eyes. Henri held up a finger and shook his head slightly to let the clerk know they were incognito.

The clerk gave a small wink to show he understood.

Valentine put down the lute and approached the display case. "Still, if I were to choose, I'd take the tuning fork. An A, if you have it?"

The clerk was only too quick to oblige and took the A tuning fork from the case. Valentine struck it on his arm, then held it against the body of a violin set on display. The sound was clear and bright.

The note twisted something deep inside Henri. He tried not to squirm in discomfort. Nor if asked would he have been able to identify why the pitch of the tuning fork ground at his insides, a blade grinding against a whetstone.

Valentine looked to Henri's face and lifted the fork away. The vibrations may have remained, but the sound was no longer heard by the human ear.

"We'll take this one, please." Valentine lifted the fork to indicate what he meant.

"Where shall I send the bill?"

Henri found the first smile of the morning. "Dr. Mikhail Stanslovich." He gave the direction and watched as the clerk carefully wrapped the tuning fork in a box as to protect the metal from becoming bent and ruining the pitch.

While Valentine finished the transaction, Henri went over to the sheet music. The man who had been looking had moved on to study a display of small harps. As he glanced at the printed sheets, he found a poster with a rather chilling coincidence included in the information.

The poster announced a concert at a local music hall.

The part of the announcement that unnerved him the most was the name of the musical conductor: William Kane.

WILHELM PACED back and forth on the sidewalk outside the Malmount. Miss Alexandre was late.

He took out his pocket watch and glanced at the face. She was getting later by the minute. If she didn't show in the next five, he would call it a day and strike her name from the book, no matter the consequences. There were too many other details to consider to bring Valentine back into the fold to waste time on a young woman who had shown as much respect as she had talent.

At four minutes and counting, a carriage pulled up to the Malmount. The driver came down off his box and helped a rather pale and listless Juliana Alexandre from the coach. Her skin had no luster, her hair limp and oily. Her skin appeared so pasty one might be capable of reading the signs on the businesses behind her, simply by gazing through her.

"Good God, woman. What is the matter?" Wilhelm pulled a handkerchief from his pocket and covered his nose and mouth in case the girl suffered from some unknown contagion.

"I am well." The fact perspiration began to bead on her forehead belied the protestation. "We can go inside and practice in the hall."

As she neared, he got the distinctly rancid scent of the *wolfsine's* bite. So that was how Azgarth chose to fix Juliana Alexandre's lack of true talent? He'd forced it on her from an external source? Did he understand the workings of his own creations so little as to believe that the *wolfsine's* bite had any effect if there wasn't some raw material there to work with in the first place?

God save him.

He took her arm and placed it through his, helping her into the music hall. Her mother followed along behind them, keeping a close eye on her frail daughter.

If Wilhelm hadn't seen it for himself, he'd not have believed one person capable of changing so materially in so short a time. Was it because in her soul she was not talented other than what might be acceptable to perform in her own music room? If so, Azgarth had miscalculated.

"We will go inside and you will take the stage. I want you to get a real feel for singing in a hall. The acoustics will be very different from what you hear in your parlor. It takes some getting used to." He relayed the information to her as they entered the Malmount and headed to the auditorium proper.

He helped her up onto the stage and placed her where he wanted her to stand.

The piano stood on the stage as well. An accompanist Wilhelm had never seen or met before held a songbook to his thin chest.

"Sir, I was sent by the master to assist you."

More like spy on him to ensure compliance.

Wilhelm merely nodded graciously and stepped to the edge of the piano. After a proper warm-up where Wilhelm appreciated a slight difference in the power and fullness of Miss Alexandre's voice, he gave a cue to the accompanist to begin the first piece.

The music was the same piece he'd heard over and again in the days he'd worked with Miss Alexandre. How the accompanist knew which music and arrangement was needed, he had no idea, unless Azgarth had relayed the information. That made him decidedly uneasy.

He gave Miss Alexandre her cue, and the sound that flooded from her body was one born of the heavens. Tears filled his eyes as he listened with growing wonder at the transformation of such power, he knew without a doubt she would make her mark on the operatic world.

She finished the song and bowed her head. Her breath came fast, and she had grown paler.

Wilhelm pulled a chair over from the wings and rather forced her to sit.

He rested a paternal hand on her shoulder. Thoughts of making money from her voice filled his head. He could almost hear the clink of coins and the soft swish of banknotes changing hands. Fear of Azgarth might make him work hard in his tasks, but money was his true motivator. Nothing in this world or the next held quite the sway of currency. Whether it was paid in drafts, bonds, bullion, or bars, he didn't care. As long as it spent, he enjoyed it.

"You have a brilliant future ahead of you, my dear. I knew God had not wasted your talent. You only needed that one small breakthrough to make you a star. And you will be."

Despite the fever raging through her system from the *wolfsine* bite, Miss Alexandre's eyes lit with joy. She glanced to her mother before turning back to him. "Are you in earnest?"

He held up a finger. "I never promise what I can't deliver."

He turned to the accompanist. "Let's practice the second number, if you please?"

This one came out even stronger than the last. Notes rang from the rafters, making the entire auditorium vibrate.

Perhaps he needed to rethink his stance on vocalists. This slender young woman might very well one day rival Valentine for fame.

Chapter Eighteen

"I still don't think this is a good idea, Henri." Andres touched Henri's sleeve as they both peered around the corner of the stage to the figures practicing for Friday's performance.

Now Andres saw Herr Maestro in the flesh, he wanted nothing more than to be away from him. Fear rose with every piano chord. If he hadn't witnessed it with his own eyes, he'd never have believed Wilhelm Kering, maestro and puppeteer to the chosen, had taken on a vocalist. A soprano, even. Many times over the years of his captivity, Andres had heard the great maestro lament vocalists were even granted the right to take the stage or call their particular talents music. His disdain for vocal arrangements was legendary and public.

One time he'd even been accused of beating an opera diva bloody during a rather heated discussion. Andres had not been in attendance on that occasion, but had tried to find the singer only to learn she had gone into seclusion in an undisclosed location. Not even his fame had gained him access to the information. If anything, his association to Herr Maestro had ensured he never learned the truth of what had become of the diva in question.

Andres stuck his shaking hands down into his pockets. Why did he no longer remember the woman's name? Had it been struck from the book?

A gentle buzz started in his head, leaving him feeling slightly dizzy and disoriented. This time he pulled harder on Henri's sleeve.

Henri turned. His eyes widened in shock, and he held out firm arms to catch Andres.

Black spots clouded Andres's vision.

"Come on. Let me get you out of here." Henri put a strong arm around Andres's waist. "I think we've done enough for one day. We'll take a carriage home."

"I need some air."

They crept out into the back alley behind the Malmount. A strong scent of urine, dirt, and garbage hit his nose in a violent stink strong enough to make him gag. This was not exactly what he meant by needing air. Nor would he find what he wanted in London.

At least he only suffered from slight nausea now. The black spots and fear of collapse had fled, leaving him with a nasty hollow feeling.

"Wait." Andres stopped Henri before they made it to the end of the alley. He took a firm grasp of Henri's jacket. "I may know of the talisman you seek."

Henri cradled Andres's face between his hands and gave him a sound kiss. "I knew you'd remember."

The love and trust reflected back from Henri's eyes was enough to make Andres want to slay dragons and defeat dark fae in single-handed combat. "It's not much. Not what you might think."

"It doesn't matter what it is. Any item can be infused with power if given the right set of circumstances."

Andres shook his head. "I will admit. I don't know what kind, if any, power this might have. It's not a stone, wand, chalice, or anything of the kind. It's a book. A ledger. Small enough to fit into a special pocket in the lining of Herr Maestro's jacket. Many times over the years I've seen him pull it out and write something down."

A slow smile spread across Henri's face. "Words are very powerful."

"Should we go back inside and try to find it?" The prospect alone made Andres heart start to race.

"No. Not today. Friday night there will be more people and lots of confusion backstage. We'll stand a better chance of being able to search his belongings without being questioned. No one will care. Today there aren't as many people around, and we'll stick out."

Andres wanted to point out they'd already been inside today and had not been caught, but he refrained. "Then we have to wait and follow Herr Maestro to his lodgings."

Henri grew concerned. His brow furrowed as he assessed Andres. "Do you feel well enough to stay out so long?"

Andres gave a broken laugh. "We don't have much choice. It's the only way we're going to be able to find where he's staying. If he doesn't keep the ledger on him, he might hide it in his rooms."

"Good point." Henri glanced off to the end of the alley. "We should find a better place to sit and watch than around the theater entrances."

"Agreed." Andres hurried from the alley and out into the street.

Across the way, between the rolling carriages and horse traffic, he spotted a small teashop.

He pointed to the storefront. "Let's go have some tea. We can sit at one of the tables by the window and watch both the entrance and alley."

Henri fell into step beside him as they navigated across the busy roadway. The teashop did a brisk business for the time of day. Andres removed his hat, but kept his face downcast. He wanted no one in the shop to recognize him. He'd have left the hat on, but feared that might call more attention to himself for his bad manners than going without.

They ordered a pot of tea and took a seat one row away from the windows that afforded them a good view of both theater egresses.

Andres watched the front of the building, ready to go into action if the need arose. He hated to be this close to Herr Maestro, even if it was behind glass and his former master had no way to see inside the tearoom. A quick glance around and he noticed there were no observers watching them. No one cared if they were two men drinking tea to pass the time or waiting for some agent of a dark fae master to leave the scene of his current crime. As it should be. For all he was a famous man, he no longer craved the recognition that came with the honor.

They sat eating sticky buns and drinking tea, letting the conversations of the other diners flow around them as a river moves between the rocks. Immovable. Quiet. He wondered how many of those in the teashop realized their world was frequented by beings that crossed over from a separate dimension. How many knew their lives could change in a blink if Azgarth deemed they had some preternatural talent he might exploit in some way?

Andres ran a hand through the front of his hair, where a few locks had come loose from the tie. Tension coiled inside him. He'd not be able to take a deep breath until he was once and truly free.

The front entrance of the theater opened. Andres put down his cup with a decided click. "Come on. He's leaving."

Henri stood and scooped up his hat. They hurried to the foyer and watched as Herr Maestro placed his latest protégée into an awaiting carriage. Even from the distance, Andres could see the cold calculation in Herr Maestro's eyes. The man, no doubt, had already spent the untold wealth he'd make from the young woman's talents. As he'd done to Andres.

"I hope he doesn't treat her as he did me," Andres whispered only loud enough for Henri to hear.

Henri cut dark eyes to Andres. "Should we rescue her?"

Andres gave a shrug. "Depends if she wants rescue or not. I have met a few over the years who had no wish to leave the comfort and safety of life within the circle of Azgarth's chosen."

Henri gave a world-weary sigh and slight nod. "I understand that feeling only too well. If one is presented with the choice between destitution and living under the yoke of a man who promises wealth, most will choose wealth."

"Especially in these times of cruel poverty and uncertain futures."

The world was changing so quickly that man had a hard time keeping up with the advances. Even tasks such as farming and weaving had been supplanted by machines to increase production and use fewer workers.

Herr Maestro got into a carriage and started in the opposite direction as the young woman.

Andres hit Henri's arm. "We're going to lose him in the traffic."

"Not if we hurry." Henri rushed out into traffic and caught the back end of a delivery cart as it started by. He jumped up onto the back end.

Andres followed. He loped his arm around the wooden slats. "Are you mad? We can't cross the whole of London like this! We can't even be sure we're following the carriage."

Henri shot him a knowing smile that heated Andres's blood and made him long to kiss him with all the passion and excitement flowing through his veins. "I spent my youth traveling in just this manner. Stick with me. I won't let us get lost."

If there was ever a soul in the entire universe he trusted, it was Henri.

They rattled down a few more streets. Henri kept his gaze on the carriage in front of them. "Jump!"

Together they hit the paving stones and ran down a side street. Pure exhilaration coated Andres's mouth and burned through his lungs. Arms and legs pumping, he rushed to the end of the street where Herr Maestro's carriage went by. Henri took a flying leap at the back. His feet landed secure on the lip where the cab ended.

Andres's heart filled with doubt he'd make the leap. There wasn't near the room on the back of the hackney as there had been on the delivery wagon.

Henri turned and held out his hand. He mouthed the word *jump*.

Andres leapt, but came up short. He fell to the refuse strewn cobbles. Dirt and horse dung painted his clothes in stinky stains. When Henri made as if to let go of the carriage, Andres shook his head, waving him on. If at least one of them were able to see where Herr Maestro stayed, it had to be good enough. Besides, Henri knew London. Andres only called it a temporary home.

Andres picked himself up off the street, brushed at his clothes, and started the long trek back to Dr. Stanslovich's.

HENRI LOOKED back as Andres stood and brushed at his soiled clothing. Love and concern welled up. He really should jump off the damn carriage and ensure Andres was all right—that he hadn't injured himself when he fell. It hadn't been too long since he'd suffered terrible injury at the hands of Herr Maestro.

Renewed purpose rose to stifle off the sweeter emotions.

For laying hands on Andres, Wilhelm Kering had to pay. No other answer would do.

Henri held on tighter to the hackney. His knuckles turned white in his grip. The carriage continued to trundle on down the street. Henri hunched lower so as not to be seen by either Herr Maestro, if he turned to look out the back window, or the driver. Not that the driver seemed too worried about anything going on around him. He was rather aggressive as he cut across the city.

The carriage finally came to a stop in front of the Imperial Hotel. Henri stepped off the back and made himself as unobtrusive as possible as he followed behind Herr Maestro into the hotel lobby. He couldn't risk following him all the way to the floor or his room, but he could sit and watch the elevator to see where the lift stopped.

It didn't take long to obtain the information. Three.

Henri hurried from the hotel and hailed a cab—one he sat inside. He watched the streets as they grew near where Andres had fallen. What if he'd gotten lost? London was a big city with so many unsafe areas, and Andres most likely didn't know his way around—at least not enough to find his way back to Dr. Stanslovich's without assistance. If he were injured badly, he might become disoriented.

A little past the area where the Malmount was located, Henri saw a lone figure walking along the street. His long blond hair had come down from its tie, his hat was pulled down on his head, and he carried his overcoat on his arm. People shuffled out of his way as he walked.

Henri beat the roof. "Stop the carriage!"

The driver pulled the horses to a halt.

"Andres!" Henri opened the door and waited as Andres turned around to see who called his name on a busy street. When he saw Henri, his face lit and he hurried over, guarding his side with his arm. "Come on. Let's get you home now."

Andres climbed into the carriage and settled in the seat next to Henri. "I'm sorry. I smell as if I've been mucking stables."

"Never mind that. Are you all right?" Henri searched for injury as the carriage pulled from the curb and back on its way to the manor.

Andres flinched and turned away as Henri pressed on his side.

Henri looked up sharply. "You have hurt yourself. Let me see."

Andres pushed his hands away. "No. It's fine. I'm so dirty. I don't want you touching me."

Henri gave an uneasy laugh. "I lived in dirt most of my life. It's not a new experience for me."

Andres relented and let Henri lift the tail of his shirt enough to see his torso. "It's looking a little discolored along your ribs." He pressed on them. The chest in that area wasn't flail, but Andres did wince and try to squirm away a few times.

"I don't suspect they're broken, but we'll bind your ribs once we get back to the manor just in case."

"Please don't tell Dr. Stanslovich about the injury. He'll not let me leave the house again."

Henri gave a snort, but there was more truth to those words than he cared to admit. "We'll keep it between us. I promise."

He let Andres's shirt fall back into place. Andres placed his hand against his ribs, bracing the tender area. He turned his attention to the passing scenery.

"I wish we were already in America without the threat of Azgarth or Herr Maestro hanging over us." The statement was made low and into the glass of the window more than to Henri.

"I'm not going to leave you, Andres. I don't think I could now. But don't despair. We will find a way out of this."

Andres turned to stare at Henri. Worry cut grooves around his mouth. "What if the book isn't the talisman you're looking for? What if there is something more that binds me to Azgarth?"

"Then we'll deal with it when and if that happens. We were never sure this was the way to sever the ties between you. If it doesn't work, we'll have to explore other avenues."

Andres let out a loud sigh. "I don't know what else to try."

"There are enough occult bookstores and vendors around the city; we could make use of them."

The look Andres shot Henri was one of extreme irritation. "I'd hate to see anyone get injured. I'm afraid Azgarth is way out of the league of any local occultist."

Henri ran a hand through his hair. Tension coiled in his gut. Hopelessness rested on his shoulders. "I'm only trying to come up with a plan in case ours fails. We have nothing solid on him. Only your observations, and so far they have not been rich with ways to defeat such a being."

"Defeating him was never in my plans, only getting away from him."

"In this case it might be one and the same." Henri placed his hand on top of Andres where it was curled on the seat between them. "I am a very determined man. Do not underestimate what I can accomplish."

Andres's gaze dropped to Henri's mouth. "I'd never be so bold as to make that mistake. Not with you."

They rode the rest of the way to the manor in relative quiet. Henri's mind churned with the promises he'd made Andres and how he was going to fulfill them when he wasn't even sure of what they faced. This wasn't the same as finding a solution to some mechanical problem, or discovering a disease of the body. Trans-dimensional travel was almost impossible to even consider. How did one go about contemplating such a miraculous thing? Hard to believe that a being existed that could walk between worlds—and yet, he'd seen it with his own eyes.

Still….

They pulled into the manor drive. Dr. Stanslovich stood on the front stairs, hands on hips and coattails back in an indignant manner.

"I think our presence has been missed." Andres opened the door as the carriage came to a stop.

"And now we get to see if our illustrious patron will aid us on Friday or if we must continue on without his assistance."

Henri doubted very much Dr. Stanslovich would even entertain the idea of helping them to find the ledger. Why should he? He believed the world was made from formulas and explainable circumstances. In order for Stanslovich to help, he'd have to let go of the idea he understood the true fabric of the world.

Henri paid the driver the fare and helped Andres up to the front of the house, despite his protests.

Stanslovich watched the carriage as it pulled away. "Did your investigation yield any results?"

"Perhaps."

"What happened to you?" Stanslovich gave Andres an inspecting glance.

"Fell from the back of a carriage."

Stanslovich started forward to assist Andres, but stopped when Henri lifted a hand. He didn't want to break a promise, but from the look on Stanslovich's face, he already knew Andres was hurt.

"It's his ribs. I think he might have bruised a few. Nothing life threatening."

"And you're not the physician here." The rebuke came as cutting as it did swift.

Henri's guts twisted and turned. "I need no reminders of the fact."

Andres said nothing, but Henri felt him tense as they entered the manor.

"Forgive me, Henri." The words were so foreign to Stanslovich, they sounded thick, as if they became clogged in his throat.

Henri brushed off the apology. No doubt it had been given for the sole purpose of proving to Andres he was a decent fellow. Stanslovich wasn't a bad man; he had just become a bit territorial over the past few weeks.

"Perhaps you should take him straight to his room. He can bathe and change."

Andres glanced down. "Yes. A bath is a good idea."

"When you've finished, we will all meet in the library and discuss what you were searching for and what it is you found."

Chapter
Nineteen

M IKHAIL TRIED to stifle his anger and disappointment. He'd never lost anything he wanted to another man. Not once. Confidence in his charm, success, and power had been his defining traits. He might not have been born English, but his adoptive homeland had always appreciated wealth and success—enough so that oftentimes a title had not been needed to open doors. At least not at the circles he traveled.

Why was the one thing he desired forever out of his grasp?

He'd saved Valentine's life, for Christ's sake. The reward should have been his, not Henri's.

"Stop brooding," Dante chastised from across the library.

Brooding seemed to be the only thing he had at the moment. Answers were a world—a dimension—away. How miraculous an existence to have seen into both worlds—the material and the fae?

Did it even really exist?

Oh God. It had to. He'd seen that damn thing come up through the fluid of the resurrection tank. It had materialized as if coming up out of some primordial ooze.

No matter what he did, he couldn't quite purge that image from his mind. The sight of scales, the sounds of the splashing liquid, the smell of fear, hunger, and desire had painted the air, clogging out all other experiences. All the senses had imprinted on his soul a photographic cell of a single moment in time.

He wiped a hand down his face and gazed at Dante, who didn't seem near as worried or upset as Mikhail felt. "I've been thinking of how to correct this miscalculation for days, and I've come up with nothing."

"Miscalculation?" Dante crossed his arms and leaned farther back in his chair. "I believe Henri and Valentine are onto something. We should wait to hear what they have to say before we give up hope."

Mikhail raised a brow. "I have never in my life given up hope. I don't intend to start now."

"Promise me you'll listen to Henri and Valentine and not dismiss their ideas or what they discovered today because it has no basis in science."

The request was akin to asking him to deny gravity.

He gave a brief nod as Henri and Valentine entered the room.

While they took seats, Dante rose and poured them both a drink. He'd always been more of a gentleman than Mikhail. The contrasts in their personalities should have made them bitter rivals, but instead had made them close as brothers.

An uneasy feeling spiraled up in Mikhail's gut, reaching up to spread out along all his nerve endings. He shifted in his seat as he watched Dante move through the room. Something unfamiliar pricked his conscience. He pushed the disquiet away and turned to Henri.

"I've been warned to hold my tongue until I hear all information, and then I may comment." Mikhail twirled his hand in the air. "You have the floor, Henri."

Henri stole a glance at Valentine, who gave an encouraging nod. "As we looked through the accounts in the book we found, it occurred to me that perhaps Azgarth's hold on Valentine came from the power of a talisman—a charm—something personal that allowed Azgarth or one of his agents to control a subject."

The unease grew, nearly choking off Mikhail's breath. "And did you find anything?"

"Not yet, but Valentine remembered a notebook, or ledger, that Herr Maestro keeps on his person and writes things down in. We don't know if it might have any ties between Azgarth and himself, but it's worth a chance to locate and at least investigate."

Mikhail rubbed a hand along his chin, thinking. "A notebook to jot ideas down is a pretty slim bit of information to go on. Even I've been known to keep one close at hand in case an idea should strike when I'm away from the laboratory."

"And yet." Dante raised a brow and made a circuit of the room. "Think of all the lines of poetry, epic journeys, or operas laid down on paper with words. Let's take the supposition that what Valentine has told us about Azgarth, his observations, are truth and that this fae master holds sway over those with musical talents. It is not a far stretch to suppose that the very words written down by poets, playwrights, and composers hold a power due to their creation. Take that one step further and place the burden of collection of such data on someone Azgarth would trust to bring more into the fold. An agent."

Mikhail watched Dante, trying to see beyond the cold calculation in his eyes and the set of his jaw. Apparently, he'd given this a lot of thought.

"And did you find a book?"

Henri shook his head. "Not on this pass, but we did find Herr Maestro."

"Where is he?"

Henri set his untouched drink on the sideboard. "He's got rooms at the Imperial. During the day he's rehearsing a young woman for a recital on Friday night over at the Malmount."

Mikhail took in his three companions. There weren't going to be any further experiments until this situation had settled. He might as well play along. "All right. What do you propose?"

Light filled Henri's eyes—a purpose that Mikhail had only seen when Henri was embroiled in creating one of his inventions. "During the performance, Valentine and I will go through his dressing room to find the book, but we need someone to go through his rooms at the Imperial. I fear we won't have adequate time to search both of them."

Mikhail smiled at Dante. "Are you up for a bit of mischief on Friday?"

Dante struck a pose by the fireplace. He pulled a cigar out of his jacket pocket and rolled it in his fingers. "Rather."

"It's settled, then. Friday, we take back our lives."

WILHELM WENT over the proposed program for Friday he felt showcased Miss Alexandre's considerable talents. The transformation was astounding. Amazing what a well-placed bite by the *wolfsine* did for a talentless girl.

He dipped his pen nib into the ink and began to scratch it across the page. As he lifted the pen to dip another time, the scratching continued. He frowned and turned to look over his shoulder. The edges of the room bled into the fae realm. Instead of the sitting room in his suite at the Imperial in London, he sat in an opulent room, under the watchful eyes of Azgarth.

"You wished to see me, my lord?"

Azgarth used a long fingernail to slide a piece of sheet music over to him.

Wilhelm glanced down at the paper. Lines swam in front of his eyes, wavering and whipping, a flag in a hurricane. He blinked a few times. For all he tried to make the staff stay in place, it danced across the page. As far as he could tell, there were no notes.

He glanced up at Azgarth's changing form. "Blank?"

"Yes."

"What am I to do with a blank sheet? I haven't time to write an aria."

Azgarth leaned forward. "It is *not* for you. Tomorrow there will be a young musician at the hall while you practice. Give the paper to him. He will not squander the opportunity."

Wilhelm tensed. Did that imply Azgarth believed *he* had? Was that the reason he'd been relegated to the role of agent? If there was one crime of which Wilhelm had never been guilty, it was squandering an opportunity. He knew damn well how to milk the most out of every turn of fortune.

"How will I know the musician?"

"You will know."

An immediate and acrid scent of smoke filled the room. Fumes rose up from between the leather covers of the ledger. Another name had been added. Anxious to see the identity of the new chosen, Wilhelm resisted the temptation as if it were of no consequence.

"You are adding names faster than I can cultivate them."

Azgarth made a low growl at the complaint. He spread his arms wide. "This is a golden age of invention, artistry, and innovation. Arts and sciences have collided to produce the most amazing and breathtaking accomplishments. I will have them under my control."

Wilhelm spread his hand across the unused sheet music. "And your latest conquest?"

"You will have to wait and hear it to understand the depth of his genius."

In all the years he'd served Azgarth, the game always played out the same. Wilhelm tried to get a small sample to work with before the unveiling, only to be thwarted by Azgarth's will. The fae master never gave secrets away—not until he was ready to unleash his chosen on the world. Not until he knew precisely how he might use their talents to honor him.

"And this new and amazing talent will come to me?"

Wilhelm wasn't prepared for the speed and violence of Azgarth's strike. Before he blinked, he was backed up to the wall, suspended above the ground, a tight hand around his throat, blocking his breath.

"You hear me and hear me well, *Herr Maestro*. I will not be mocked. Not when I hold your very life in my hands. Not when you live by my whim. Never forget that." Azgarth gave one final squeeze before he let Wilhelm drop to the ground in a heap.

Cold suffused his neck, icy fingers that never seemed to let go, even after the physical threat was gone. Frostbite bled into the skin of his neck layer by freezing layer.

Wilhelm scrambled to his feet, holding a hand to his burning throat. Bottles and assorted toiletries flew off the shaving stand as he knocked them asunder while trying to pull himself up to the mirror.

The feeling radiated down his chest, seeping its way around his sides and across his back. He removed his hand from his throat, looking at the bright red flesh. Perfect impressions of long, thin fingers wound around his neck. How much longer must he endure this torture to see his reward?

Quiet—save for the harsh sounds of his own breath—enveloped the room. Wilhelm turned from the mirror, once again alone. Relief poured through his body, but the signs of his quick and intense punishment remained. He knew from experience the marks might be there for days.

It would serve Azgarth right if Wilhelm tore the sheet music in half and burned it in the fireplace. He stalked to the desk to pick up the paper. The sheets had fallen to the floor when Azgarth had slammed him against the wall. He reached down to pick them up. His hands went to the edges. He made a motion to rip them apart, but nothing happened.

The pages might look and feel like paper but were constructed of fae magic.

A cold laugh came from everywhere and nowhere. It seeped from the walls, oozing around the room, thick as honey.

If the paper didn't tear, he doubted burning it would do much good either. He set it back on the desk and took his seat.

Looking over the program, anger rose. He crushed the paper into a ball and began to write again. This time he filled the list with only those songs the most celebrated of sopranos would dare attempt. See what Miss Juliana Alexandre made of these songs.

He chuckled, though there was no one to share in his dark mirth.

Sleep tried to claim him a time or two as he wrote, but he fought off the sweet arms of oblivion, only to wake up hours later with the indentation of the pen in his cheek and drool across his list.

He shook his head to clear the muzzy images from the night before. His throat remained sore, but the skin felt better to the touch.

Movements were slow, almost drugged. Judging from the clock, he was going to miss his rehearsal with Miss Alexandre if he didn't put a bit of pep in his step.

He quickly washed, shaved, and changed, then gathered up his belongings before heading out of the hotel to find a carriage. He wasn't going to wait for the hotel transport. There wasn't time. And despite his blatant defiance the night before, he had no intention of inciting more of Azgarth's ire.

The Malmount's doors were open, and Miss Alexandre was already on the stage warming her voice with the accompanist when Wilhelm arrived.

He threw the sheet music across the top of the piano. "Here. We are changing the program."

Panic covered Miss Alexandre's face. She exchanged a glance with the accompanist. "Isn't it too late for me to learn new songs?"

Wilhelm gave a negligent shrug. "That all depends on you, my dear, and your ability to retain notes and lyrics."

"The concert is tomorrow night."

"Then you had best be a quick study."

From the audience seating, Mrs. Alexandre stood. "Really! This is unacceptable."

Wilhelm turned on the doting mama. "Who is the maestro here? You or me? I suggest you sit down and keep yourself occupied or I will have you removed."

She gave a great harrumph and sat back down.

Juliana turned fearful eyes Wilhelm's way. "Can I at least hear the songs before I sing them the first time?"

"I don't see why not." He placed a piece of music on the stand in front of her. "Follow along, if you will."

The music started, a few piano chords. Wilhelm watched as Juliana tapped out the time with her foot, her head made a steady bob with each note. Concentration shone in her eyes, but her expression was one of serenity.

When the song ended and the last note died on the air, she glanced up from her copy. "I can do this."

"I am pleased with your confidence."

Her color was decidedly improved today. An air of fortitude surrounded her. Perhaps she would not let him down.

He tapped on the piano. "From the top."

The intro filled the hall. Notes floated up to the rafters, then fell back down on them, a gentle rain of sound. Juliana opened her mouth to sing. A tone born of the heavens released. Wilhelm's knees weakened, nearly buckled. How was it possible that her tone and pitch had improved even more in the course of a night? Yet the song filling the empty theater was as pure as if a heavenly host had come to earth to sing praises. No doubt Azgarth would find that thought blasphemous to his reign over the arts. He'd not even allow God to take credit for talents, even if they weren't improved by a well-placed bite of a *wolfsine*.

Wilhelm gave her no break when the song ended. He went right into the next, letting the accompanist play through the tune, giving Juliana the feel of the music before she joined her voice with the strains of the piano.

By the time they had completed the entire program, day touched evening. Mrs. Alexandre squirmed in her seat.

Wilhelm turned from his work and studied her. "I will allow you and Miss Juliana a brief repast. No milk for your tea and do not gorge yourself on sandwiches or biscuits. We will resume practice after."

Miss Juliana gave a poised bow and hurried off the stage. Wilhelm watched after her, only then noticing a young man in the audience, whose total attention and adoration followed her up the aisle to the exit.

The book in his inner pocket warmed. So this was the young man whose name had been added to the ledger.

Wilhelm made a calling motion with his hand. "Do not be shy, young man. You came here specifically for something, and you will not be served if you do not speak up."

He dipped his head, holding a ragged hat in his palms. "If you please, sir. My name is Edwin Divine. I am a composer."

Divine? Wilhelm raised a brow. "What have you written, Mr. Divine? Have you any samples of your work with you?"

"Yes." Mr. Divine touched his hand to a battered leather satchel. Though his clothes were clean, they were threadbare in places. Pride showed in the way he presented. Edwin Divine might not have money, but he was not one to let a mere condition such as poverty stop him from presenting in the best light possible.

This young man had decided potential in that area. Great potential. Now if his talent was even close to acceptable before a *wolfsine* bite, Wilhelm might have something to work with.

Mr. Divine reached into his satchel and pulled out a finished piece of music. He walked up to the stage and held out the piece.

Wilhelm took it and skimmed a glance over the page, sight-reading as he went. The music was good, not great, but the man before him had potential.

Wilhelm reached into his inner pocket and pulled out the blank sheets provided by Azgarth. "Take this paper and write me an aria. Dig deep and find the source of your inspiration."

Mr. Divine turned to stare over his shoulder to where Juliana had gone. "When do you need it returned?"

"When it's finished, of course. Not until."

As Mr. Divine took the paper, his expression changed. A light scent of burnt cinnamon and almonds filled the space between them, emanating from the pages.

It was only after Mr. Divine had gone that Wilhelm reached into his jacket and opened the ledger to the last page. There at the bottom was the burnt entry of the name Edwin Divine.

Chapter Twenty

FRIDAY EVENING proved an awful night for weather. Thick fog had rolled in, sealing the city in a cocoon of shifting mist and echoing sounds. Mikhail studied Henri and Valentine as the carriage slowed to allow them to alight close to the Malmount without being seen in front of the building. Not that much of anything was going to be seen in the curtains of heavy vapor. Still, they'd come this far with the plan, and Mikhail would hate to see it thwarted by even one observer.

The faces of his companions showed nothing but determination to complete the task of searching Herr Maestro's dressing room and locating the book. Reservations that the search would yield anything of value continued to turn over in Mikhail's mind, but he kept those opinions to himself. The others seemed to believe this search important to fighting off the bonds of Azgarth and his agents. His intellectual side told him they were chasing a ghost. And ghosts hiding in fog were never easy to find.

"Be careful," he urged Henri and Valentine as they slid from the carriage seats and out to the cobbles. "At the first sign of trouble, I want you to hightail it to the rendezvous point. Understood?"

"Yes." Henri's reply was clipped and tight. His jaw clenched hard in the carriage lights.

Valentine glanced up at Mikhail and gave a curt nod. "We will."

Henri closed the door, and Mikhail rapped on the driver's box. In motion once again, the forward momentum seemed a crawl. At this pace they'd reach the Imperial about the same time the concert ended.

Dante reached over and covered Mikhail's hand with his own. Sensation shot up Mikhail's arm and across his chest. He turned his hand over and squeezed Dante's fingers, glad to have a friend who understood him so completely, knew his faults on a grand scale, and accepted him all the same.

"Have you thought of what you are going to do if Henri is correct?"

The question caught Mikhail off guard. He slipped his hand from Dante's and turned to him. "I suppose I will deal with that eventuality when it occurs. If it occurs."

"You know that's not what I mean, Mikhail." Weary resignation put a discordant note in Dante's voice.

Yes, he did know, and he did not care for it in the least. His entire worldview—that which he knew without question—the realm of the physical, tangible, would be ripped from underneath him. A constant and unbreakable anchor gone.

"I can't think about that now."

Dante held up his hand. "All right. I won't press, but we do need to discuss it soon. I don't want you to withdraw even further than you have from society."

Surprised, Mikhail studied Dante. "As often as we've traveled the world together, gone to theaters and museums, you dare say I'm withdrawn from society?"

Dante's gaze slid away. He looked out at the fog-shrouded night. "You only went on those trips to see Valentine."

Something unspoken hovered in the space between them. The inside of the carriage suddenly felt too confining.

"Say what you mean. Don't sit there and allude to it."

Dante frowned. "It's of no moment."

Mikhail wanted to argue the point but decided to retreat into his own thoughts. The last thing he wanted was to bicker with Dante. Fights between the two of them usually ended with offense and hurt feelings, neither of which they could afford at such a time.

They rode the rest of the way to the Imperial in silence.

Traffic had crawled to a trickle in this fashionable section of town. Mikhail and Dante left the carriage. The driver pulled to the side of the hotel as he'd been instructed.

Zero hour had arrived.

With trepidation burning a hole in his gut, Mikhail gave a nod to Dante as they began to climb the stairs that fronted the Imperial. Mikhail carried his black bag filled with medical equipment. Not that they had need of any of the instruments inside, but it gave credence to their claims. Now the only obstacle was if the hotel staff had seen Herr Maestro leave.

However, the only sure way to appear above reproach was to act as if they had every right to be there.

They approached the concierge's desk.

Mikhail pulled out a card. The name that appeared on the front was that of a Viennese colleague he'd met at a symposium four years before. They were enough alike in coloring and height that no one who knew the physician in question would doubt the identity if a description was given to them.

"I'm Dr. Frelingheuser, and this is Dr. Alberti. We've been called by William Kane to attend him."

The concierge placed a finger on his lips and gave a nod. "I promised I would not call a physician myself, but seeing how he has seen fit to do so himself…. He is in suite 315."

Mikhail tried not to react with shock. Instead he acknowledged the concierge's discretion. "You cannot be too careful in your position. You are to be commended for your vigilance in protecting the privacy of your guests."

The man seemed to grow two inches in height under the praise. His chest bowed out. "Will you need me to see you to the room?"

"No. We would hate to take you away from your duties. Mr. Kane or his associate will answer the door. Thank you for your assistance."

Mikhail slipped the concierge a few sovereigns for his trouble when he shook the man's hand.

Dante slid Mikhail a sly glance as they crossed the lobby to the elevator. "I had no idea how good you were at subterfuge."

"I only did what I needed to buy us time undisturbed."

"Good work, Dr. Frelingheuser."

They were quiet on the lift, only giving the operator the floor they needed. When the doors opened and they stepped off, strange music filled the hallway, originating from suite 315.

HENRI LED Andres through the backstage area, putting up a hand to stop him whenever one of the stagehands appeared. As they walked by a music stand, Andres grabbed it and hurried along the corridor, changing positions to let Henri follow him.

"If we act and look as if we are supposed to be here, then no one will question us." Andres scooped up stacks of sheet music in his other arm. "Don't stand there and gawk. Pick up something."

Henri let out a sigh. He saw the point but really only wanted to get into the dressing room, check it, and then get the hell out. The last thing he wanted was to spend the evening answering questions from the constabulary about why he was ransacking Conductor William Kane's dressing room. Not that he'd keep quiet on Herr Maestro's true identity. On the contrary, that would be the first words out of his mouth as he was arrested.

Luckily there weren't as many people backstage as Henri would have imagined. Most were engaged in operating the curtains. No scenery changes were needed during a musical performance of this particular type. A small orchestra sat onstage behind the singer, none of whom could see backstage from their positions. At least not as far back as where Henri and Andres walked—he hoped.

Andres navigated them away from the stage area and down a hallway that led to the dressing rooms and, farther back, storage. Music swirled down the corridor, coming from the stage. Power radiated from the singer's voice, an almost mesmerizing quality that compelled the listener to bond to her.

He shook off the dazed feeling and hurried forward.

Andres abandoned the music stand and sheet music outside one of the dressing room doors. "This has to be his. He'd never allow a first time headliner to take the larger dressing room. His ego is too large for such a thing."

Andres tried the knob. "Locked."

Henri pulled out a small hook and needle from his pocket. "This shouldn't take long."

Before he had a chance to put the device into the lock, there was a decided click from inside the room, and the door eased open, a silent entity granting invitation to enter.

Henri glanced up at Andres. "I suppose it doesn't get any easier than that."

They stepped inside and closed the door behind them, but first Henri took a piece of paper and placed it between the door and lock. If odd circumstances were going to take place, he'd rather they weren't locked in the room.

Andres stood in the middle of the space and turned, arms outstretched. "Do you feel that?"

Henri moved closer, trying to sense anything unusual on the air. Heavy atmosphere shifted, the coming of a large storm. The laboratory had that same eerie feel before all hell came calling. "Let's just search and get out of here."

Andres took a small bag out of the wardrobe and began to rifle through the contents. "Clothes. Nothing else of note."

Henri searched the drawers on the dressing table. Bottles, jars, and containers of cosmetics, pomades, and perfumes. Nothing that looked or was shaped like a book. Most of the articles appeared old, used as if they had been permanent fixtures in the drawers.

An overcoat hung on the rack. Andres went through the pockets, both inner and outer. He shook his head in defeat. "Nothing."

"Keep looking." Henri shut the drawer he'd been searching and opened another one. This had hair pieces, fake mustaches, and false noses. He lifted the props out of the way and searched underneath. Nothing.

Not willing to give up yet, he moved on to the next drawer. Spirit gum, removers, and lotions. Again nothing of value or note. He closed the drawer with a frustrated bang. That's when he noticed the music had stopped—but so had all the other sounds from the theater. No applause thundered down the hallway, no sounds of people moving about, even the clomp of horses' hooves from the street failed to filter into the room.

Henri turned to Andres and held up a hand. "Do you hear that?"

Andres stilled and cocked his head. He waited a beat or two before frowning. "I don't hear anything."

"Exactly. Don't you find that unusual for a theater during a performance?"

Color drained from Andres's face. "Not when that performance is in another dimension."

Henri stood. Fear climbed up from his belly to lodge in his throat. He held out his hand to turn the doorknob, his fingers shaking. Andres put his hand in the middle of Henri's back, giving encouragement.

The knob turned easily in his hand. He pulled it open and looked out. An odd patina settled over the interior of the hallway. Where it had been bathed in gold from the gaslights, it had now taken on a gray washed-out appearance, chalk paintings on a rainy sidewalk.

Shapes became sketchy and hard to distinguish. Henri walked down the hallway, hands raised to help him maneuver to the end. Had he turned in the right direction? Nothing about the corridor looked even vaguely familiar.

"Find the back door into the alley." Andres followed him, turned sideways. He patted the walls as he moved. "Do not venture into the theater proper."

Henri stalled. "Why not?"

"Easier for us to become trapped in there."

"If you haven't noticed, we are trapped. I have no idea how to get us out of here."

Andres appeared to breathe a little faster.

"Do not hyperventilate on me. We have to get out of here and see if we can find a way back into our world." Henri took Andres's hand. "Stay close."

Laughter rolled above their heads. A feeling of being watched, evaluated, and taunted oppressed from every angle. Henri picked up speed, nearly dragging Andres behind him.

No matter how loud or hilarious Azgarth found their fear, Henri wasn't about to give in to the feelings. Wasn't going to even listen to the sounds that pursued them.

They turned down a corridor Henri thought for sure led to the stage door and ended up coming out stage right on the other side of the building from where they'd entered. He stopped and looked around. "How did we get here?"

"It doesn't matter. We'll end up where Azgarth wants us to be." Andres gave Henri's hand a squeeze before stepping out in front of him. He looked ahead, and the way they had come.

Henri followed Andres's gaze and didn't like what he saw. Ropes and pulleys used for stage sets tangled in the rafters, a row of hangman's nooses waiting for the condemned. He blinked a few times to clear the vision.

In the distance, a singular voice raised in song penetrated the layers of the space between worlds. Henri tried to question what his heart knew to be true. The theater proper was empty. Sounds from the street didn't leak into the room. Someone might have been stationed in another place within the structure, but he doubted the fact. The ghostly voice lilted through the halls, behind the curtain, along the rafters. A wind of unknown origin billowed through the room, bringing the voice closer, until it faded again, moving by on the breeze.

"Come on. We'll try this way. Go to the front of the theater." Henri walked out on stage and started down the stairs. He was almost to the floor when he turned around to notice Andres was no longer behind him. As a matter of fact, he didn't see him at all.

Cold dread seeped into his bones.

"Andres." Henri hissed the name in better than a stage whisper. Why he did that he wasn't quite sure, other than not wanting to alert Azgarth to his position—not that the fae master didn't know already.

Where did Andres go?

He stood still, trying to hear if there was any violin music. If Andres had been taken, then how was Henri supposed to get him back?

"Andres."

Noise from the catwalk had Henri looking up. In the dim light, it was hard to see who was walking on the upper level. "Andres?"

"Shhh. I thought I heard something."

"Up there?"

"Better vantage point to see the entire theater."

The man had a point. Henri hurried to the ladder and started up to the catwalk. Never one to fear heights, each step he took felt an invitation to peril. The ladder moved in a rickety shuffle across the boards. He gripped the sidebars hard. His body shifted. This was not going to work. He wasn't supposed to go up there.

Another jolt to the ladder and his feet slid off the rung. Sweat coated his palms making it impossible to hold on long enough to regain purchase.

"Help!"

He let go, dropping to the stage with all the grace of a bag of flour. He hit hard.

"Henri!"

Henri sat up, trying to catch his breath. He heard Andres scrambling along the catwalk, but hurt too badly to look up to watch his progress. He'd rather Andres stayed put for now instead of negotiating the ladder, but the words of warning were coiled in his throat, unable to make it out with any force.

Above him the ropes began to sway and the creak of pulleys came alive. Andres rode down as a pirate might aboard a storm-tossed ship. He hit the stage and ran to Henri.

"Are you injured?"

"Only my pride. Got the wind knocked out of me too."

Andres rubbed a firm hand along Henri's back. "What happened?"

"Someone didn't want me to follow you." He tried to get up, but took a few more minutes to regain his equilibrium. The fall had made him a bit dizzy when he turned his head a certain way. "What did you hear?"

"Whispers. The language of the fae."

"What did they say?"

Andres pushed back the hair that had fallen from the tie at his nape. "I do not understand the words. I only recognize the sound. I can only describe it as strains of spoken music."

Henri had heard French spoken in such a manner. The voices so soft and sweet they resembled a song. However, he was sure someone as well traveled as Andres Valentine would know French when he heard it.

Andres helped Henri to his feet. He brushed off the back of his pants as a matter of course, not because he felt they were dirty. His head still pitched and rolled with the regularity of a ship at sea. A step away from Andres and he realized how unsteady his gait had gotten.

"Maybe you should rest a bit more."

"No. We have to get out of here. I don't think I'll feel right until we are back in our own dimension." By rights even saying the words out loud should have made him look insane. But the situation was real and true. A theater didn't empty itself in a matter of seconds during a performance. Someone would have been left behind.

Eerie music began to play in a loop. Violins. A song that Henri knew well—one heard on the streets the night he'd met the *wolfsine*.

Andres put his arm around Henri's waist and helped him along the back of the stage. "We have to move. This is not the place we want to be caught by a *wolfsine*."

No. Indeed, it wasn't.

Henri's heart began to hammer. Sweat broke out on his back, running down to lodge in his waistband. His lungs almost hurt to draw in the thick air.

As if by mutual agreement, they turned right, down the passage where they had entered. Almost free.

Hot breath bathed his neck. The stench of something wicked hit his nose. Gorge rose.

The *wolfsine* was gaining.

He looked behind them but saw nothing, save that odd watercolor shimmer all around them.

Henri found the stage door. He gripped the knob, expecting resistance and found none. It swung open to reveal the alley just as they'd left it.

Normal sights and sounds returned. He sagged against the outside of the building.

Another foggy night in London.

Chapter
Twenty-One

A HEAVY feeling filled the hallway. As Mikhail and Dante approached room 315, the door opened in a slow, creaky sweep. Fear pressed down on Mikhail's shoulders, but he continued forward.

Strange lights in all the colors of the spectrum floated and popped above their heads. Soap bubbles, buoyant and free. The door slammed shut behind them. Dante jumped and turned with disdain toward the commotion.

"You've got our attention." Dante's tone was hard, confrontational. Perhaps not the best course of action, but then, they were not the aggressors here. If the accounts from Dante were accurate, Azgarth had been the instigator when he'd had them attacked on that dark Paris street.

Mikhail moved around the room, checking the wardrobe, bureau, desk, anywhere a book might be hidden. Music wound its way around his body, gentle as a lover's caress, but at the same time menacing. Hateful. The touch turned clingy, sticky as a spider's web. He twisted, trying to pull free.

The bands wrapped tighter. He tried to force the ligature away from his torso, but the harder he pushed, the stronger the bonds grew. Lights flickered on and off. All matter seemed to blend together then, as if a giant hand smeared paint across a canvas. Up and down no longer held meaning. He reached out a frantic hand for Dante, but he was no longer beside him.

"Dante!"

His panicked voice echoed back to him.

The world tipped up again, this time giving him a violent shake. He put his hands out to break his fall and fell through the floor down and down. He hit the ground with an impact that forced the air from his lungs.

He gasped, trying to breathe.

Slowly, air began to fill his lungs again. The scent of fresh grass and rich dirt tickled his nose. He blinked a few times, looking around him.

He turned his head. Pain shot through the back. He'd hit harder than he thought. A moan came from somewhere above him. He rolled and found Dante, looking much worse for wear.

"Are you all right?"

Dante's gaze found his. He rubbed a hand down his face. "What in the hell happened to us?"

"I think we fell through the floor." But grass—dirt?

Mikhail sat up and took in their surroundings. This was not the hotel. Above them an endless blue sky reached far enough to touch the heavens. No clouds marred the expanse.

It had been night when they had entered the hotel.

"How long do you suppose we've been here?"

Dante stood, brushing the dirt from his clothes. His expression grew hard, jaw set. "We've been here before."

Mikhail stood as well. "Really? When?"

"Paris."

Always their troubles began and ended in Paris. He wished he'd never stepped foot on those streets with their exotic absinthe and messy painters. But he'd been drawn there to the music and amusements.

"How did we get out then?"

"I don't remember. I only remember awaking in my bed and having the bite marks of the *wolfsine* and a few other images out of time and place."

He swallowed down the rising panic.

All around them colors appeared exaggerated—an artist's palette more vivid than he'd ever seen. Details were fuzzy, the edges blots of paint rendered by the hand of an Impressionist. Lines shifted and became fluid. Form had no substance, only the suggestion of shapes. He recognized trees and flowers, grass, and beyond the hill, a lake. Sunshine sparkled off the water, not in the usual manner, but as stagnant dots of white.

"I feel like we've fallen into a painting." Mikhail tried to touch the trunk of a tree, but his hand passed right through it. "Interesting."

More than that, it was damn alarming. He tried to keep calm, to not show how profoundly this unexpected side trip affected him. The thing that scared him the most was the fact Dante had begun to take on the waving lines and hypercolor of the world in which they'd been plunged.

Mikhail lifted a hand and touched his own face. "Can you see me clearly?"

"No. I can see the color of your hair and suit, the color of your skin, but not your features."

"Then it must be the environment. It's created to give that effect. Light and colors, mirrors used to create an illusion." He looked around him. The possibility existed that they hadn't fallen through the floor into this alternate realm, but through a door into another room in the suite made to look this way in order to disorient anyone who might trespass in Kering's rooms. Special lights and mirrors procured from the stage could offer such an effect.

"It's possible." Dante didn't sound convinced.

"Think about it. All it would take was someone who was well versed in the art of stage magic or even set design for a play."

"Going on that theory, we should be able to walk a short distance in any direction and come to a wall. Follow the wall around until we find the door."

"Good idea." Mikhail raised his arms in front of him and started walking forward. He encountered no obstacles as he moved. No bed or nightstand tripped him. No washing basin rim touched his fingers. Under his feet, the ground sloped downward to the lake.

Sounds of water lapping the shore and the cry of sea birds tickled his hearing. Either the suggestion of both was so strong his mind created the sounds, or they were real.

He stopped. "Do you hear that?"

Dante tilted his head. "Birds. Water."

So it wasn't his imagination. A gramophone maybe?

They kept walking toward the lake. On the far shore, a man sat atop a huge bolder. Strains of a lyre filtered out across the water as he strummed. Bells tinkled when he moved.

He stopped playing. "I wondered when you'd arrive, but hoped you'd stayed on the hill awhile longer. Seeing you react to your environment is most enjoyable."

"Who are you?" Mikhail challenged.

"Don't you know?"

Mikhail was afraid he did.

ANDRES TOOK a deep breath and leaned against the adjacent building. He'd never been so scared in all his life, but didn't want Henri to know. He risked a sidelong glance at his lover. Henri stood glaring at the stage door as if he'd be able to bring Herr Maestro from the theater by the force of his anger.

And Henri was angry.

Andres didn't have to read minds, he only had to look to the set of Henri's jaw and the clench of his fists. He was ready to do battle and throw consequences to the wind.

"Do we wait here or go to the front of the building?"

Henri took off his hat, wiped at his brow, then replaced his cap. "Which way does Herr Maestro usually exit a theater?"

"Depends on the theater and size of the crowd. He's been known to exit the front if there were adoring fans waiting to praise him. A theater this small, no matter how triumphant the act, he will sneak out the side. Not only that, but he might wish to do so in case the authorities are waiting out front." Andres looked to the end of the alley. "Though it seems the fog is still quite thick. No one would see him."

Henri nodded and took a position that mirrored Andres's. "That works to our advantage. No one will see us either."

Andres swallowed. "Are you sure you want to do this?"

"Yes. I do. More so now that we were trapped in that horrible transdimensional space."

Andres pulled his coat closer. Cold penetrated his body right down to his bones. He always associated that deep kind of frozen insides to crossing over into the fae realm. The sensation didn't go away on its own, but lasted until the body was submerged into a hot bath.

"I wonder how much longer we'll have to wait."

Henri took his pocket watch out and stared at the face. He tapped it a few times. "My watch stopped."

"Not surprising. There is no concept of time in the fae realm."

"Then how does Azgarth know when and how to find his chosen?"

Andres sent his hands down into his pockets. "I don't know the answer to that. Perhaps he is bonded by the *wolfsine's* bite to those he's chosen and can sense them and where to come out of the realm."

"Like the homing instinct on a pigeon." Henri slipped the watch back into his pocket. "It could be very much like that."

Noise came from inside the building. A thunderous applause that vibrated the very cobbles under their feet. Shouts of *bravo* filtered out into the street.

"Is that the end of the concert or only that particular number?" Andres didn't expect an answer since neither of them knew the program or proposed length. "I'm going to the end of the alley. I'll signal if I see anyone coming out of the front of the theater."

"Whistle. I might not see a signal in the fog."

Andres indicated he'd heard, then hurried to the mouth of the alley. He poked his head around the front of the building. He couldn't see anything but heard the burble of voices—many excited ones—the sounds of moving feet.

Better than whistling, Andres turned and hurried back to Henri. "I couldn't see a thing. Fog has grown thicker. I did hear the sounds of a crowd leaving the theater."

"All right."

Having no idea of Henri's intent by that answer, Andres stood watching the stage door, hoping it opened soon and they could jump Herr Maestro and retrieve the book. Only then would he feel as if the night had been a success or worth all the turmoil. Whenever he'd been stuck in the fae realm, he'd always bartered his way out by playing a song or two for Azgarth. Sometimes he'd return days later only to get a beating from Herr Maestro for being gone so long, even though it was Azgarth who had kept him.

So many injuries Herr Maestro needed to account for.

Rage burned up into Andres's throat. He turned away so Henri wouldn't see his expression, and noticed something shining out of the fog. A sense of unease settled over him, the feeling of being watched and weighed.

He leaned in and whispered in Henri's ear. "I don't think we're alone in this alley."

"We haven't been for some time. I'm trying to ignore it. I suggest you do too."

Henri might as well have asked him to walk to the moon or make gold from straw. Both would be an easier proposition than waiting for whatever it was to show itself, and for all the *wolfsines* were horrible creatures, they weren't the worst in Azgarth's arsenal.

The stage door opened, and people began to flood out into the alley. Musicians with their cases in their hands, laughing at their triumph. A taste of euphoria spilled into the air. Andres knew that emotion well. Nothing proved as intoxicating as playing to an appreciative audience and feeling their love and approval in return.

Well, perhaps nothing.

He turned a loving gaze to Henri. The love of the man beside him made all other performances and music pale in comparison.

"Valentine?"

Hearing his name made him turn his head in reaction. He should not have given in to the reflex, but it was too late.

"Christ. It is you."

Andres stepped forward with his hand outstretched, manners taking precedence over prudence. He regretted the action immediately. "Lorenzo. How are you? I haven't seen you since… Paris?"

"Yes. Paris. Five years ago." Dark eyes searched his face. "I thought you were dead."

"Exaggerated tales by gossipmongers. Nothing more. As you see, I am well and whole."

"So you did come to London for treatment. I thought that the fantastic part of the tale."

Andres shook his head. "No. The fantastic part is that I am no longer on the stage."

Lorenzo frowned. "Do you ever plan to return?"

"I don't know. Not in the immediate future." Andres sent a pleading glance toward Henri, hoping for rescue. To his surprise, Henri was no longer there; he'd taken off to follow a dark-clad figure.

"Excuse me, Lorenzo. It was nice seeing you again."

"Perhaps we can meet for a drink while I'm in London."

"I'd like that," Andres called back as he took off in a run to catch up with Henri.

Murmurs trailed in his wake. Other musicians who had known and worked with him over the years. Or those who knew him by reputation. He put them from his mind and continued his pursuit.

Henri moved fast when called upon, but what surprised Andres more was the speed with which Herr Maestro appeared to move. Ice sliced through him.

"Henri! No!"

Henri didn't slow or stop. He kept plunging forward, getting lost in the fog as he turned the corner out of the alley and into the street. The fact Henri ran straight into a trap choked Andres. Panic pushed him onward, even as his lungs burned and his heart pounded, and he refused to stop. He had to save Henri.

Mists swirled and swallowed people, horses, and carriages. Even the buildings were cloaked behind a wall of white so profound it seemed endless. Gaslights were odd glowing orbs that only became visible when an arm's length away.

The clatter of hooves on cobbles alerted him he'd gotten too close to the street. A carriage brushed by him, wind and the sharp musk of horses swirled around him. Henri was lost in the fog.

Andres stopped and turned in a circle, trying to filter through the ambient noise, pungent smells, and shifting mist. Nothing indicated Henri's presence.

Something moved past him, touching his hand. Scales, warm and silky, fluttered against his fingertips. He looked down to the *wolfsine* that walked beside him. It raised its massive head and sniffed the air, searching. Andres followed the beast, feeling for sure he'd find Henri at the end.

The *wolfsine* picked up speed. Rippling muscles and sturdy bones moved under the surface of the scaly hide as the animal stalked through the city street. No one passing them appeared to see the creature.

Screams came from the next street over.

The *wolfsine* broke into a run. Andres followed in its wake.

They ran for almost a block before turning into another alley. Then the *wolfsine* leapt. It came down on one bent over a human bleeding from a rent in his side.

Blood ran through the man's fingers as the fighting, snarling mass of teeth and talons rolled off and began a fight to the death.

"Andres."

He fell to his knees and placed a hand over Henri's side. "Dearest Christ. I don't know how to help you."

His own bite from the *wolfsine* hadn't been this dramatic, this deep.

"Take some fabric and put it over the site. Hold pressure."

"I need to get you help."

"Please. Just do this, or I'll bleed out and there will be nothing for you or anyone else to help."

Andres swallowed. Amid the sounds of a harsh conflict of two large predators, he ripped the sleeve off his shirt and rolled it up to stanch the blood free-flowing from Henri's side.

His hands shook. A warm, wet rush ran over his fingers. "Oh, Henri."

"Shh. Don't say it."

Sobs tore at the back of his throat. He bit his lip to keep them at bay. His lover was going to die in front of him, and there was nothing he could do to stop it.

He'd seen several injuries in his years serving as one of Azgarth's chosen, but he'd never seen one like this. Death was not the goal of the *wolfsine*; it was to initiate. This was an attack of the worst kind. Vengeance for trying to steal the book or for trying to corrupt him away from the fae realm? If he'd been asked, Henri had no part in that—Azgarth and his agent had done the damage all too well.

Henri's breath grew labored. His eyes began to close.

"No. Stay with me. Stay awake."

"Green, warm valleys."

"What?" Andres leaned closer to hear the ramblings falling from Henri's lips.

"Sunshine. Music."

Impotent rage filled his heart. He threw his head back and howled as a wounded animal might. "I will come back into the fold, just don't let him die. Do you hear me? I swear I will live to serve you."

Henri placed a bloodied hand on top of Andres's. "No. Live and be free."

The sounds of battle died. Andres turned to see the hulking form of one of the *wolfsine* lying on its side. Still. The other *wolfsine* stalked over to the fallen Henri. It sniffed around the injury. A deep whine emanated from its throat.

This one was the protector.

It whined a few more times, then nudged Andres's hand out of the way. He looked down in horror as the thing began to lick away the blood from Henri's body.

"Stop that."

"No. Let her."

Her?

Andres shuddered but moved his hand over a bit while still applying the necessary pressure. The *wolfsine* began to make a humming sound as it worked around the wound with its long tongue.

Henri reached out a feeble hand, stroking the beast's massive head. He made no sounds, only the harsh rasp of his breath. Helpless, Andres leaned back on his heels. When the *wolfsine* finished, it sat back and licked its lips, then gave Andres a steely gaze.

"I don't know what you want, so staring at me is a wasted effort."

The *wolfsine* nipped at his remaining sleeve.

"Do you want me to follow you?"

The thing turned its head, pulling at Andres.

"I can't leave Henri."

Henri moaned.

Andres leaned down and placed his hand on Henri's forehead. Already the fever was upon him.

"Henri, I'm going for help now."

The *wolfsine* continued to sit vigilant by Henri's side, on alert and muscles coiled and ready to defend if the need arose. Andres couldn't have asked for better protection for an injured Henri.

With a last, lingering look, he hurried from the alley.

Chapter
Twenty-Two

Mikhail did not intend to antagonize the person before him, be it human, elf, ghost, faerie, or other. Until he knew all the particulars of his and Dante's current circumstance, he'd use caution in his interactions.

"Well, are you not even going to venture a guess?"

If Mikhail had been able to see the voice bearer clearly, he might have seen a smile. The emotion came out in the timbre, but the sincerity of the words left him flat. Much like most of society. The surface only showed the most basic of emotions, but not the true heart of the person. It seemed no different with this man of shifting lines and blurry features.

The man laughed, a hollow, tinny sound. "You certainly do play cards close to your vest, Mikhail."

When Mikhail startled at the use of his name, the man laughed again.

"What? Did you think I didn't know you? That you were not one of my chosen? It appears I need to take a firmer hand in your life. Show a greater presence."

Resentment bubbled to the surface. He bit his lip and locked his jaws.

"And Dante Savoy." The being turned. "Treading a line you haven't quite decided you yet want to cross."

Mikhail frowned and studied his best friend.

Red slashes appeared high on Dante's cheeks as he took a menacing step toward the rock. "Not content to bring us here when time is of the essence, but you have to mock us as well? Must be quite boring to be a powerful being if you have to meddle in the affairs of men."

Shame was a malignant force. Mikhail should have said that—should have confronted Azgarth. Oh God in heaven. He'd fallen through the looking glass and ended up in some world where reality was a nightmare and dreams were haunted things.

Azgarth canted his head. He tapped a long, slim finger against his chin. "Interesting."

After a few moments in silent contemplation, Azgarth slid off the rock and started to walk away. "You'll find what you're looking for when you wake up."

Mikhail started after him. "Wait. I have questions."

Though Azgarth had blended into the subtle watercolor of the scenery, his disembodied voice floated back to them. "Should have thought of that before."

"He was less than helpful and not as impressive as I'd imagined." Dante slid his hands down in his pockets. "Are we supposed to lie down and fall asleep, or did he mean when we eventually get out of here and make it to our beds?"

"He's toying with us, and that makes me more apprehensive than if he'd used a full frontal attack."

By silent agreement, they started around the lake. Did it matter which way they walked? Space within a space, without dimensions or edges, how were they ever to find their way out? No map, compass, or sextant would ever be able to navigate the way to the other side of this no-man's-land. Mikhail failed to wrap his mind around the fact such a place existed alongside the mortal realm. How was that even possible? How had science and reason not known this?

A mile into their journey, he stopped and looked around. The scene had changed; they were no longer in the Impressionists' meadow. Light leached from the colors, bleeding to more of a grisaille. Trees morphed into buildings. A meandering path had turned into rain-soaked cobbles.

"I'm not positive if we should keep heading in this direction and hope we find the Imperial or if we should turn back and try to exit where we entered." Though they hadn't entered the meadow in a conventional manner.

"Let's keep going." Dante yawned. "My apologies. I seem to be getting sleepy."

No one walked down the streets. For all intents and purposes, they were the only people alive. If Azgarth had legions of chosen, they were not present and accounted for; as a matter of fact, Mikhail wondered at there being any.

"I wonder if this is merely a diversion to keep us occupied and off the trail of this mystery ledger or an actual exercise to prove our worthiness somehow." Dante's speculation was punctuated with another loud yawn.

"Does it matter? We're here now, and we've met the man himself, and I have to say I'm not impressed."

"Each time you say that I want to duck my head to ensure I am missed by the lightning strikes."

Mikhail raised a brow. "And yet you were brave enough to say what I could only think."

"Bravery. Stupidity. It garnered us no results save walking in this endless field… or cityscape." Dante let out a sigh. "Let's get walking and hope this test either begins or ends soon."

True. They didn't even know if Azgarth meant to test them or where it might take place. All the endless walking might bring them deeper into the fae realm where they would spend their eternity.

Why hadn't he listened more closely to Valentine when he began to tell of his experiences with Azgarth? Maybe one day he'd learn that having his nose in his experiments and discounting the fantastic until proved otherwise was detrimental to his pursuit of scientific discovery. However, the one thing in all this he could not shake was the fact Azgarth had called both he and Dante his chosen. Were their lives controlled by subtle manipulations, preparing them for a future only Azgarth knew? He'd pushed, prodded, and moved their chess pieces across the board of life until they came to the point in time where they were able to save Valentine as he fell from the window?

What to do now?

If they were being manipulated, how did they stop it?

By finding the book and destroying it, the same as Valentine wanted to do.

"We aren't going to get out of here until Azgarth decides to let us leave." Mikhail hated being dependent on another for his survival or care. Even worse when the one in charge was an untrustworthy member of an alternate race heretofore unknown by humans.

No, that was untrue. Some cultures had spoken of the fae for hundreds of years and knew to be leery of their friendship. Fae were tricksters by nature.

Dante glanced up and down the abandoned street. "Azgarth has no reason to keep us here. Think about it. If we're here, then whatever master plans he has for us are forfeit. We only do his bidding by working in the human world; otherwise why give you powers to resurrect the dead?"

The question pulled Mikhail up short. He pivoted to look at Dante fully. "True."

"Unless he only means to stall us here, bidding time away from Valentine and Henri."

"Perhaps." Mikhail canted his head, watching as the shadows of the fading gaslights changed the shape and look of Dante's face. It made him look a stranger, and maybe he was that and more. "What power did you get from the *wolfsine*?"

Dante lowered his head and turned away. "It's not as grand as yours, but it does make me a most effective doctor."

Which probably explained why patients found Dante—indeed, no matter where he traveled—and asked for treatment. They'd been accosted more than once in a foreign city when someone came seeking him. Mikhail hadn't given the interruptions much thought at the time, other than Dante's reputation as a skilled physician preceded him.

"You aren't going to tell me?"

Dante lifted a shoulder, dismissing the question. "There's not much to tell."

"You did get something from the exchange other than torment and having to live with my skepticism all these years."

Dante laughed; it sounded rusty, not like him. "I did."

Hurt that Dante refused to share his manner of power given by the fae, Mikhail turned away and studied the buildings around them, trying to find even one edifice that looked familiar.

Strains of a lonely concerto filtered on a gentle breeze. The tune wrapped around his body as the other one had, this one pulling him forward, toward the dark structure at the end of the street.

"I think we are supposed to go this way."

Dante fell into step beside him. Voices from passersby filled the air around them, yet there were no shapes to suggest anyone else inhabited the dimension.

They continued on, up to the stairs that led to the building's entrance. Mikhail placed his hand on the knob and swung the door, expecting to find the lobby full; instead they found the inside of Herr Maestro's suite.

Henri lay in the alley, riddled with pain. Cold ate away at his limbs, starting at his toes and fingers, then spreading with each heartbeat. He fought to keep his eyes open, to not succumb to shock.

The *wolfsine* remained by his side. A low rumble, not unlike a cat's purr, came from its throat as it snuggled near his injured side. He reached out and ran a hand down its scaly head. The purr grew louder. It comforted and lulled him into a restful calm.

He closed his eyes.

A low growl alerted him to danger. He cracked one eye open and saw nothing but a shimmery shadow. Light from the end of the alley shone across the silhouette in the shape of a man. The figure moved forward. Heavy fog that had permeated the area earlier dissipated.

Henri sat up, brushing the hair off his forehead. "Are you here to help?"

The figure reached down and quieted the *wolfsine* with a pat on the head.

"In a manner of speaking." The voice was lyrical, almost singing, but not quite.

"Where is Andres? Did he send you to help me?"

A light laugh filled the alley. "You might say that, though I've watched you since birth. A bright light in a dreary world."

The man squatted down over Henri, clucking his tongue as he pulled Henri's bloody shirt away from the site. "This will heal nicely. I believe my pet might have been a bit overzealous in marking you with his bite."

Henri turned to the man. "Azgarth?"

"In the flesh."

"Ha. What do you want with me?"

"Anything you wish to give. Your machines marvel and confound me. I've not seen a more remarkable man since da Vinci."

"What if I don't want to build for you? If I decide not to indulge that side of my nature?"

Azgarth huffed. "As if you even possessed the strength to refuse. You might be a physician-in-training, but in your heart, you are an inventor. And you will change the world."

Henri turned. The lines of Azgarth's face shifted and changed, never really giving him a good sense of Azgarth's features. "I'll make you a deal."

Azgarth looked up sharply. "And that would be?"

"I'll do your bidding if you agree to release Andres."

Azgarth pushed to his feet. He said a few words to the *wolfsine* in a strange dialect. The beast rose and licked Henri's face before turning and trotting down the alley, disappearing into nothing.

"I will consider your proposition."

"No. I want reassurance." He reached out, but his hand passed through where Azgarth's body should have been.

"I can give you none."

Henri closed his hand. Tingles erupted from fingertips to elbow. "Then I'll rescind the offer."

Azgarth laughed. "Oh, Henri. You do delight me more than you'll ever know."

"Glad I can amuse you."

"You do."

Henri's eyes grew heavier. He fought the urge to sleep. Without the vigilant *wolfsine* guarding him, he didn't want to drift off in the alley. "Why did you send my friend away?"

"Because you need no assistance. I will look over you."

"Isn't that kind of like the fox watching over the chickens?" Henri touched his side. "Though in this case the chicken has already been feasted on."

"The drama!" Azgarth clapped his hands together. "I should have marked you for the stage."

"How would you enjoy someone pulling your strings? Deciding your life was no longer your own?"

Azgarth batted the argument away. "And what difference does it make if your life is controlled by a jealous God or a demanding fae? Humans have no free will. Everything they do is controlled by one higher being or another. It is only a matter of which one takes control of you."

The very idea made Henri want to vomit. Gorge rose to the back of his throat. God the Father, Son, and Holy Ghost he might not necessarily believe in, but he was familiar with the concept—had lived and worked alongside people who had deeply religious convictions. Meeting a being of another realm, one with godlike powers who could control the destiny of a human, and hearing that same being talk as if some great battle was fought to gain control of individuals, well that was enough to tip the world off its axis.

How did that work exactly?

If he had been a devout man, would Azgarth have gotten a foothold? Or did religion and beliefs even play into it?

"You've gone quiet. Ah, it's just as well. Human minds are too small and segmented to expand their thinking to include alternate versions of what they perceive as a deity."

Henri cracked one eye open and considered the shifting form of Azgarth. "Are you declaring yourself a deity? Should I bow and genuflect in your presence?"

"A certain amount of respect is appropriate, but then you would not be as engaging."

Silence stretched out for what might have been hours, Henri lost track of time.

"Let Andres go."

No reply came. Azgarth had left.

Chapter
Twenty-Three

ANDRES STOPPED and looked around him. The fog had lifted. Visibility returned to normal. People moved by on the sidewalks, passing him by and speaking in whispers. Had he become recognizable to the London masses? He doubted the average passerby would ever give him a second look, especially when he didn't have a violin in his hand.

He didn't see the carriage with Drs. Stanslovich and Savoy and hesitated to venture too far away from Henri to find help. The kind of help they needed was not present in most of the faces he saw. Perhaps if he went to find the Imperial, he'd be able to bring the doctors to Henri and explain what happened. The gash on Henri's side had healed enough it had stopped bleeding, but Andres didn't know if he trusted the amount of blood loss. Henri might be too weak to defend himself should another *wolfsine* appear.

He tried not to think of the greater implication: that Henri was now a servant to Azgarth. His life was no longer his own. They would have to figure out a way to free them both.

It occurred to him, as he stood on the street corner, he no longer knew where he was or how far away from the alley where Henri lay. Someone bumped against him. He turned to apologize, and stared into the face of all his hatred and fear.

"You!"

Herr Maestro's eyes rounded. His lips flapped. "You really are alive."

"Thanks to Dr. Stanslovich bringing me back from the dead."

Herr Maestro took a step back. Andres advanced.

An odd sense of power came over him. No longer did he fear this man who had once held his life and career in his hands. Andres cast a sweeping gaze over Wilhelm Kering. There was nothing left to fear in him. He'd been cast aside by Azgarth, and he didn't even know it. That shining halo of power was now muted, putrid, and pale. Kering might still do Azgarth's bidding, but only to stay alive. He was no longer marked as a favorite, and it showed.

Andres took another step forward, backing Kering into the mouth of an alley, away from the watchful eyes of the public. Rage filled his heart and soul. He'd been so long abused and tortured by Kering, the hatred bubbled up in a geyser of emotion. "Give it to me."

"Give what to you?"

"The book."

"What book?"

Andres reared back and hit Kering in the face, knocking the maestro's head back. Kering grabbed at his cheek and turned frightened eyes to Andres.

"Give it to me."

"No. You don't know what you're saying. There is no book."

"Liar!"

Andres hit him again, this time knocking him to the ground. He grabbed for Kering's coat and got his hands slapped for the effort.

"No. Azgarth will kill me if I lose control of it."

Andres balled up his fist and punched Kering under the jaw. The maestro's teeth clacked together. Blood came from his mouth, nearly hitting Andres in the face. Kering went still.

Quickly Andres searched the inside of Kering's coat and found the book. He held it to his chest, then lifted it and kissed the cover. There was no time to look and see if it was the one he searched for, he had to vacate the area. Let Kering wake with a headache and sore mouth. At least Andres left him in better condition than Kering had left Andres.

He stood and ran the opposite way, out of the back of the alley and to the next street. Lights cast streams as he ran past.

Please let me find Henri.

He still hadn't found help, but he had located the book. Wasn't that enough? He'd get him home—back to Dr. Stanslovich's manor—and have one of the servants find him and Dr. Savoy. It had to be enough.

Everything went quiet around him. Only the sounds of his harsh breath and heartbeat sounded in his ears. Even his footsteps on the paving stones were gone. Oh dear God in heaven, had he fallen once again into that shadow world between worlds? Had taking even a minor revenge on Herr Maestro caused him to come under Azgarth's scrutiny?

He kept moving forward. Running. Searching.

Something caught his eyes as he ran past an alley. He skidded to a stop and doubled back. Three shadows were visible in the middle of the alley. One held a hand torch, the other was bent over a prostrate figure lying on the ground.

Light caught the face of one of the men—Dr. Savoy.

Andres ran to them. "How did you find him?"

The doctors exchanged glances. Tension filled the alley.

Dr. Savoy gave a grim nod. "It wasn't easy. We got lost a couple of times. Good God, what happened here?"

"He went to follow Herr Maestro and was attacked by a *wolfsine*." Andres squatted down, taking Henri's fevered hand in his. "I went for help and got lost."

Dr. Stanslovich tied off some bandages he'd placed on Henri's injury. "We were unable to locate the book."

"I have it."

They both looked up at him. "He had it on him?"

"I don't know if it's *the* book, but it is *a* book." Andres rubbed a hand down the side of Henri's face. "He's too warm."

"We'll get him moved to the manor."

Andres glanced around them. The body of the fallen *wolfsine* was no longer in the alley. Neither was the live one. "I don't know what's real anymore."

"You either? We've had a rather interesting evening ourselves." Dr. Stanslovich bent down and put Henri's arm over his shoulder. "Get on the other side and help me get him to the carriage, Dante."

Andres started to step in, but Dr. Stanslovich shook his head. "You have injured ribs. I don't want you to carry anything."

The pain in his ribs was nothing compared to the one in his heart. "Is he going to be all right?"

"He's had quite a lot of blood loss, but I don't see that Azgarth will let him die. It doesn't seem to be the way he works."

Those words coming from the ever skeptical Dr. Stanslovich chilled Andres as nothing else had. He sounded like a firm believer now. What had happened to them to cause such an about-face? Andres didn't ask. He walked ahead of them so he could clear the way through the milling crowd at the front of the alley.

The driver spotted them and dropped down off his box to open the carriage door.

Once they were all inside and trundling toward the manor, Andres reached into his pocket and opened the book. The stench of burnt paper filtered up to his nose. Columns of names were scrawled across the pages. Some of them Andres recognized, others were a mystery to him.

"Is that it?" Dr. Stanslovich gazed at the leather-bound ledger with hate-filled eyes.

"It is."

"And have you found anything of interest?"

"Hundreds of names. All musicians, singers, composers."

"May I see that?" He held out his hand.

Andres handed the book to him. Dr. Savoy leaned in as they began to look through the entries.

Dr. Stanslovich glanced up from the pages. "I wonder how far these go back."

"I'm not sure. Some of those names I've never even heard in the music world. I certainly never worked with them."

"Do you think this book has been in Kering's possession the entire time? That he made all the entries?" Dr. Savoy turned a page and scanned the list of names.

"I'm not sure, nor do I think it's important. I only wish to destroy it." Andres turned to Henri, who slept on the seat beside him. He tucked a carriage blanket up higher around his chin. "Henri's name isn't in there."

"No. Neither are ours."

A haunted look passed between the two doctors.

"Do you suppose there are more agents out there? More books?" Dr. Savoy posed to his colleague.

They both turned to Andres.

"I think there is a real possibility. Music isn't the only art Azgarth covets."

Dr. Stanslovich went back to the book, and they all lapsed into silence.

WILHELM WOKE to a stench he'd only smelled in nightmares.

He rolled over and his hand landed in a viscous liquid with a rancid scent that rivaled decomposition. Where in the hell was he? He shivered with an unbearable cold. Looking down at his body, he realized he was naked and submerged into the pool. Darkness pressed in on him from all sides.

There were no sides to the tub or vat, at least none he could discern in the dim light. A figure appeared above him.

"Help me."

A laugh filled the air around him, echoing in a way that reminded Wilhelm of an empty tomb.

"You've lost the book." The accusation sealed his fate.

He tried to find a way to push the blame to another, but his mind refused to work. How had he lost the book? When had he been brought here? Holes filled his memory. The only clear memory was that of the thunder of applause. Somewhere in his life, he'd been showered with accolades.

Now he lay in a stinky goo, unable to recall the places or faces who had been instrumental or important in his life. All his memories were dissolving into the thick pool that surrounded him. Cast off and floating in the tarry substance, he could almost pick them out one by one as they became absorbed into the liquid.

"Valentine." The name fell off his lips unbidden. A face was no longer attached, only the vague knowing that he had somehow been wronged by the person.

A low growl filled the room. Anger pressed down on him from the being standing at the edge of the pool. Something bubbled and bloated near him. A hand rose into the air, skin peeled back to reveal the skeletal fingers beneath. A leg brushed against his. Oh God in heaven, there were others in the pool with him. Dead ones. The stench wasn't imagined; it was real and came from the flesh and fumes of the decomposing bodies stuck beneath the liquid's surface.

Panic kicked his heart rate and filled his lungs. He rolled over to try to swim to the edge, but came face-to-face with a horror so unimaginable, he screamed.

Eyes hardly recognizable as belonging in a human skull stared into his. Blackness, emptiness, all lived inside that skull. The jaw was unhinged, open, breathing fetid breath into his face. Wilhelm gagged and almost lost consciousness but for the fear that propelled him forward. He batted at the thing. The head snapped free of the exposed spinal column and landed in the goo with only a slight splash. It gurgled and burped as liquid displaced the air in the empty spaces. It sank below the fluid line.

"Escape is futile. You've displeased me for the last time."

Something grabbed for Wilhelm's leg. He kicked, trying to fight off the pull that brought him dangerously close to submerging in the gross remains of those who'd gone before him—of those who had been punished by Azgarth.

This was not the end.

His life had not come down to this, would not be dissolved in so much human filth.

The rancid fluid touched the bottom of his chin.

No!

More skeletal hands joined the first, wrapping their bony fingers around his calves. An arm wound around his upper thigh and yanked. His face went under. Wilhelm held his breath and closed his mouth.

Down and down they dragged him. His lungs burned, fair to bursting for want of air.

A face floated by on his memory as spots exploded behind his closed lids. A golden god with long flaxen hair, playing a violin with passion and talent enough to move the heavens to tears.

The vision glanced up and pointed his bow at Wilhelm accusingly, as if to say this was a fitting end to one as wicked as he.

Fires ignited along all his nerve endings. Lesions opened on his torso and back, stinging with the full force of an acid bath. Was this how the others lost their flesh? Were they all subjected to the same painful demise?

Even with his life ticking down and death certain, he tried in vain to fight his captors.

He gasped and his mouth filled with the taste of death.

His tongue swelled, closing off any chance for him to break the surface and draw air. Panic made him claw at his throat. Hunks of skin fell away, leaving holes where his fingers worked.

Take me! Please allow no more of this terrible end. Deliver me from the pain and agony.

But no angel or God listened to the pleas. The torture continued, slow, unrelenting. Even past the point he should have lost consciousness. He floated on a sea of horrific sensation. Each pain an arrow through his system. A lack of breath and heartbeat didn't seem to matter; he'd passed from the realm of the living to that of the damned. The torture unending.

Chapter
Twenty-Four

PAPER, INK, leather—it was only a book made of materials that were not special or magical in any way, shape, or form. Mikhail turned the ledger over in his hand again, trying to find something that might set it apart from all other books. Nothing caused panic or alarm. He felt no rush of adrenaline or current when he ran his hand over the cover.

No matter how much of the fantastic his mind saw, his intellect still failed to comprehend that this was real, not fantasy. More than anything he wanted to find a rational explanation when none had presented. Even after falling through the world into one populated with watercolor landscapes, he maintained there was more to the situation than met the eyes.

Senses could be confused, altered due to stress, fear, or other medical conditions. Hallucinations were a common condition of fevers, infections, and mental disease.

The only problem with that was none of them currently had a fever, save for poor Henri, who writhed on his bed, twisting the sheets and soaking the linens in sweat.

He and Dante had already given Henri something to combat the fever. The medication only needed time to work. Worry put him on edge. Made him short and curt with those who had as much to lose in this game as he.

Mikhail rubbed the ledger's cover. The intricate detailing felt rough against his palm. "Are you sure this is the right one?"

Valentine looked up from where he fussed over Henri. A frown creased his brow. "I can only assume. It was on Herr Maestro's person and contains my name and that of other musicians. If it's merely a ledger listing all the musicians he's worked with over the years, then it won't help us either way."

"So you explained on the way home, but it doesn't hold that this book doesn't *feel* special."

"That fault can hardly be laid at my feet."

"I wasn't assigning blame." Mikhail thumbed through the crinkly pages, attempting to find something that might make the book seem more than it appeared.

Dante held out his hand. "If it's nothing, then toss it into the fire. It will burn and we'll be rid of it."

Mikhail touched the cover one last time and gave a nod. Since there was no fireplace in Henri's room, he had to go find a place to pitch the damn thing away. Henri mumbled nonsensical words from the bed as he left. Mikhail hesitated, trying to process them but couldn't place them.

Dante was close on his heels. "I think we need to take that to the laboratory and destroy it there. We can't anticipate what will happen once it contacts fire. What if the pages were soaked in a combustible fluid to prevent someone from attempting such a thing?"

Mikhail's appreciation for Dante grew. Sometimes a bit of paranoia went a long way to ensuring safety. "All right."

The laboratory hadn't been used since the destruction a few days before. No fire lit the cavernous grate.

"We'll need to build one up first." Mikhail stalked to the fireplace and started laying in materials to make the fire.

"That will take too long." Dante took the book from Mikhail's possession and crossed the room. He took a heavy cast-iron cauldron from a shelf and set it on the floor. "All it takes is a bit of alcohol and a match." He put words to deed and filled the cauldron with isopropyl alcohol, then threw the ledger in.

A strike of the match filled the laboratory with a chilling finality. Flame grew to life, and Dante dropped it into the cauldron. Fire shot up, burning the alcohol. Screams came from the center of the heat. Faces composed of the lapping tongues of flames twisted and turned. A shout filled the house.

Mikhail and Dante exchanged looks and took off in the direction of the servants' quarters. They found Valentine doubled over, holding his stomach. His handsome face was contorted with the grimace of pain. Blood ran from his lips.

"Good Christ!" Mikhail waved to Dante. "Go put the flame out!"

Dante left the room, his shoes striking the floor hard as he ran.

Mikhail helped Valentine to sit in a chair. "Try to take a deep breath. Holding it isn't going to help."

"Can't. Help. It. Pain." Valentine wiped at his lips. Blood smeared across his teeth and hand.

"Let me see your belly." Mikhail tried to pull Valentine's hands away, but he guarded the area too well. "Please. I want to see if there are any external lesions."

"No. Please." Valentine panted between tight lips.

Percussion from an explosion rocked the manor. Valentine's head snapped up. Terrified, he looked to the door.

For a moment, Mikhail's heart stopped. Visions of Dante lying dead filled his head, and his stomach dropped. Torn between duty to Valentine and the safety of his best friend, he had no direction. Didn't know what to do first.

Tears leaked from the sides of Valentine's eyes. Each breath seemed to come a bit easier.

Slowly Mikhail stood. "Will you be all right? I need to go check on Dante."

Valentine nodded. He grabbed for Mikhail's hand and squeezed it. "Azgarth."

Mikhail swallowed down the bilious terror flooding through his veins. In all his days, he never expected to battle a supernatural being in his own home. Nor did he know precisely how to achieve such a goal.

Servants scurried out of his way as he ran down the hall to the main foyer where marble had been blown outward from an impact site that resembled a cannon blast. The door to the laboratory was blocked, Dante nowhere to be seen.

Instead of the shifting form of Azgarth in a pastoral scene, the dark fae master now stood as a towering bastion of limitless power. Anger rained down on Mikhail from above.

"Give me the book. You have no use for it." The melodic tones had been replaced by a low, menacing growl.

Determination swam in Mikhail's veins. He wasn't going to let Azgarth intimidate him this time, no matter the consequences. Death would be preferable to knowing he owed his breakthroughs to this being who bound souls to him with impunity.

Mikhail pointed to the sealed doorway. "You cut off the access to it when you destroyed my home. That's your own fault and none of mine."

A roar loud enough to rattle the windowpanes blew over him. Mikhail stood resolute, stubbornly refusing to cover his ears to the onslaught.

"You tried to destroy it. That is *your* crime."

"Is it a crime to want to be free from a higher being's machinations? Is it a crime to want to live in peace and not be hounded by *wolfsine* and turn corners to find oneself in an alternate dimension?" Mikhail took a step forward. "Is it a crime to know in your heart that all your inventions and innovations were the sole work of your own skill and intelligence? I believe it is that very knowledge that makes us human. If you would rather we dance like puppets on a string only you control, then you haven't dealt with the strongest of the species."

"Ungrateful human!" Azgarth started to reach for Mikhail, but he danced out of the way.

Mikhail didn't even comment on the slur. Oh, he was more than ungrateful at the moment. He was downright offended. With one step, he turned and picked up an ancient sword some long-ago resident of the manor had left behind.

Azgarth laughed at the puny human weapon. At the moment, it was all Mikhail had, and he'd taken fencing like most young men of his social class. As a matter of fact, he was pretty good with a blade. Granted, this one was a bit rusty and unbalanced, but it might do the trick to inflict some injury.

Azgarth, however, did not appear in the least afraid.

Still, Mikhail tightened his grip on the pommel and stood his ground. "I will defend what is mine until the death if need be."

Azgarth took a menacing step forward.

Mikhail remained resolute. He raised a brow at the implied threat. His mind whirled with ways he might send Azgarth back to his realm and seal the portal. It might be the only way to be rid of him. At least it might give them time to find a way to destroy him for good.

Violin music came from the direction of the staircase. Mikhail didn't let his gaze off Azgarth for even a moment. Valentine must have taken the servants' stairs and collected his violin. What he thought to do, Mikhail didn't know. It did make for a lovely distraction.

Azgarth turned his head to search for the sound.

Valentine came into view, looking pale as death, but he played with all the heart of a man with nothing to lose. He played the song he'd debuted in Venice. His fingers flew over the strings, his bow danced, and he moved as if to hypnotize the fae master.

With his attention diverted, Mikhail brought up the rusty sword and thrust it straight through Azgarth's side.

Thunder shook the manor. The yowl of pain and betrayal blew out the windows, sending glass flying in all directions. Mikhail hit the floor, holding his hands over his head.

The front door blew open. Dante stood in the doorway looking like an avenging angel. He held the cauldron in his hands.

"You want the book, Azgarth, you can have the bloody book!" With that, he threw the contents of the cauldron into the wind. Ashes scattered on the breeze. Bits of the binding and cover not consumed by the flame fell to the floor.

Valentine continued to play, laughing as his hands moved faster, freer than they had been before.

They might have enraged Azgarth, but the night was far from over.

A TERRIBLE cacophony woke Henri.

He lay on his bed alone and soaked in sweat. Strange sounds filled the house. Were they trapped in a storm, or had war come to London?

He tried to roll over onto his side, but pain shot through his body, taking his breath but leaving memories in its wake. A *wolfsine*—he'd been bitten. Looking down at the bandage on his side, he saw no blood on the dressing. The flow must have stopped, or Dr. Stanslovich had stitched him up when they arrived home.

Where were they now?

Music filtered in from the main house. Andres was playing. Loud and passionate, the strains filled the servants' quarters. A loud yell of pain and misery hung on the air.

God in heaven, he needed to get out there and see what was happening. Help in some way.

Gritting his teeth in pain, Henri rose and held his side as he started for the main house. Sweat cooled on his skin as he moved. Breeze from open windows whipped through the rooms, bringing a cold wind with it. He shivered but kept moving, not allowing even a little discomfort to stop him.

He took the stairs one at a time. The climb more difficult for the want of speed. Whatever the *wolfsine* had done to him had zapped him of all strength.

When he came to the hall, he took in the scene as one would watch two trains about to collide. No way to stop them, only to watch the horror to come.

Andres played as Azgarth danced in pain. White fluid leaked from his side. Fae blood? An old rusty sword lay on the floor covered in ashes. What in the blazing hell did they think to accomplish? The scene reminded him of a circus of the damned.

Yet from observing the tableau, Henri knew there was one way to seal the void. Music worked on sound frequencies. Oscillations created heat and friction in the atmosphere. If he could only get to the laboratory to retrieve his compression device he might be able to marry the two together to seal the portal. Only then he noticed the laboratory doors were blocked by debris. So he had heard what sounded like an earthquake; he'd not imagined that in his sleep.

His plan might not even work, but it was worth a try. At this point anything was worth a try.

Had they even managed to free Andres?

Dr. Savoy glanced up, locking gazes with Henri.

Henri made a motion, letting Dr. Savoy know he'd return in a moment and that he had an idea. Dr. Savoy gave a nod and went out the front door.

He turned from the scene, praying they could hold off Azgarth a little while longer.

First he needed to find a tuning fork. The only one he knew of he'd bought for Andres a few days before. He climbed up to the guest rooms, moving as fast as his decreased and weakened state allowed. His side pulled and pinched with each step. For every two stairs he climbed, he had to stop to catch his breath. Sweat beaded on his upper lip and pooled at the small of his back. He wiped at his face.

Andres's room was neat and tidy. The tuning fork lay on the desktop. Henri grabbed it and headed back down the stairs.

He'd have to find another way into the laboratory. He'd also need a few other pieces of equipment to augment the oscillations of the tuning fork. By rights he needed one about the size of a city block, but barring that unlikely scenario, he'd have to make do with what he might rummage from the laboratory.

And he knew precisely the thing to use to boost the power.

Going out the back of the house, he edged his way around the manor and to the laboratory windows. One of the boards was missing where the broken windows had been covered after the storm. Dr. Savoy waited for him in the laboratory. He held out his hands to assist Henri through the frame.

"I expect you have thought of some way to close the portal." Dr. Savoy continued to hold on to Henri's arms until Henri was steady on his feet.

"A theory, but I'm willing to go on faith here."

"So what have you got?" Dr. Savoy rubbed his hands together. His dark eyes were bright with anticipation.

"A tuning fork." Henri held the musical calibrator up in front of his face. He watched as the excitement turned to disappointment. "It's an instrument that uses vibrations to make sound waves. Amplify it enough and it can work."

"Perhaps, but I doubt you'll get the frequency of oscillations you want with that alone."

"I won't. But I'm going to use something that will keep the vibrations at a constant high frequency." Henri set the tuning fork on the table, then made a beeline for the resurrection tank.

"What do you propose?"

"I need the generator."

Dr. Savoy started for the platform where the generator still sat. "I'll get this; you gather whatever else you might need."

Oh, and he did need other pieces in order for his plan to work. If it even worked. Right now he had only a vague idea of the mechanism. As with most of the inventions he made on the spot, the vision grew clearer the more he worked, the deeper into the task he delved.

Across the laboratory, a row of drawers held all manner of washers, nuts, bolts, bits of string, wire, and other goods. He hadn't the time to solder anything in place. All he had time to do was to take copper wire and twist it around the handle of the tuning fork. Now, he only needed something to keep the oscillations going at a constant ultra-high frequency to effect a change.

Next, he took the compression device and turned a screw, adjusting the amount of percussions per minute. A change in frequency in conjunction with the generator would shoot through the copper wires and excite the tuning fork, keeping the pitch and tone playing at a constant level.

Insane? Perhaps, but he had no other ideas. None. Other than sending an arc of electricity through the portal.

Henri turned back to look at Dr. Savoy. "Remove the grounding wire."

Dr. Savoy glanced up with a question on his face, yet he didn't bother to give it voice. He leaned over and plucked the wire in question from the base. "I hope you know what you're doing."

"Not entirely, but then we're so far out of our depth at the moment, I really don't believe it matters." Quickly he fixed the compression device to the tuning fork, feeding the copper wires through the body to complete the circuit.

Dr. Savoy slid the generator over the floor. "Hook it up. I'll remove the debris from the doorway."

Judging from the sounds coming from beyond the laboratory, they were running out of time. Sweat ran down his forehead. He wiped the back of his hand over it and unwound another length of wire. This he fed into the body of the generator, to connect to the compression device.

When he finished, he dragged the entire ensemble over to the door and started to help Dr. Savoy remove the debris.

They used neither care nor finesse, but chucked the pieces into the laboratory proper without thought to where it landed. Little by little a hole began to form, and he could see into the foyer. The sight was enough to stop him cold—but he couldn't let it.

A black shadow eclipsed the opening. Pressure pushed down on the top of Henri's head. He tried to shake it off. That odd dizziness that had grabbed hold of him in the theater returned.

He'd be damned before he'd let the fae world take over the material.

Henri hurried through the passage. He launched the oscillating fork through the doorway and into the heart of the portal. Electricity arced outward, sending sparks showering around the foyer. Azgarth roared in outrage. He spun on Henri, arms outstretched to the side.

The portal closed, sucking the fae master through the entrance. It slammed shut, sending a column upward to burn a hole into the ceiling.

"Get some water!" Dr. Stanslovich was up his feet. He pulled the curtains off the rod and began to beat at the flames that started to consume the ceiling.

"Fire! Fire!" Andres shouted down into the direction of the servants' quarters.

Henri moved as fast as he could to the stairs and hurried to the next floor. Already the carpet smoldered, sending a horrible stench through the rooms. Smoke began to accumulate. He'd not intended to burn down Dr. Stanslovich's house.

A vase of flowers sat on the table at the end of the hall. He hurried to it and threw the blooms to the floor. A quick splash of the water and the smoldering from this side went out. A sizzle hissed as the water sank into the carpet.

He leaned back against the wall and gave a deep sigh. This part of the battle might be over, but the war had just begun. Valentine was free, but as long as the rest of them were beholden to Azgarth, none of them were safe. He only wondered how and when the dark fae master might next manifest.

Sensing he was no longer alone, he opened his eyes and watched Valentine cross the length of the hallway to him.

Valentine stopped a few feet away from him. "It isn't over."

"I know." Henri dipped a shoulder. "At least you're free. I did make good on that promise."

"Yes." Valentine's gaze skimmed down Henri's side, landing where the *wolfsine* bite lay hidden by a simple cotton shirt. "But now you are under his control."

"I am."

"What are we going to do?"

"What do you want to do?" Henri threw the question back at him, wanting only to hear the words he longed for.

Valentine rubbed his chin. "I will stay and fight with you. We must find the other books. Set you and others free."

Despite their miserable state, both injured and standing on soaked carpet, Henri smiled and closed the space between them. "I hoped you'd say that."

CASSIE SWEET lives and works from her home office in the New Jersey Highlands, where she shares space with her overly affectionate Golden Retriever and artist husband. Her writing takes her to many destinations, both real and imagined.

Website: www.mystickat.com

Facebook: www.facebook.com/MKMancosKScott

More from DSP Publications

The Godhead Epoch: Book One

No one can outrun destiny or the gods.

In Epiro, a kingdom in Greece, Perseus is prophesied to be a great demigod hero and king, with a legacy that will shape the world of Gaia. When he was born, his grandfather exiled him, and his mother brought them to Seriphos, where she created an academy for demigod youth. Perseus trains there and waits for the day when he will be able to take the throne of Argos.

Despite potential future glory, Perseus's fellow students think he is weak. By the time he reaches manhood, he has given up the hope of having any real friends, until Antolios, a son of Apollo, takes an unexpected interest in him. Perseus and Antolios fall in love, but Antolios knows it cannot last and leaves Seriphos.

Perseus, grief-stricken and lonely, rebels against the Fates, thinking he can avoid the prophecy and live his own life. But when the gods find him, he is thrust into an epic adventure. With his divine powers, he fights gorgons and sea serpents, and battles against his darker nature. Perseus strives to be his own man… but the gods have other plans.

www.dsppublications.com

More from DSP Publications

Reawakening: Book One

For a thousand years, since their defeat of the Shadow at Eyr, the dragons have slept under the mountains. Now their king, Tarnamell, has woken. Driven mad by loneliness, he hurls himself south until he finds and tries to claim the Alagard Desert. Unfortunately, the desert already has a guardian spirit, and he doesn't want to share. Amused by the cocky little desert spirit, Tarn retreats, planning to return in human form.

When his caravan enters the desert, however, Alagard is missing. Rumors fly of a dark power, and soon Tarn's caravan encounters the living dead and an amnesiac mage called Gard.

Forced to take refuge in the Court of Shells, a legendary fortress in the heart of the desert, Tarn, Gard, and their allies decide to seek out the Shadow before it destroys the desert. But to confront the Shadow, Tarn needs to gather his strength. A dragon's power depends on the love and loyalty of his human hoard, but Tarn's original hoard has been dead for centuries. Before he can face his most ancient enemy, he must win the trust of new followers and the heart of a cynical desert spirit.

www.dsppublications.com

More from DSP Publications

Blessed Epoch: Book One

For the past few years Yarroway L'Estrella has lived in exile, gathering arcane power. But that power came at a price, and he carries the scars to prove it. Now he must do his duty: his uncle, the king, needs him to escort Prince Garith to his wedding, a union that will create an alliance between the two strongest countries in the known world. But Yarrow isn't the prince's only guard.

A whole company of knights is assigned to the mission, and Yarrow's not sure he trusts their leader.

Knight Duncan Purefroy isn't sure he trusts Yarrow either, but after a bizarre occurrence during their travels, they have no choice but to work together—especially since the incident also reveals a disturbing secret, one that might threaten the entire kingdom.

The precarious alliance is strained further when a third member joins the cause for reasons of his own—reasons that may not be in the best interests of the prince or the kingdom. With enemies at every turn, no one left to trust, and the dark power within Yarrow pulling dangerously away from his control, the fragile bond the three of them have built may be all that stands between them and destruction.

www.dsppublications.com

More from DSP Publications

Wolf's-Own: Book One

Untouchable. Ghost. Assassin. Mad. Fen Jacin-rei is all these and none.

His mind is host to the spirits of long-dead magicians, and Fen's fate should be one of madness and ignoble death. So how is it Fen lives, carrying out shadowy vengeance for his subjugated people and protecting the family he loves?

Kamen Malick means to find out. When Malick and his own small band of assassins ambush Fen in an alley, Malick offers Fen a choice: Join us or die.

Determined to decode the intrigue that surrounds Fen, Malick sets to unraveling the mysteries of Fen's past. As Fen's secrets slowly unfold, Malick finds irony a bitter thing when he discovers the one he wants is already hopelessly entangled with the one he hunts.

www.dsppublications.com

More from DSP Publications

Book One of The Wode

The Hooded One. The one to breathe the dark and light and dusk between....

When an old druid foresees this harbinger of chaos, he also glimpses its future. A peasant from Loxley will wear the Hood and, with his sister, command a last, desperate bastion of Old Religion against New. Yet a devout nobleman's son could well be their destruction—Gamelyn Boundys, whom Rob and Marion have befriended. Such acquaintance challenges both duty and destiny. The old druid warns that Rob and Gamelyn will be cast as sworn enemies, locked in timeless and symbolic struggle for the greenwode's Maiden.

Instead, a defiant Rob dares his Horned God to reinterpret the ancient rites, allow Rob to take Gamelyn as lover instead of rival. But in the eyes of Gamelyn's Church, sodomy is unthinkable... and the old pagan magics are an evil that must be vanquished.

www.dsppublications.com

More from DSP Publications

When Sheyn, a headstrong young aristocrat, disobeys his parents and travels to the far east, he passes through Kandaar, an isolated country of strange customs. He is abducted, transformed by a mysterious ritual, and sold to a barbarian king as a pleasure slave. When the king is killed by Kashyan the Bastard, dispossessed prince of Clan Savaan, Sheyn becomes Kashyan's possession.

The Bastard expects Sheyn—now called Pearl—to behave as an obedient pleasure slave, but compliance is not in Sheyn's nature. Nor does Sheyn's ordeal stop at being held captive by people he considers savages. The Red Temple covets Sheyn as a living gateway to the demon realm and plans to use him to summon the God of Death.

Kashyan loathes Sheyn, and Sheyn despises Kashyan, but when the Red Temple kidnaps Sheyn, honor compels Kashyan to rescue his slave, and he starts a war in the process. If they hope to stop the Red Monks from bringing hell to earth, Sheyn will have to accept Kashyan is more than an uncivilized brute, and Kashyan will have to admit there's more to his Pearl than a pretty, arrogant exterior.

www.dsppublications.com

www.ingramcontent.com/pod-product-compliance
Lightning Source LLC
Chambersburg PA
CBHW070451120726
47910CB00003B/1007